# Christmas Cherry Auction

## 5 Reverse Harem Romances

# Christmas Cherry Auction

## 5 Reverse Harem Romances

Sylvie Haas

Ebook ISBN: 978-1-950166-57-2

Paperback ISBN: 978-1-950166-56-5

Cover Design: Masque of the Red Pen

# Table of Contents

Sparkles and Spanking..........................1

Presents and Praise.............................85

Tinsel and Teasing.............................162

Holidays and Handcuffs...................258

Wishful and Wanton..........................361

More by Sylvie Haas...........................419

Sylvie Haas QR code..........................420

About the Author..............................422

# Sparkles and Spankings

## A Reverse Harem Romance

Sylvie Haas

# Blurb

**My sassy mouth has gotten me in trouble more than once. Then I meet three guys who understand how to handle it!**

I'm participating in a charity auction to raise money for the local fire department and I'm doing it right.

Wasting no time identifying the 'money guys' in the room, I taunt them into a bidding war. It works—possibly too well. When the bidding gets out of hand and the auction is halted, the three highest bidders come to me with a private proposition. They'll triple the top bid if I'll commit the required four hours to each of them...and not just for the suggested tasks like cleaning or gift wrapping.

Will they change their minds if I tell them I'm not experienced in those other types of tasks?

Logic tells me this is a bad idea, but the Christmas season has me in the mood to believe this can work. Will my decision become a regret? I have twelve hours to find out.

If you love dirty-talking men who have over-the-top ideas of how to please their woman and want to give her babies, enroll yourself in the Christmas Cherry Auction!

# One

## Roxy

Adjusting my top to maximize my cleavage, I'm going with the adage that 'sex sells', or in my case, hopefully a hint of sexiness will start a bidding war. I've already identified three men who look like they have cash to spare.

The fire department needs a hefty chunk of change, and I convinced my two best friends to do a charity auction with me.

The idea took off when we convinced Jefferson, one of the wealthy men of Eggplant Canyon, to emcee the event. He, in turn, got three bikers from his security company to also put themselves up for bid. The three employees also happen to be firefighters so it made a lot of sense.

Other people volunteered by setting up a silent auction, and others organized a soup dinner. I'm tickled at how well the broader community has stepped up.

Turning my attention to Jefferson's voice over the loud speaker, I pause to make sure I heard correctly. Maggie, my first friend up for bid, was won at the price of twenty thousand dollars...our entire goal. Wow! Who in Peach Bottom Valley would pay that much for four hours of general help?

Her prior nervousness about the possibility of no one bidding on her can be put to rest.

I flash a smile at Maggie as she leaves the stage and joins me in the wings. Out of sight of the audience, her smile morphs to despair.

Did I misunderstand? "What's wrong? That was insane."

She retrieves her glasses from the counter beside us. It's a shame that she thought they would make her look too brainy to draw a good bid. She's adorable with them. "It turns out that *not* getting bid on *wasn't* the worst possible thing that could happen."

"How can that be bad? You raised the full twenty thousand on your own. Now there's no reason for anyone to bid on the rest of us."

"Next up, Roxy!" booms through the PA system but I ignore my cue.

"You'll do fine," she says.

"They can wait. Do you not like the person who bid on you? You only have to do four hours of chore-type stuff."

"Not like the bidder? Ha! My sinfully gorgeous and wealthy, asshole stepbrothers took it upon themselves to give me a pity bid."

The bidders are identified by numbers so I hadn't realized who won.

The auctioneer calls for me again. "If you've met Roxy, you know she likes things big. Let Roxy know how excited you are."

Applaud erupts and I question Jefferson's word choice, but he's not wrong. I'm bold and love excitement.

I squeeze Maggie's hand. "Your stepbrothers just covered our entire goal. Think of all the good you're doing."

"Fine. Go work your magic, this is your baby." She squeezes my hand back and forces a smile.

"Better go tease the masses, Roxy," I hear from a few steps away. Isadora, the other friend I roped into auctioning herself blows a kiss at me. I have the best friends ever.

Turning to the stage, I pull back the curtain, throw my arms out presenting myself, and strut to the center. It's a small, high school stage, and I'm only on it because I organized the charity auction, but I'm alive. The renewed applause, the lights, and the energy I'm absorbing from the crowd invigorate me.

Making my way to the auctioneer at the far side of the stage, I motion for him to hand me the microphone.

"What do you think?" he asks the crowd. "Should I let her take control?"

"If you don't, I will," an unfamiliar voice calls out from the side wall.

My gaze shifts to the impeccably tailored stranger. He's one of the guys I've had my eye on. He and my two other targets exude money. I don't recognize them so they must be from the city. My hope was to get them in a bidding war to fund a big portion of our goal, which is now taken care of by Maggie's stepbrothers.

That won't cause me to back down. We'll raise every penny we can.

"What's your name, sir?" I say loudly since Jefferson hasn't handed over the microphone.

"Finn, and whoever's keeping track can go ahead and write the number thirty-seven down because I'll be winning you tonight." He holds up his bidder paddle.

Am I having a hot flash at the tender young age of nineteen? Fanning myself, and hamming it up for the audience, I yank the microphone from Jefferson's hand. "Well Finn, I see a few other guys who look prepared to give you a run for your money."

Shifting my attention to the other well-dressed man who's bidding on an item in the silent auction, I say, "You in the back. Is an autographed sports poster all you hope to take home tonight?"

He sets the pen down, faces me, and says, "If the record keepers already wrote thirty-seven, be prepared to turn that seven to an eight." He picks his paddle up, displaying his number.

Going into this auction, I'd done a fabulous job keeping my mind out of the gutter, but the way both of these men stare at me—into me—I'm not so sure they'd have me clean their house, wrap presents, or any of the other mundane services we suggested.

"No one needs to write any numbers down just yet," another low, growly voice says from the front row. The equally handsome, but slightly younger man is staring straight up at me. His deep blue eyes captivate me, or maybe it's the way he points at me when he says, "I have plans for you."

I force a huge breath into my lungs. It's showtime, and these guys are my leading men.

# *Two*

# Finn

Roxy. While she taunts my business partners, I ponder if it's just a name she took on for the charity auction. She's playful—it was obvious the second she owned the stage, and furthered by the way she's toying with us.

I can't take my eyes off her. She's a vixen. The thought gives me pause to wonder why that name was given to one of the reindeer in the classic Christmas poem. Isn't it for children? Vixen is hardly kid-appropriate.

I shake off thoughts of children. Where did that come from?

Roxy's high heels accentuate the curve of her calves, and my gaze travels up her toned thighs. The fluffy white bottom of her skirt hits me like a cock block, but it's pretty short. If she bent over, I could confirm that her ass is as shapely as her calves.

This isn't one of *those* auctions, but I can't stop thinking of making her mine.

The top of her skimpy Santa costume has me itching to find out if I could pull it down with a single finger. I stroke my tongue across my lower lip at the thought of taking her nipple into my mouth.

My efforts to clear my mind fail.

Fuck. I'm going to win her. Too bad my business partners don't understand how serious I am. Even though we're technically bidding on four hours of assistance like cleaning and helping with Christmas tasks, that's not what I need. I have assistants for all of those things. I'll use my four hours to convince her that she's mine.

My business partner, Macalister, just moved to Peach Bottom Valley and saw the flier for the charity auction, so it was his idea to come. That doesn't mean I'm going easy on him if he bids on her. Then he brazenly says he has plans for her.

I draw attention back to myself. "Yeah, his plans are to help you off the stage and escort you to meet me at the winner's table."

She turns to the emcee. "Why don't you go get a drink? I'll handle these bids."

He salutes her and says something I can't hear. Whatever it is, it makes her laugh, and jealousy rages through me. I want to be the one to do that. I want to be the one close enough to see the sparkle in her eyes when I make her happy. I want to be close enough to feel her tits press into me with each bubble of laughter.

Not that the emcee got to, that's just my fantasy addition to the moment.

Roxy brings the microphone to her lips, sparking another pang of jealousy. I want her breath on me.

"Alright boys, who's ready to bid?" She bends one knee and swivels her hips.

I jerk my auction paddle up and an unexpected desire hits me to bend her over my lap so I can swing it down onto her ass. What has she done to me?

She giggles into the microphone, amplifying her laughter through the room...through my thickening cock. Her happiness is the cutest damn thing I've ever heard.

"Perhaps you don't understand how this works, Finn. You're supposed to let the auctioneer—" She points to herself. "—say a dollar amount, and then you raise your paddle."

Lowering my paddle, I step away from the wall, but stop myself from rushing to the stage. "Maybe I'm reading your mind, Roxy, and I already know what you're asking for."

The slight pause before she parries is enough to ensure she understands she's met her match.

"Well Finn, the mind-reader... What was I going to ask for?"

"Not enough."

She narrows her gaze. "Hmm," comes through the PA system as her lips purse. "You're awfully sure of yourself."

"Always." Except when it comes to her, but that will be my secret. I'm not sure what I'd do if someone managed to outbid me. I make a mental note that three guys pooled their resources for the first woman.

"What do you suggest?" she asks.

"Multiply what you were going to start with by ten?"

"What if I was going to start at a thousand?"

I'm certain she would have started her bid at one hundred dollars like the auctioneer did, but this speeds things along. "Do you need me to do the math?"

She silently studies me, so I raise the bidder paddle again.

She worries her lower lip. Everyone else fades away while I find out just how bold my Roxy is.

"Alright Finn, the bidding starts at ten thousand dollars."

I stand stock-still with the exception of twisting my auction number back and forth.

Murmurings roll through the room.

"Perhaps you don't understand how this works, Roxy. As auctioneer, you should read my number and escalate the price."

"Bidder number thirty-seven for ten…thousand…dollars. Do I hear ten thousand one hundred, two hundred, three hundred…"

She shifts her attention around the room as Daxton, and Macalister, my business partners raise their numbers in turn.

Her eyes return to me and I say, "When the bids are hot like that you're supposed to use larger increments."

"Are you telling me how to do my job?"

"No, I'm telling you how to do the auctioneer's job."

She huffs and turns her entire body away from me, focusing on my partners. No one else dares jump into this bidding war.

"What do you say we cut bossypants out of the bidding?"

From the front row, Macalister cautions, "My bank account would thank you, but Finn's not going to take lightly to being called bossypants."

I can't decide if I should laugh or offer a hundred grand and close the bidding.

She mock whispers into the microphone, "Between us, I don't think bossypants is man enough to do anything about it." She raises her voice. "What do you say? Are you ready to outbid the other guy back there and go for eleven thousand?"

The banner in the back of the multi-use area makes their twenty-thousand-dollar goal clear. It's already been met by the first woman who was auctioned. I motion for Daxton, who's still at the back of the room, to meet me up front.

Thrusting my bidder number in the air, I say definitively, "Twenty thousand. Stop the bidding."

Roxy's speechless for a moment but as I move between the stage and the front row to meet with Macalister and Dax, she finds her words.

"And if I keep calling for bids?" She dead stares me. The woman has sass.

"Don't." I'm used to my word being gold, but Roxy's challenges fire me up.

A grin plays on her lips. "Are you going to make me stop?"

Playful antagonism. I love it. Shooting a glare at her, I turn to my friends. "We can outbid each other all night long, or we can—"

"Do I hear twenty-one thousand?" Roxy asks the audience.

Tamping down my laugh, I keep my tone as serious as possible. "I said to stop."

"I asked if you would make me." She's toying with me in front of everyone.

I don't care what anyone else thinks. I don't care that she's at least ten years younger than me. This is what is missing from my life. Fun...and Roxy.

Closing the gap between the front row and the stage, I'm within reach of being able to touch her silky legs when she steps back. She shrugs and gives me a sly grin.

"I'll bend you over my knee and spank you if I have to." Did I just say that out loud? My need for her is getting out of control. I never lose control. And while my words can't have been loud enough for everyone to hear, everyone up front did. Laughter and scoffs and conversations break out until Roxy raises the microphone to her mouth.

The room falls silent as if she's about to speak the word of God. She does even better. The challenge is in her eyes before her lips move.

"Twenty-two thousand...going once..."

If I wasn't caught in a moment with her, I'd have jumped onto the stage. Out of respect for common decency, I'll consider it a good thing that the emcee races to her and rips the microphone from her hands, positioning himself between the two of us.

"Okay, ladies and gentlemen, please take a minute to support our firefighters by bidding on items in the silent auction and buying refreshments. We'll resume the live auction in ten minutes." He nods and waves at the crowd, then motions for me to follow him.

Macalister grabs my arm when I start to move.

"What the fuck was that?" he asks.

"I want her."

Mac and Dax talk over each other, pointing out that I can't just end the bidding. They want her too. Then just when I think a woman is going to be the first thing to ever come between us, Mac offers the voice of reason.

"Hold on. This is only for help with cleaning and Christmas stuff."

"I'm convinced she's game for more." At least with me.

"I'm pretty sure we each feel that way. What if we each donate twenty k, and share her?"

"Like a gang bang?" Dax looks way too excited.

Mac clarifies, "I believe the more politically correct term is reverse harem."

She's supposed to be mine, but rather unexpectedly, I like the idea of sharing her with the two people I trust most in the world. Glancing at the stage, I catch her watching us.

It's a risk, doing a joint bid, but it's the only way I can be certain I have contact with her after this evening.

I spell out a plan. "All right. We each drop twenty grand. It's for a good cause that she cares about. No promise of anything other than four hours of help with shopping or whatever."

"No sex?" Dax asks.

"Not unless she's game, but we pay first. No pressure."

Instinctively, we fist bump. There's no actual plan for how we'll carry this out or why I have the slightest notion it will work. We haven't even discussed that I want a lot more than four hours from Roxy. Yet, my gut tells me to let fate guide me for once.

# Three

## Roxy

Jefferson escorts me backstage despite my protests. His concern for my safety is genuine. It's probably why he's so good at running a security company with his twin brother.

Logically, I should be concerned that strangers showed up at our small-town fundraiser auction and bid exorbitantly on me. Logic has never been my strong suit. I'm more of a Polar Express kind of girl. We should all be dreamers and just believe.

*Express* seems to be the key. It's crazy how quickly my interest in Finn and the other two is growing. Attempting to get my imagination in check, I imagine myself wrapping a pile of presents for them. I barely center the first package on the paper when my fantasy shifts to the three of them centering me on a bed for a mind-blowing sexual experience. And since I have nothing to judge it against, why not believe it would be magical?

That's better than most of my friends say about their not-so-great first sexual encounters.

Jefferson's in the thick of grilling me about stranger danger, and it occurs to me that he chose to emcee the auction so he could assess the bidders. His wife, Natalie, is a lucky girl—double lucky since she's got him and his identical twin brother.

Their wild ménage stirs up curiosity of what these three guys would like to do with me. Would I dare?

As if on cue, the men round the corner and my mind absorbs them in slow motion. Their arms and legs move back and forth with deliberate swagger. Their fitted shirts hug their sculpted pecs. They look from each other to me in turn.

My panties melt like an icicle on a sunny spring day.

Jefferson steps in front of me. "I don't know what's going on guys, but Roxy put a lot of work into this auction. Don't make a mockery of it."

"Hold on." I wiggle to get in front of him, which puts me within inches of Finn's firm body. He's so much bigger than when I was on stage. He exudes even more power, and the subtle hint of his cologne only serves to speed up my melting panties. What is that scent? Musk and money?

Jefferson protectively sets a hand on my shoulder, which draws Finn's gaze.

Finn says, "You can let go of her. She's able to handle herself."

I appreciate Jefferson's kind gesture but Finn's belief in me earns bonus points. I shrug my shoulder free.

Craning my neck up, I ask. "Are you really going to donate twenty thousand dollars to the Peach Bottom Valley Fire Department?"

"There's been a change of plans."

Crap. My heart slides out of place. If I have to get on stage a second time, it won't be the same, but I'll do it. All for the cause.

I'd been working a shift as Santa's helper at the mall when one of the kids asked Santa to bring his dad safer fire-fighting clothes. It didn't take much snooping for me to find out that the department wanted to upgrade their gear but it was going to take some time to raise the money.

What a burden for a kid to worry about his parent's safety. The auction is my answer to that child's request.

A finger tucks under my chin and lifts. I hadn't even realized I'd looked down.

"Changed in a good way, Roxy. Daxton, Macalister, and I are each donating twenty thousand." He motions to each man and they nod their agreement.

"Really? "I light up like the moment someone plugs the Christmas tree in.

They all say some version of yes. I have to force my eyes from Finn to the other two, but its Finn's hand that caresses my cheek. His thumb stays wrapped around the other side of my jaw. I'm pretty sure that he understands I'm his about the same time I figure it out. Maybe before.

Is it shameless that I lean in a little?

He speaks to Jefferson. "Why don't you get the auction going again and see how much more you can raise? We'll take care of Roxy from here."

Jefferson's terse. "If you're each donating then you each need to fill out your information at the winner's table. And if you do anything—"

"You don't have to worry about us." Mac's calm tone mirrors his words.

Jefferson mutters warnings as he walks off.

"Maybe you do need to help me with the math? I can't believe you're donating sixty thousand dollars?"

"We're each set on winning so we came to an agreement."

"Does that mean I have to help each of you for four hours? I will. It's just that my schedule is busy this time of year."

Finn trails his fingers to my shoulder, down my arm, then takes my hand between both of his. "We understand that you're only obligated to give us four hours and that we're supposed to limit our requests to things like general chores."

His words hang in the air. Can this really be happening to me, or am I reading too much into it?

"We have something else in mind." Dax's jaw flexes and just when I think he's going to reach for me, he crosses his arms. Darn.

"Okay," I say far too quickly. This is insanity. "I can't promise anything."

It's highly unlikely that I misunderstand their intent. What's harder to understand is that I'm seriously considering choosing my first time to be in a three-way—correction—there are three of them, so that makes this a four-way. A foursome? A bod quad? Does it even have a name?

I fight down the tingles of excitement that have my skin eager for their touch. If I don't control myself, I won't be able to walk in my heels. My Santa's helper costume doesn't leave much room for error. One slip of any kind and I'll be falling out of my red and white outfit.

Mac guides me by the elbow toward an exit. "We should go somewhere more private to talk."

Jefferson's keeping an eye on me.

I say loudly enough that I'm sure he can hear. "Let's get your information on file first."

Jefferson gives me a grateful nod. I'm not sure if I fully comprehend the surreal moment.

Isadora pulls me aside when I send the guys to do their paperwork. "Are you sure it's safe to go with them?"

"I know it's hard to understand, but I feel safe with them."

"I'm not saying you shouldn't do it. Lord knows if a dream team bid on me, I'd be tempted to go for it, but be careful."

"I will. Now get on stage and see how much you can raise."

"Probably not as much as the three firefighters will. I heard that Sasha is going to use her inheritance to bid on all of them."

"I love it. I'll cross my fingers for you and her," I say as Isadora prepares to take the stage.

Will Finn, Dax, and Macalister use credit cards to cover their bids? Must be nice.

Dax snags my wrist when I walk past. All I was going to do was watch Isadora's bidding, so I do it by his side while he's hunched over the table filling out all of his personal information and letting them make a copy of his driver's license.

A few locals give me the side-eye. Less bold temptresses might let the judgmental glances bother them. I take it as a sign of jealousy.

More interestingly, the three mountain men who had revisited the soup line several times, suddenly pay attention to more than their bowls when Isadora slinks onto the stage. The men sit upright, directing their attention to her every move. Whispers between them result in a bunch of head nodding. Are they going to bid?

I don't know a lot about them other than they live remotely in the Cherry Ridge Foothills and never cause any trouble. And sure enough, the second Jefferson opens the bids on Isadora, one of the mountain men raises his bidder number.

I kiss my crossed fingers and wave them at her.

"All set," Mac says quietly.

They grant me a minute to enjoy the bidding war that breaks out over Isadora. Not as verbally charged as my bidding war since the mountain men are pretty quiet, but it's clear from the start, they don't intend to let anyone else win.

I'm tickled that we've raised more than enough money to make sure our firefighters have proper gear. I'm even more excited that Isadora might have a little fun headed her way, just like me. Poor Maggie though, her stepbrothers ruined it. Who would have guessed those protective older brothers would be such a problem?

Surveying the room, I don't see Maggie or her brothers. I text her a thank you since my guys are ready to start the timer. But before we do, I have a little bit of explaining about not being able to promise anything.

Mac's gentle pressure on my arm becomes more insistent. I grab my purse and coat, and thank my lucky stars that after my girlfriends and I came up with the charity auction idea and we recruited Jefferson, his wife and the others of Eggplant Canyon took it on. They even scheduled people for cleanup. All I had to do was sell myself. Ha!

The four of us navigate the dimly lit parking lot behind the high school, and it dredges up memories of friends who made out back here after school events. I'd been *in a mood* in high school and didn't date, went with Maggie and Izzy to the dances, and generally thought my girlfriends would be enough for all of eternity.

Then they both ended up with boyfriends, although they never got serious. It's all for the best. We realized we can still be besties even if we date.

"How does this work?" I stop a few feet away from the SUV we're headed toward. "Should I drive my own car?"

"Do you have four-wheel drive?" Mac asks.

"No, where do you live?"

"I moved to the Cherry Ridge Foothills last month. Finn and Dax live in the city, just came for a visit this weekend. Why don't you ride with us since it's going to snow tonight."

I give this serious consideration. Beyond the thrill of hooking up with three super hot rich dudes, it's like the universe is telling me this is okay. They hadn't even flinched when I said I wasn't promising anything beyond the expected. My brain flicks through several moments these guys could have triggered a red flag. So far, they're all green.

Clasping my coat closed, which does nothing for my bare legs, I say. "I don't mean to sound...well...humor me, please."

They huddle around me like I'm designing a championship-winning play in a football game.

I wait for their agreement then continue. "Since you mentioned that you have something *different* in mind for how I'll spend my hours, would you mind elaborating?"

My mind plays with the possibility that if I go home with them, I'll be walking into a kinky sex den.

Finn grabs the back of my coat and pulls me into his chest. "Your sassy little mouth earned you a spot on my knees. Don't think I forgot."

The potential for a sex den increases. Have they done this before? I squeeze my thighs together and lean into him. He's thick and possessive. I wonder if he'll really spank me. Why does that turn me on so much?

Dax tucks his fingers inside the opening of my coat. The warmth of his hand contrasts against the tops of my boobs which were slightly chilled from the brisk evening air. His pinky dips into my cleavage.

I swallow hard. I want this so badly it's ridiculous. It also validates that I'd told myself I would know when the time was right.

"Roxy, if we have to explain what we meant by different, you might not be ready for this."

Oh shit. Don't mess this up. I say the first thing that pops into my mind. "You're not taking me to a red room of pain or a torture dungeon or anything, are you?"

The men stare at me incredulously before Mac laughs, followed by Dax, then Finn. I sag in relief and join them.

Mac comforts me. "It's a fair question. You don't know anything about us, and consent is key." He glances at Dax then rubs his brow. "Let me be clear. What we're offering is sex, with all three of us. If that's as crazy to you as it sounds to me now that I've said it out loud, I understand if you want to slow things down. These guys will understand too. I promise."

It can't be a coincidence that Maggie and Izzy both got bought by three guys in the auction, even if Maggie's scenario is decidedly not as fun. I embrace the Christmas spirit and believe.

"It is crazy, but it's just four hours, right?"

Finn clears his throat. "What if we—"

I wave him off. "Sorry. I forgot to do my math. Four times three is twelve. Looks like we've got until tomorrow morning boys!"

A scream escapes my lips as my feet are swept out from under me. Then I'm cradled against Dax's chest and all is right in the world. Why have I not spent more time snuggled into men's chests? It's so comforting and protective and...I don't even have a word strong enough for the emotions enveloping me.

His face is shadowed against the moonlight. "You're the cutest fucking thing ever, Roxy. I can't wait to make your blonde ringlets bounce when I slide you up and down my cock."

Does my surprise show? I'm paralyzed by his statement. I didn't know guys really talked like this. Not only have I missed out on chest snuggles. I've missed out on...conversation.

He presses his lips into mine and lingers his tongue over my lips as he pulls away. "I can't wait to lick that innocent look right off you."

Oh no. I got caught up in their sexiness and forgot why I stopped a minute ago. "So...about that..."

My heart's banging in my chest. Dax has to be able to feel it through our coats. They wait silently.

"The licking the innocent look off me thing...you can kind of actually do that." Jesus, that was a horrific ramble.

Are they catching on? Have I confused them?

"I've never had sex." The words tumble nervously from my mouth. I hope Dax's nerves don't cause him to lose hold and send me tumbling to the ground.

His grip tightens. "Don't fuck with us."

Mac looks away. Is he irritated?

Finn says, "Actually, fucking with us is exactly what we're hoping for."

Dax shoots him a glare. "Seriously, Roxy?"

I nod. "Please don't let that be a deal breaker. At least take me home and let's explore those spankings, Finn."

They exchange glances and must know each other pretty well because it seems to solidify a decision. Duh, they're willing to do this *bod quad* thing so I guess they're comfortable around each other.

Finn drags his thumb over my lips. "You heard the lady, let's get her home. We'll start with her sassy mouth and see where we end up."

# Four

## Mac

Finn likes to drive because he has a thing about being in control. Dax does too. I'm more of a go-with-the-flow kind of guy. In a rare turn of events, I overrode them because I have snow tires on my SUV.

My white knuckles on the steering wheel aren't because the road has gotten bad though. Everything happened so quickly tonight, I still can't believe we won a girl at the auction and we're taking her back to my place.

If I'd won her independently, I planned on spending four hours getting to know her and seeing if I could morph it into something more. Paired with Finn and Dax, this won't move slowly. That's not necessarily a bad thing.

I grip and regrip the steering wheel as I navigate the switchbacks that are illuminated only by my headlights. Cloud cover moved in, stealing the moonlight.

Dax and Finn are snuggled up to Roxy the Virgin in the backseat. What no one knows is that the front seat is also occupied by a virgin. I roll my shoulders to ease the tension.

Not saying something when Roxy did was probably a dumbass move. My partners don't know I've never been with a woman though. In the guy world, you just play along, say the right things, and tell anyone to fuck off if they press you for details.

Will Dax and Finn think differently of me as a business partner if they find out I've never had sex? It shouldn't matter. Our company sells a monthly subscription box of men's hygiene products. Sometimes companies ask us to include sexually related items, but it's not our focus, and I've never nixed something they wanted to offer.

The decision of whether or not to say something tightens itself around my chest. The three in the backseat are too absorbed in touching and kissing to worry about me. They've even covered that Roxy's on the pill and everyone is disease free. I could hardly believe everyone consented to unprotected sex.

The only bummer is that Roxy's on the pill. I'd love to lock that woman down as my wife and mother of my kids. It seems rash, but I felt it the moment I laid eyes on her. I suppose that's not the kind of thing that happens with this type of scenario. I'll talk with her afterward.

The crunch of gravel under the tires as I turn off the main road onto my driveway causes the trio to quiet for a moment.

"Almost there. One more mile." It satisfies my need to say something.

"It's so pretty with the snow decorating the trees. Hard to believe we're only twenty minutes outside of town." Roxy's admiration of my property makes my chest swell against the tightness.

"With fifteen minutes of that being uphill, it's a big elevation change. When we get to my house, you'll be able to look out over the town."

Dax scoffs. "I'll let you guys admire the lights while I rail Roxy from behind."

"If she decides to go that far." My defense of her could have sounded gentlemanly or considerate. Instead, it sounds clipped.

A delicate tap on my shoulder sends a jolt of excitement through me.

"Thanks Mac, that's sweet, but I want this. I'm not totally inexperienced. I have a vibrator."

How can she sound so confident that a vibrator prepared her for three guys?

Parking under a covered driveway that loops in front of my door, I hop out. The back doors of the car don't open. Are they going to have sex in the car?

Giving one last consideration to whether I could attribute my likely early ejaculation to the four-way, I trash the idea.

"Get out," I demand, opening the door, my clipped tone returning.

"Yes, sir, kiddo," Dax mocks me. Our age difference has never been an issue, and I probably read too much into his response. He helps Roxy out.

I shake it off so I can focus, and pause at the front door. That's my do-or-die trigger moment. Turning around with my eyes on the rich colors of the stained concrete driveway, I take a deep breath.

Lifting my gaze, I meet Roxy's.

"Everything okay?" She's so sweet. The notion of keeping her in my life, making a future with her, and imagining a boatload of kids piling out of our SUV washes over me. Totally wrong vibe for a four-way fling.

Clearly, everything is not okay. "Yeah, there's just something I should have said earlier."

She tosses her hands to the sides. "Can you top me announcing to three strangers that I'm a virgin and want them to take me home and have wild sex for twelve hours?"

My nervous laughter is drowned out by Dax and Finn cracking up. The mood quickly sobers when they notice.

Dax says, "Do you need to go in and pick up your underwear and socks?"

Finn bumps my arm lightly with his fist. "What's up, man?"

In one fell swoop, the same as when I'm convincing myself that public speaking isn't terrifying, I suck in a deep breath, wring my hands together, and look past them.

"I can outdo Roxy." I shift my gaze down to hers. She's raised her eyebrows. I get it out. "I've never had sex either."

Her eyes pop wide, there's a suspended moment where I swear the world stops, then she claps her hands, squeals, and hugs me. "Oh my god, that's so amazing. We could have our first times with each other...and these guys."

She angles her head to each side, smiling adoringly at Dax and Finn. "Did you guys know?"

Absolute confusion plagues both of them.

Dax finds words first. "You better not be lying."

"Oh, I take that as a no," Roxy says and turns to Finn.

He shakes his head. I can see his wheels turning as he's bound to be replaying every mention of sex, every opportunity he had to pick up on something, and wondering how he missed it.

"You better not be lying," Dax reiterates.

"I'm—"

Roxy's hand stroking my straining cock chokes my words. I shift my hips away to keep from blowing.

"That makes this even more special." She lifts up on her toes and kisses me. Her soft lips, her sweet scent, and her excitement test my ability to hold back.

Maybe I should go ahead and nut so I can get one out of the way. It might buy me a few seconds when I'm with her.

"I'd appreciate it if you guys could keep jokes to a minimum."

The guys grumble with hints of laughter threatening.

Roxy saves me. "I tell you what, if they make a joke, I'll be the one spanking them."

Her joke breaks their laughter free. It was all I could do to ask. I'll deal with the rest in the moment. Turning to the door, I pull my key out. I'm about to unlock my world.

# Five

## Roxy

Mac was so nervous, he had to be telling the truth. Poor guy. As soon as he lets us inside, he tells us to make ourselves at home and he vanishes. Finn and Dax plop onto the couch.

Before I can do the same, Finn grabs my wrist and pulls me onto his lap. "Ready?"

My mind is a whirlwind, but a gentle tap on my backside is enough to clear that up. The reality of what's happening sets in and if it wasn't for the feeling that something is incredibly, naturally right with these guys, I'd question if this decision would have better been based on logic than dreams and believing.

I can't stop the grin from spreading over my lips.

Dax notices and says, "Dude, she's ready."

My nervous giggle could make me come across as immature. Wanting to own my role in the evening, I kick my heels off and reposition my knees on the couch next to Finn. Leaning over him, holding myself up with my hands placed on the other side of his lap, I strategically expose my bottom toward Dax.

Honestly, it's easier than looking into his eyes while I let his friend spank me. I'm sure my little Santa's helper skirt rode up and my red and white striped panties are visible.

The groan that comes from Dax lets me know I've made the right choice. Finn's hand slides up the back of my thigh stopping just below my butt cheek. The tips of his fingers wrap around my inner thigh and have to be within millimeters of my sex.

He might as well be holding my throat. I can barely breathe.

When I wiggle my hips to try to get him to touch my sex, he yanks his hand away. A sharp, light tap on my bottom is paired with a gravelly, "You're a naughty girl. I'm starting to think you want discipline."

Isn't that obvious? I'm confused in the funniest way. Sitting back on my heels, I say, "Okay, maybe you don't need to explain math, but this sexy discipline thing would benefit from an explanation."

"Oh, sweet Roxy. You are innocent, aren't you?"

"Well, depending on how this is supposed to work... I don't tend to lie, so yes, I am innocent. But since that won't get me spanked, I'm kind of wanting to lie right now." Without thinking, I say, "I'm so sorry Daddy. I've been a very bad—"

The clatter of glass breaking causes all of us to turn to Mac who's standing in the doorway from the kitchen. He'd gotten wine and glasses but they're shattered all over the floor.

Good news...it wasn't a red. Less chance of stains.

I jump up and rush to him, but he thrusts a hand out. "I don't want you to get cut. I'll clean up, but what the fuck did you just call Finn?"

Mac can't even bring himself to say it. I blush.

"Daddy." Finn's voice is low and possessive, and coming from right behind me. His hands slide around my waist and onto the tops of my thighs. His thumbs extend onto my sex. If he wiggled them just right, I would be a very happy girl, but he's not doing that. He's pulling me backward.

"I'll help," Dax says.

"I've got a shop vac in the garage." Mac steps that direction then turns again and faces Finn and me. "Whatever the fuck that Daddy thing was...hold that thought. It was hot."

He heads to the garage and Dax gathers the larger pieces of broken glass.

Finn, or should I say, Daddy scoops me up, carries me to the couch, and sets me on the middle cushion.

"Sit right here, Little One."

My heart does a flip that he gave me such a cute nickname.

Still towering over me, he says, "Don't try to make me discipline you. You'll get it when you need it."

36

I'm not a cat, so I run with my curiosity. "What happens if I do?"

The extra big grin I flash at him is met with heavy breaths that cause his chest to rise and fall noticeably.

He hooks one of my ringlets and strokes his fingers down the length. "If you purposefully do things you think deserve spankings, that makes you a brat."

He doesn't elaborate any further, and something about the way he says the word 'brat' excites me.

Does that mean I'm being a brat? I like the fun push and pull dynamic. Do I want to be called a brat though? That's even worse than wanting spankings. Worse in the very confusing way of why things that I thought were negative are intriguingly positive coming from Daddy.

How did these three men unleash this side of me?

I catch sight of Dax staring at us, no longer picking up broken glass. Finn clears his throat.

"Yes, Daddy?" My hands are tucked between my thighs and I lower my head slightly. I don't want him to see the smile playing on my lips as I decide I *am* a brat.

"Wait here, Little One, I don't want you to get cut."

Given a moment to think, it occurs to me that I like to instigate things. That's what was happening on stage. That's why I wanted to taunt them. It's all part of how I knew I would start a bidding war and identified those three men before I ever got on stage. This is a match made in heaven.

When Daddy decides that I'm going to behave and goes to help the other men, I hatch my plan. I take in every clink of glass, the scent of the leather furniture, and the slight kiss of warm air over my skin as the heater kicks on. I'm alive. Vividly so.

My skin prickles, eager for their touch. There's so much permission to play. I'd always thought sex would be more serious and I don't know...methodical?

Of course, there are many flavors beyond vanilla, not that I've explored them, but I didn't think it would be so fun. This beats the hell out of the hand-holding and lingering glances I've pined over when I see couples doing them in public.

I check myself. Okay, in public I'm not going to call Finn 'Daddy' or let him spank me. Our age difference would make that extra interesting. And with three of them...

Suddenly, I realize the floor is pristine and the men have disappeared into the kitchen and garage.

Oops. No time left to make a plan. I'll rely on instinct to be a brat. Daddy told me not to move. Easy, I hop up, scan the room, and rush to the small Christmas tree Mac has on a corner table. My heart pounds to the point I worry it's out of control.

Calming myself by focusing on details, I note that the tree is about three feet tall and has built-in lights. Mac doesn't have any presents under it and no ornaments, so I don't have much to look at. But it provides the perfect outlet not to be sitting where Daddy told me to.

My heightened senses have me tuned in to every footfall as the men cross the tile kitchen floor. The footfalls that stop on the carpet sound like Daddy's. A little heavier than Dax's and I haven't heard the garage door close so Finn hasn't returned.

I close my eyes and try to imagine what he's thinking...and that we both understand the game we're playing. I'm all in.

A guttural growl breaks the silence. "Little One."

A shiver runs up my spine in the split-second pause. He hasn't crossed the room yet.

"What do you think you're doing?"

For starters, I'm pretty sure I'm ovulating at the thought of an impending spanking.

We talked about sex stuff in the car. I'm on the pill. The reveal seemed disappointing to them, but hey, this girl didn't know she was going to meet her future daddies at the auction.

Firm deliberate steps draw closer to me. The heat of Finn's body overtakes me. The essence of his masculinity sends all of my feminine parts into a tailspin. One of his hands clasps mine, and without turning me, he walks to the couch.

There's no getting my tiny hand out of his large firm grip. It takes a couple of steps to get my bearing. I can't complain. I'm being a brat. This is part of it, and it takes everything in me not to laugh.

He guides me back to the same position on the couch as before, points, and I shake my head.

"I said to sit and wait for us. Do you understand what it means to have a Daddy?"

I can't answer because the *Roxy* version of me is about to crack up at how silly this scenario is and that it turns me on so much. I have to let go of Roxy and embrace my inner brat.

I angle my face to look at him. Dax enters the room and the garage door closes, so Mac will be here soon. My body's shaky with excitement.

Daddy's eyes lock with mine. It occurs to me that it's bratty not to answer, so I don't.

With steeled calm, he adjusts his pants as he sits on the couch.

He's already sporting an erection, which is mighty impressive. Is he as turned on by my brattiness as I am or just because I've basically agreed to trade in my V-card with them?

His face reveals nothing. Quite the controlled daddy. "Little one, do you understand what happens when you don't listen to Daddy?"

I shake my head. It seems like the right thing to do. He wraps his fingers around my hand and pulls me to sit next to him.

"Daddy's going to spank you."

Keeping up the ruse that I don't care, I meet his gaze. "Are you hard because you get to spank me?"

Dax suppresses a chuckle. Mac may have nearly passed out. In my periphery, he steadies himself against a chair then sits on the arm.

"Fuck." Finn guides my body over his knees, and because he's sitting on the edge of the couch, I'm literally dangling over his legs. My blonde ringlets drape around my face, obscuring my view.

Although the heater provided warmth a moment ago, my body is so hot that when he lifts the back of my skirt, cool air tickles my bottom.

"Dax, do you want to do the honors of getting these panties off?"

I swallow my mortification, reminding normal Roxy that bratty Roxy has this under control. Not the time to employ logic...just believe that this will work. It's okay to do something I'm not going to talk about in public. I've heard of these things. It's not that weird. It's just hard to believe that I'm doing it with three guys for my first time.

Dax steps closer. "Are you sure we shouldn't let the virgin do this?"

"We're gonna spread this out. I'll be the first to spank her. You get to be the first to undress her. Then the two of us will offer guidance while Mac is the first to fuck her. Sound like a plan?"

I've never been so wet in my life. And for the first time since I was a toddler, someone other than me is going to remove my panties. I know enough about sex to know that my wetness should be a huge turn-on for the guys.

# Six

## Dax

I glance at Mac. His Adam's apple bobs. Only one of us will get to fuck her first, and I'd expected it to be Finn, who now goes by Daddy. Letting Mac go first probably puts me last, but I'll make it work.

Roxy's plump ass taunts me.

An unexpected struggle breaks out in my head. I'd love to have a woman call me Daddy—the power dynamic, the look in her eyes, the way she's being a brat. It's a game. It's the best game I've ever seen played. The interesting thing is that I like watching it.

My cock is hard as a rock. Without a doubt, the only reason I can't actually imagine a scenario where I'd ask a woman to call me daddy is that I'm pretty sure Roxy is the only woman for me. And not just for me, but for the three of us. And Daddy has already been designated.

I'm generally game for the wild shit, but there's more to this than a wild romp. I think. I'm sure as hell not going to be the first one to say it though.

You don't just buy, or rather win someone at a charity auction and find out you're soulmates. Or do you? We've got twelve hours to figure it out, or suffice it to say, we've got her till morning.

I turn back to Mac. "If you weren't a virgin, I'd fight you for who gets to go first, but I agree with Finn. You do the honors. As long as we're all here, it's fine."

"Um...Yeah... I'm good with that plan." Mac's clearly shell shocked. Most people don't have their first time in a group setting complete with pointers.

"Yay!" Roxy says from her vulnerable position.

And now that we're all in agreement, I have some panties to remove. Instead of heading straight to Roxy's ass, I play out the moment, kneel in front of her, and push the curls from her face. "You're in control here, Baby. We're not going to do anything that requires a safe word." I glance at the two guys who nod agreement. "But if you'd feel better making one, we can."

"I can take it."

Her fucking sass makes my cock twitch. "I'm being serious, Roxy. This is your first time. If you say stop, we stop. We can talk about it and regroup if needed."

"You're so sweet, but Daddy told you what to do, so I think you're kneeling at the wrong end of me."

Damn this woman. I lean in and kiss her. I'm not gonna ask if she's kissed a guy before. Presumably, she has. It's a far cry from having sex, but my heart shreds a little bit just thinking about her kissing anyone other than the three of us.

I plunge my tongue between her lips, and she leans into me a little harder. Her tongue explores me, hungry for more. God, she tastes so good, like sex with a sprinkle of holiday spice all rolled into the brightness of a star, which I realize isn't a flavor but that's what she is.

Roxy isn't like any woman I've ever been with. Mac won't be the only one to nut embarrassingly early if we keep this up, so I pull back quickly—fast enough it takes her a second to regroup. I watch that second where she's wanting me. It's fucking glorious...angels sing...Santa becomes real... Am I the only one in the room who understands this isn't going to end in twelve hours?

Roxy is my future.

She slow blinks, and I stand before she can say anything. Assuming my place behind her, I set my hands on her bare feet, gently caressing. I take my time as I work my way over her ankles, up her calves, along every silky inch, shifting my gaze from one leg to the other. It's the only way I can keep from looking at the sweet endpoint. I'll enjoy it when I get there.

"Are you going to play your part or do you need help?" Finn asks.

"I am doing my part. Mac has lessons to learn."

I make sure Mac is paying attention before I continue. "You never just jump in and get straight to the point with a woman. I mean, you could just toss her on the bed, spread her legs, and shove your dick inside of her. That would make it about the guy, right? It's a surefire way to leave her thinking about walking out the door so she can give herself an orgasm."

"That's excellent advice. Always make sure she comes first, and a few other times," Finn adds.

"Take your time and enjoy her. Look at these shaved legs. She may not have known that she shaved them for us, but they deserve to be enjoyed. She's trusting us, and I sure as hell want to spend as much time in her trust as I can."

From such a short distance behind her, I glance at her panties. "She soaked, guys."

Groans fill the room, and she fidgets.

Her pussy juice is the most addicting scent in the world. My cock hurts and there's a serious risk I'm gonna lose control. I don't worry too much since I'll recharge quickly around her.

"Always make sure she's enjoying the moment." I wink at Mac then slide the back of my fingers over her silky red and white striped panties. "I've never been much into candy canes until this moment."

I lean in and lick the striped cloth. Immersed in her scent, I nip at her ass, making her flinch and squeal.

"Did you bite me?"

"Did you like it?"

She huffs. I lower my face, nuzzling against her backside, and lick the wetness of her panties. Merry Fucking Christmas. I've never tasted anything so sweet. I double down until her moans fill the air.

Desperate to remove the barrier between us, I tuck my fingers into the waistband of her panties, and slide them halfway down her thighs before running my hands back up. Spreading her round cheeks, I dip my tongue into her tight pussy. She's so sensitive, her cries escalate from my tongue alone.

I question if she's faking it. Is she being a damn brat? I'm trying to decide if I like the brat thing when her body shakes and she comes apart on my face. Her juices coat me as she comes. Drinking and lapping, there's no question that I am the first one to make her come. It takes everything in me not to say, "Who's your daddy now?"

When she's limp, I sit back and ease her panties the rest of the way from her legs.

"How was that, Baby?"

Her voice is soft as if she's still drifting through the climax. "I'd hate to vote you a ten out of ten since that wouldn't leave room for evaluating the other guys. I'll have to reserve judgment until everyone's made me come."

Roxy is a fucking brat. And I have my answer. I love it.

# Seven

## Roxy

Draped limply over Daddy's lap, I can't believe my first male-provided orgasm happened like that. I'm tempted to ask Mac where the bedroom is so I can splay myself on the mattress and tell them to get busy. I need to gather data for my rating system.

I truly need a minute to gather myself.

The warmth of Daddy's thick hand covers my butt cheek and makes slow small circles. Am I finally going to get that spanking that was promised, what seems like ages ago at the auction? My breaths quicken in anticipation.

Dax told Mac not to jump right in. Make her wait. Yes, anticipation. I've been waiting for the spanking, and Finn hasn't given it to me. The urgency must build for them as much as it does for me, an assumption proven true by their erections. Seems like a perfect opportunity.

"What's a girl gotta do to get spanked around here?" I sass them. This game goes both ways, and now Daddy can't spank me.

His hand pulls back from my ass and slaps so quickly, I don't have time to brace myself. My sex tightens in the strongest Kegel imaginable, but my sex is empty despite three erections in the room.

I guess I was wrong about him being able to spank me after I challenged him. And if there was any question if I was going to like it...that has been answered.

"What's that you're saying?" Daddy asks.

"I was beginning to think you were just a big tease."

He cracks up and his hand shifts to the other cheek, rubbing a little patch. Then the next smack, harder this time.

The sting leaves me hoping he made a handprint. The beginnings of another orgasm tighten as my walls clench around nothing. The euphoria of the previous spanking is already buried deep in my past. This gives a whole new meaning to the term Spank Bank.

His hand slides onto my upper thigh inching inward until he's stroking my sex. My hips shamelessly push into his finger, desperate to have him inside of me. He said Mac would be the first to fuck me, and I assume that means with a penis. Nobody was assigned to a finger fuck.

The tips of his fingers part my pussy lips. Wanton lust unfurls inside of me. This is happening. I need more. I wiggle further back.

Then damn him for pulling away. I'm left hanging for a moment and scramble to push upward, holding onto the couch so I can turn to him. I'll try the same approach that worked for a spanking.

"What's a girl gotta do to get finger fucked?"

I'm in for a shock when he's dragging his glistening finger across his lips. His eyes are closed as if enjoying the aroma of a fine wine, presumably not the one Mac dropped earlier. Then his mouth opens and he slowly drags his tongue along his digit.

"Jesus, Dax. How could you take your mouth off her?" Finn says.

"Team player, dude. We've got twelve hours. And trust me, every breath I take fills me with Roxy's essence. I'm not missing out on anything. Why don't you see how good it feels when she orgasms on you."

Daddy looks down and catches me staring in disbelief.

I point awkwardly in Dax's direction. "What he said."

Finn laughs. I bet you taste yourself every day, don't you?"

"I...no...well...uh..."

"I'll take that as a yes." He's so damn smug. "Were you going to lie to me again?"

I can't think of anything sassy to say. I'm wound too tight. His fingers skim ever so lightly over my exposed bottom. All I can think about is the trail of fire his touch leaves as he slides back into position, the tip of his fingers parting my intimate lips.

He pushes farther this time and my walls tighten around him. It's like he belongs inside of me. Like we're destined for a lot more than twelve hours. I check myself...I have to remember this for what it is. They won me and now we're all winners, for the night.

It would seem that if I'm lying, I shouldn't get to climax, and yet his fingers are doing an excellent job of rewarding me. I play along.

"Oh, no Daddy, I wouldn't taste myself. I'm a good girl."

His free hand wraps around my chin, keeping my head angled. We stare into each other's eyes. I'm lost in the best of ways. This is so much bigger for me. I'm a fool for thinking I could guarantee a wild ride of a first time and not feel something.

Every word. Every touch. Every look is so intimate. I'm going to need a lot more practice before I can separate sex and emotion. Yet I don't want to. I have the sense that it would be wrong to separate the dynamics existing here.

My eyes get weak and my body starts to flinch as he brings me closer and closer to release.

"That feels good doesn't it, Little One." How can he be so sweet and tender if he's separating sex and lovey-dovey feelings?

The only thing I can ensure is that this continues to be spectacular for the next eleven or so hours. I won't let this turn into a crappy 'first time' story.

I don't bother to open my eyes. "Look at you trying to make me say you're better than Dax when my orgasm is at your fingertips."

"There's nothing wrong with admitting you like it."

"I didn't realize Daddy would need me to stroke his ego before he lets me stroke his cock."

"You're twisting my words, Little One."

"I'm sorry, Daddy," I wiggle on his lap, the promise of release is unbelievably close. I'll get to come on his fingers—my first time to come with something other than a dildo inside of me. My walls tighten.

One more stroke of his—his fingers are gone. My body is caught in suspended animation waiting for something that's not there. I squeeze my thighs together but it's not the same. The ache is all-consuming. Did he misunderstand my moans?

"I didn't finish."

"That's the trouble with being a little brat. You're at Daddy's mercy." His voice is low and sincere.

I almost want to tell him I'll stop being a brat. Almost.

Then a sharp slap stings my bottom and his hand stays in place as if trapping the warmth in my skin. My walls clench so hard it's almost enough to trigger my release. Everything is so close and yet so far.

He's good at this game, and while I may not understand the rules, I have all night to learn them.

"Are you ready to tell the truth, Little One?"

"About what?" I'd confess national secrets if I knew any.

"Do you taste yourself?"

I opt for an answer that should create more questions. Because, yeah, I really like this brat thing. "It's true. I taste myself and I really, really like it. I'm so glad you like it too, Daddy. I can't wait to taste myself on your lips."

There's shuffling and groaning from both of the other men. Finn's expression goes dark for a few seconds before his thumb that's holding my chin brushes over my lips.

"That's right, Little One. These lips should never speak lies to Daddy. Good girls get rewarded."

I'm working up a bratty comment about where spankings fall in that continuum when there's pressure on my face to turn away from him.

I hadn't noticed Dax kneel in front of me. He leans in slowly. He's offering what I just asked for—the taste of me on his lips. If Finn touched my sex right now, I'd instantly unravel.

My scent hits me as Dax's breaths carry across the inch that's left between us. I part my lips, licking them, overeager. Then Finn's finger slides up from my chin, intercepting the kiss. His fingertip dips onto my tongue as Dax's lips make their own effort to find mine.

Dax's tongue slides over the digit. We're a sloppy tangle. We're in sync. We're—

Thoughts escape me as Daddy slides two fingers of his other hand inside of me, where they belong. The sabbatical my orgasm had been on is over. I can't see Mac but just knowing that he's watching pushes me headlong into the hardest orgasm of my life. My body convulses around Daddy's fingers. I gasp against their joined finger and mouth. We're no longer separate.

With no idea of how much time has passed, would I have ever come down from the high if they hadn't freed my mouth? I tighten my walls around Daddy's other hand, taking comfort that he's still inside me.

He acknowledges my efforts with a twitch of his fingers then slides them out, cups my sex, and says almost imperceptibly, "Only twelve hours?"

A lament? Purely out of physical need, or is he tapped into the emotional side too? Unsure if I was supposed to hear it, I tuck the comment away.

He lifts me with a little maneuvering and keeps me from crushing his erection. He must be in agony. Why am I the only one who has any of their clothes removed?

He holds me tightly into his chest, kissing the top of my head as I curl into him. It's so sweet. It's so intimate. It's so much more than a quick fuck. Is it the older guy thing? They know how to please a woman? So many of my friends talk of their

53

same-aged boyfriends offering little more than enthusiasm or porn-fueled ridiculousness.

I expected these three to be ravenous beasts rutting into me when they found out I was a virgin. It's not like that at all.

"Mack, why don't you strip down while she takes a minute to rest," Dax says.

"Um...yeah...okay...right, my turn. Got it." The poor guy has a lot to live up to. With his inexperience, this is likely to be closer to my friends' experiences. I'm too snuggled in to look, but the sounds tell me clothes are hitting the floor.

The rumble of Daddy's voice through his chest soothes me. "Little One is more than ready for a cock."

Should I thank him for managing this situation?

The couch dips beside us. When I peek my eyes open, I smile at Mac. Energy flows into me, pushing the exhaustion away. The tingles in my sex heighten. Shifting a little, I lower my gaze to Mac's erection. Are they all this big?

Dax has taken a seat next to the couch and strokes the outline of his erection. It seems they've all got my vibrator beat.

Still secured in Daddy's arms, I return my eyes to Mac's. "Are you ready?"

"As long as you are, Roxy." He caresses the back of his fingers down my shin. I wiggle to sit up and Daddy helps me, even gives me a little nudge to straddle Mac's lap. It's insane how Daddy handles me with such ease.

I glance from Mac to Daddy. "On the couch?"

"Anywhere you want," Mac says.

I toss away the earlier thoughts of being splayed in his bed. Unsure if Mac is ready to handle a brat, I opt for clarity. "Okay, right here."

Reaching for his cock, I stop and ask, "Can I touch you?"

Was that weird? It's currently trapped between his naked, rock-hard abs and my dress, and presumably, I'll be doing a lot more than touching it.

"You can do anything you want, Roxy. I'll tell you if you somehow manage to find something I don't like."

We exchange smiles and a moment of tenderness. This doesn't feel like it should end in twelve hours.

Trailing my finger over his tip, I'm surprised by the smoothness of the swollen head. My tongue slides over my lips. His shaft is more textured, veiny, but so freaking hard. I shift on his lap as my sex begs to find out how he'll feel inside of me. Way better than fingers is my guess.

He lifts the furry white edge of my skirt. "Can I undress you?"

"Wait! That's my job," Dax interrupts. No one objects as Dax unzips the back of my dress and gathers the bottom, especially not me. Fitting with his comments about going slowly, he takes his time peeling the fabric over my body.

Finn and Mac look like they're about to drool as my sex is exposed, then my tummy. I lift my arms overhead and don't get to see their expressions when my breasts are revealed, covered by a bra. Maybe that's not as exciting.

I don't know what becomes of my dress, but Mac shifts his eyes from my tits to my face. Does he feel guilty for ogling me?

The brat can help with that. I cup my hands over my bra, pushing the girls together. "Go ahead and look. I do it even more often than I taste my naughty sauce."

*Naughty sauce*? Not sure where that came from but it warrants choked laughter from each of them. Finn's reaction morphs into a throat clearing, and since I'm in brat mode, I ignore him and keep my eyes firmly planted on Macalister the Virgin. I'd never thought I'd be someone's first.

Dax's hands are back on me as he unhooks my strapless bra and carefully guides it around my body.

Mac swallows hard. The muscles in his neck flex. I trail a finger between my breasts, down my belly, and into my curls. Jesus, I'm even wetter than I thought.

I'm not generally the type of person to get nervous, so it's not entirely weird that I'm oddly comfortable. I can't say the same for Mac. Stress is etched in his features. Lifting my finger, I tap it on his lips.

"Since you're the only one who hasn't had a taste..."

His tongue darts out, licking my fingertip and his hand grips my wrist, maneuvering my finger into his mouth. After he's sufficiently gotten me funneled toward my next orgasm from sucking my finger, which I didn't know was possible, he looks at Dax then Finn.

"If you guys are going to offer some pointers, you better hurry."

His attention turns to me. "I need to do this right now."

I brace my hands on his shoulders and lift on my knees, allowing him to notch himself at my entrance.

Daddy offers, "You have to remember this isn't all about you. It's about her. So, before you blow your load, take it down a notch."

The sternness in Daddy's last statement feeds my brat, but before I can say anything, Daddy wraps his hand around Mac's cock. Mac and I gasp in unison as Finn pulls it out from under my needy sex, and presses it against Mac's stomach. What the heck?

"Sit back, Little One."

"I don't want to."

"You can't just jump on every guy who gets a dick out for you. He's got to make this right."

"Please Daddy, it would be really, really right to do this." I'm apparently not above begging. My body's thrumming with desire. My sex is literally tightening around nothing, practicing its primitive programming to milk a cock.

Daddy looks toward my butt, and while I'm tempted to stick it out and taunt him, I have an even stronger desire to have sex.

I obediently sit on Mac's strong thighs. Finn shifts sideways on the couch, letting go of Mac's shaft in the process. The heat of his length slaps against me. If I had more skill doing this, I'd pop up and sink onto it, but I don't want to mar this evening with a trip to the ER.

"You've got the most perfect set of tits." Mac's breaths are ragged.

"She's sitting right there and you haven't even touched them." Daddy lifts Mac's hand and cups it under my breast. The mingling of their thick fingers into my soft mound makes my breaths match Mac's.

Daddy frees his hand and trails it lower. "And look at that belly. It's a little flat for my taste. I'd like to see—"

"See it swollen with a baby?" Mac shoots a nervous glance at Finn.

I tuck that odd comment away with Finn's lament about twelve hours. And yet... Nope. Not going there. Thankfully Finn resumes his suggestions.

"She's perfect. Look at those cute blonde ringlets. Why aren't your hands in those pulling her in for a kiss? You're gonna get to fuck her. We all know that. Do it right." Finn pauses. "And since I know you're almost ready to blow since your dick swelled when I touched it—"

"I...it... No, it didn't," Max stutters.

"Don't worry, Mac. It's all good. I'll let you repay me."

Does that mean what I think it means?

Finn keeps going. "But when you get inside that tight pussy you're not going to last. You better have her on the edge of climax before you stretch her around your tip. You got that?"

"Yes, sir."

Flutters wisp through me at Mac calling Finn "sir". Why is that so hot? Why is any of this so hot? I don't know. But I'm pretty sure I'm ruined for any kind of normal sexual experience.

# Eight

## Mac

"I'll slow down, Roxy, and make sure you enjoy this." I'm nervous. I glance at the other two guys. No pressure. I return my gaze to the gorgeous woman in front of me. It's her first time too. I guess I shouldn't be surprised by her confidence after her stage performance during the auction.

For a moment I question whether the whole thing's a ruse. They could have hired Roxy to take my virginity, for all I know. But there's no way the guys could have found out. And she's intensely sincere.

Instead of Finn's dominant approach, I go for a gentler one and address her.

"I figured my first time would be special. And here it is. I didn't expect it to be with someone like you."

Her gaze narrows and she tilts her head. "I don't think that came out quite how you meant for it to Mack. Maybe you should stop talking."

Fuck. I'm gonna screw this up. I cup both of my hands around her jaw. "Roxy, you're the most beautiful woman I've ever laid eyes on. You're sweet. You're sassy. And it turns out your bratty in a really hot way. You're everything I ever dreamed of."

She winks at me. "You're one lucky guy."

I lean forward while I pull her toward me. The kiss verges on too much. My cock and balls are teaming up for release. It's a shame to pull away, but it's the only way I can keep from covering her belly with my cum.

I don't want it *on* her belly, but *in* it.

Building the anticipation, as I was instructed to do, I caress every one of her curves, memorizing them.

My earlier comment about getting her pregnant had blurted out of my mouth, and I'd assumed the guys would rake me over the coals for getting attached. Nobody said a word.

There was simply a hint of a smile on her lips.

I can't explore that though. Can't risk scaring her off. I also can't shake the swell of my chest that I'll be the first to mark her as mine. Her first ever. And like a total asshole, which I'm usually not, I hope to get her pregnant.

It's not an idle thought though. I've done a deep dive into it. With all the planning she's put into the auction and the general busyness of the holidays, maybe she didn't take her birth control pill one day, or she messed it up somehow and it's not effective, and there's nothing stopping my seed from shooting into her womb and putting a baby inside of her.

My heart might as well be in her hands as I lean away because I can't exist without her. Finn and Dax may be fine with walking away in the morning, but I plan on showing her where to put her toothbrush. I don't see her as a fling in my past, or even just in the present. Roxy is my future.

I memorize the contours from her lips to her chin. The dip at the junction of her neck and shoulder and the soft slope of her breast. Her rosy nipples are beaded, teasing me more than any Christmas present ever has.

She's my Christmas cherry, and I'm hers. We're swapping the most intimate gift. Trust.

I smooth along the curve of her waist until I lower my thumb to her center. Her little gasp and the wiggle of her hips when I find her clit save me from embarrassment. She's the only woman I've ever touched like this.

Porn has provided a vague semblance of what to do, although I don't expect it to play out like those fabricated marathon sessions. Her body is my best guide as she gently rocks and moans.

My mind is put at ease that I am going to give her an orgasm. Isn't that every man's worst fear? Well, maybe just every good man's worst fear.

"Roxy, I want to take my time exploring every inch of your body and I will, but right now, I need to get you good and ready.

I need to be one with you." My last comment might be too intimate. Fuck if I know, but she seems to like it.

Her expression is soft yet aroused. She does some kind of whimper moan and I can't wait any longer. I ease a hand under her ass lifting her, and god, her ass is fucking luscious. No wonder Dax took her the way he did.

She follows my lead and neither of us has to touch my cock to get it into place. Although secretly, I wish Finn would slip a hand in to assist. It's not necessary. The damn thing has a mind of its own and positions itself with innate skill.

She eases down. The wet heat of her curls drowns me in heaven. I don't even need a fucking orgasm it feels so good. I could exist inside of her forever. But this won't get her pregnant. I resume the circles on her clit while she cautiously lowers herself. We alternate between locking eyes and sharing the moment of becoming each other's firsts, and watching my cock sink into her.

"Does it feel good to have him inside of you, Baby?" Dax asks while he comes over and sits on the edge of the couch. Finn is on the other side of us. I'm aware of them. I figure they're both jealous of me right now, but my world is centered on Roxy.

Dax strokes the side of her face when she gives a breathy agreement.

Her hands feel small as her fingers dig into my shoulders. I can't imagine what it's like for her, but for me, sliding into her is like being surrounded by perfection.

My cock swells harder and thicker with each tiny movement of her body. Every time she clamps around me, I fear it's going to be the movement that sends me over the edge. I'm so close. I've never ridden the edge for so long. Even when I've strung myself out it wasn't like this.

When she's fully seated, both of us gasp for air. Had we been holding our breaths?

"Were you being a brat, Little One? That was the slowest fuck I've ever witnessed." Finn rubs his fingers over her nipple.

I move my hand from her clit to her hip. The other hand is already holding her. I don't trust my body to take any timing requests. I might start unloading cum at any second.

"No, it was just that hard to get him in." Her laugh sends dangerous vibrations to my cock.

"Damn, Mac. Don't ruin her for us."

I don't understand the thought forming in my mind. I've never been attracted to guys before. Never had even the slightest inclination to touch or be touched by my business partners. I go with my instinct.

It's killing me not to move, but the allure of having Finn and Dax included buys me time. I meet Roxy's half-lidded eyes. "Would you be okay with them joining in?"

"What do you mean?"

I better be reading this right. "You could touch them while we finish. They could touch you, or me."

The wickedness in her smile makes my balls tighten. "We'll be a *bod quad*."

"A what?"

"I don't know what we're supposed to call it since there are four of us."

I laugh. "Bod quad it is."

With her eyes locked on mine, she says, "Would you let Daddy kiss you?"

Damn. She went for it. I beg myself not to come. Distraction...I think of all the new subscriptions we've gotten for our monthly men's boxes. Snow shoveling. Dropping the four-hundred-dollar bottle of wine. Nope, that one doesn't work. That's when I first heard her call Finn "Daddy". My cock twitches inside of her.

She gasps and grips my shoulders harder. This is torture. This is also possibly the end of my business relationship with Finn and Dax if I miscalculated.

"Yes." My answer hangs in the air. Nobody moves.

In my periphery, Finn nods.

Roxy's grin grows. "Can Dax take over on my clit?"

"Did I do it wrong?" I ask too quickly.

"Not at all. Just so that everyone has something to do in the bod quad."

"Once I start pumping you on my shaft he can."

"Works for me," Dax says.

Roxy licks her plump lips. "Then you boys better get naked because we're about to do this."

The guys jump up, stripping their clothes. I pull Roxy in for a kiss, and the slight shift makes my cock swell. My fingers tighten on her hips.

"You're mine, Roxy." I can't control myself any longer. Pumping her up and down, I watch her tits bounce as she fuels what will be my biggest release ever.

The shine of her juices on my shaft is a sight I'll never forget. I want to bathe in her sweet scent. I want to watch her as she comes. I lift my gaze and a bond settles between us. This isn't just sex. Fuck. Not for me. I hope it's not for her either.

Whatever the other two guys think, I want them in on this. But if they're not all in, I'll run off with Roxy and never look back. She can be sweet and tender or play the brat role. I love everything about her. I thrust hard against her pumps.

Dax and Finn hurry into place. Dax's arm rests on mine as he reaches for her clit. Electricity emanates from our contact. Finn grips my chin and lands his lips on mine. He's hard and demanding, leaving me stunned when he pulls away.

His focus instantly shifts to Roxy. He pinches her nipple. "Now come for us, Little One."

She strokes each of their cocks but can't keep hold as I control her body on my shaft.

Her eyes flutter shut and her pussy tightens so hard around my cock, I don't have a choice but to release, to relieve the pressure consuming me, to fill her with my seed and put a motherfucking baby in her so that she's mine forever.

She's the epitome of beauty as she comes on my cock.

The growl that fills the room may be mine. It may belong to the other two. Hard to tell since all I can focus on is Roxy, and the streams of cum hitting her from each side.

She looks good in white.

She looks even better falling limply into me as my body pushes every last drop of my seed into her womb. My cock doesn't go soft. It has to keep her full so nothing leaks out.

I hold her, stroking my fingers through her hair as her breaths drift into sleep.

# Nine

## Roxy

Mac probably has a nice house, but I wouldn't know since the only place I've been other than the living room is the bathroom. The rest of the night was spent in a tangle on blankets on the living room floor.

The tiny Christmas tree offered the only light for each of our subsequent love-making sessions—sex sessions. I need to remember it was just sex and our twelve hours are over.

The weight of someone's leg over mine, a hand on my chest, and bodies all around can't last forever.

When I allow my eyelids to flutter open, sunlight fills the room. The brightness is contrasted by the peaceful sounds of slow breaths and light snoring coming from the guys.

I debate whether I should get up or wait for them to wake up. My body's exhausted and exhilarated all at the same time. My mind is in complete chaos. The only thing *bad* about my first sexual experience will be that it can't last forever. Overall, I'm more than pleased with the choice I made.

How to move forward is a bigger question. What will sex be like with a normal guy?

Sex...such a simple word. It doesn't seem like enough. It was so perfect. There's something about the dynamic of the three of us, which of course is ridiculous. Other than the weird thing going on in Eggplant Canyon that SmorgasSmut, the social media gossip group, has been lit up over, I don't know of anyone who has a relationship like this with so many people.

I scoot free from Daddy's arm, Mac's leg, and the hand that Dax has resting in my hair. They don't wake as I step away. They're bound to be exhausted too. This will give me a chance to leave without the weird morning-after thing.

I breathe a sigh of relief when there are no messages on my phone. A glimmer of worry flashes through me and I check that I have reception. Yes. Hard to schedule a rideshare without internet access.

Studying the guys sprawled on the blankets, I take a photo. I'll never share it with anyone. It's my private reminder of a night that was too good to be true. Wanting nothing to mar the pleasant memories, I open the app and order a ride.

The guys won't have to thank me for not making this awkward. While Daddy, or probably Finn this morning, Dax, and Mac sleep peacefully, it's hard to imagine any of us feeling weird about what we did.

And yet, my friends who do hookups say it's just part of the deal—better not to sleep over, just leave after the sex. Since our last session was only a couple of hours ago, I suppose I am.

Honestly, I can't take any more sex right now. My feminine bits need a rest.

Tearing my eyes from the trio, and looking out the large picture window, the thick blanket of snow sends worry through me. Will any of the drivers be able to make it this far into the foothills? I can barely tell where the road is.

I tiptoe across the living room to gather my dress, bra, and underwear, which is not still wet, thankfully.

The morning after thing hits me. It's the walk of shame, getting a ride share from a rich guy's house in my Santa costume. Ugh. I don't want to be that girl.

I'm saved by the vibration of my phone as it alerts me to a driver who will be here in twenty minutes.

One more glance at the sleeping beasties, and I decide to raid Mac's closet. I come up with a t-shirt and a pair of sweat pants with a drawstring that allows me to basically bag myself. Then I have a debate over my heels, which are decidedly impractical in the snow, and a pair of Mac's flip-flops, which are expressly too big. I go for them. Mac isn't likely to miss them in this weather.

Besides, I plan on washing everything and sending it back. As I cross his room and pass his bed, I fight the temptation to splay myself.

My time is better spent washing my face and taming my wild hair in the few minutes before the driver arrives.

Not wanting the slappy sound of flip-flops to wake the guys, I carry the shoes as I sneak to the front door. The huge glass center of the door allows me to watch for the driver. The sparkles of the snow light up like tiny prisms. There's nothing as beautiful as when the snow sparkles.

That's what I thought until I met these guys. I move a few steps away from the door that I can still easily see through, and position myself so I can peek around the corner and watch the three wise men sleep. They're at least wise as far as sex is concerned. I'm so ruined.

An extra sparkle from outside catches my attention. A big beefy truck is here. He seems to have no trouble navigating the snowy road as I tiptoe back to the door.

Gently turning the handle, I inch the door open, and step onto the porch. I'm delicately pulling the door shut, wondering if it's even worth it to slip the flip-flops on because they're definitely not good footwear in the snow. My feet are freezing but it might be easier to go barefoot.

The door catches and I give an extra tug, hoping not to make a sound. Then the knob flies out of my hands.

Finn's standing there in his naked glory. I don't have to turn around to know that the rideshare driver can see him. Finn's eyes are on me. They shift to the truck then back.

"What the hell is going on?" He uses his Daddy voice.

The other two guys rush behind him. No one bothers to fuss with clothes.

"Who's that?" Mac and Dax say at the same time.

"I ordered a rideshare." I hop back and forth from foot to foot. Should I run to the truck? This is a higher level of awkwardness than my friends warned me about.

"Why?" all three of them ask.

I try to position my hands and use my dress to hide their private parts from the driver.

Daddy catches my hand. "That's one hell of a bratty move."

I roll my eyes.

Daddy's eyes get bigger and his grip tightens. He didn't like that.

"My twelve hours were up."

"So you were just going to wreck us and run?" Finn asks.

"You don't want to spend more time with us?" Mac sounds hurt.

"I was trying to make the morning after less awkward."

"Hey, lady, do you need a ride or what?" the driver calls out.

I turn around and raise a finger. "Hold your horses one damn minute, Scrooge."

"Look, I don't get paid unless—"

"I've got cash for you to drive away." Mac interrupts.

"I'm not supposed to take cash."

"I've got five hundred dollars that say you do." Mac makes a grand offer.

"Are you getting in or not?" the driver asks.

I chuckle but when I turn back around and see the stern look on the men's faces, my chuckle is gone.

Daddy says, "The only thing awkward right now is the fact that you're trying to leave."

"And that you're standing here naked?" I try to lighten the mood.

"We're not joking. If you're sneaking off, it means we sucked so bad you want to get out of here without a goodbye." Mac steps away.

"No, you didn't suck at all...well except when you sucked on...never mind. It was great."

Dax says, "Okay, since you didn't rate us last night, do it now. Let's see what kind of numbers yield a hit and run for our hearts."

Aren't their dangly parts getting cold?

Mac returns, waving five one-hundred-dollar bills. "Come get it. I'll drive her home if she wants to go."

While the driver steps through the snow, Mac says to me, "Come inside so we can clear this up."

Before the stranger gets to us, I whisper. "I think I overdid the sex. I need a break, so if that's why you want me to stay..."

The driver mutters something about the guys using some money to buy clothes as he rips the bills from Mac's hand. He wastes no time hurrying back to the truck. Mac clarifies that he should leave.

It's my last chance to go with him.

"We don't just want sex. We want you." Mac says.

"Seriously?" I watch as the driver pulls away.

Daddy steps to the side and swats my ass. "Get inside you little brat or we'll freeze our balls off."

"We wouldn't have to worry about protection." I wink at him.

"I wasn't joking about getting you pregnant," Mac says. It's the first time any of us have addressed his previous comment.

"But—"

Daddy scoops me up. "We'll talk about this inside, Little One."

Dax kisses my shoulder. "What the big lugs are trying to say is that we love you and don't want you to ever leave."

I glance at Mac.

"I love you, Roxy." He kisses my forehead.

My gaze shifts to Daddy, who's cradled me into his chest. "I love you too, Little One. Even when you're bratty."

Can I believe this is real? A faint sound in the distance catches our attention. Looking over Peach Bottom Valley, I catch the sound again. It's a train horn. The steam from the locomotive leaves evidence of its path. I smile and give thanks that instead of being logical, I just believed.

"I love you guys too. Now we can either go inside and talk or we can practice making those babies."

"Or if you still need to rest, Mac could pay me back for how much he liked it when I touched him earlier," Finn says.

"Rest it is!"

# Epilogue

## Roxy

**Six Years Later**

I'm about ready to pop with our third and fourth kids. As seductively as possible, which is more like a strained waddle, I stroll out of the bathroom in a red and white bra and panty set I bought years ago for frisky Christmas adventures. With twins in my belly and bigger boobs than ever, the poor bra has its work cut out for it. A nip slip is practically guaranteed.

That's fine. Anything to help with my hidden agenda.

The guys are in the bedroom pulling on wool socks and winter boots, getting ready to take the kids outside to decorate our living Christmas tree.

"Whoa, Little One." Daddy's continued use of the nickname is ridiculous given my current state, which is no longer *little* or *one* since I'm an incubator for two babies. I suppose it's just as crazy to keep calling him Daddy. He continues, "You're going to need more than that to go outside."

"I was thinking we could have a little fun first. The kids' movie won't finish for another thirty minutes."

Dax discards the boot he's about to slip his foot into. He backs me into the dresser for support then drops to his knees in front of me. His hands roam over my belly. "Are you sure?"

"I'm horny as fuck. Yes, I'm sure."

"Then let me do the honors." He tugs my panties down, spins me around, bends me over, and licks my pussy from behind. It's become a Christmas tradition, reminiscent of our first time together.

The motion causes my boob to fall out of my bra. When I scramble to unhook it, he helps.

I swear my guys would keep me in orgasms 24/7 if I'd let them. I rest my arms on the dresser and widen my stance as the orgasm winds tight. Making no effort to delay it, I come undone on Dax's face.

The euphoria that envelopes me takes away all of the pregnancy aches and pains, but I'm on a bigger mission.

Dax slides his hands up my legs, rubs them over my butt cheeks, and pushes his tip against my intimate lips.

"Oh my God, I need this so bad."

"I didn't think it was possible for you to be greedier than normal, but you're almost insatiable when you're pregnant."

His thrusts tighten the knot in my core, making me feel sexy despite my blimp-ish state.

"I don't hear anyone complaining."

"No complaints here. Are you ready for this?"

I reposition my hands on the dresser, bracing myself. My belly is always in the way so I have to be careful. "I'm ready."

"Holy fuck. How do you feel so good?"

"Can we cut the small talk, mister? I need each of you and we have limited time." What I don't tell them is that I'm ready to have these babies. I've made it past the goal date my doctor designated.

The guys make sure I don't stress myself, and they're great with the kids. It's just that I'm huge and achy, every possible internal organ has been kicked, and I'd like to have control over my bladder again.

My secret plan for today came about after I read a bunch of stuff on the internet about sex and semen inducing labor. The doctor confirmed it's real. So for the last few days, I've held off from having sex. The guys should have plenty of cum stored up. I'm considering it the triple espresso of sex.

I shift my hips backward, encouraging Dax to let loose.

"You're so fucking beautiful." He slaps my ass. That causes me to clench, which was apparently a dangerous move for him. His fingers tighten around my hips. "Shit, Baby. You feel too good. You still feel too good after all this time. I gotta go. I gotta come."

"Do it. Give me everything you've got." I smile as he thrusts into me. My body comes undone around him. As my orgasm takes hold, he swells, and in seconds, his cum fills me. Attempt number one out of the way.

When he pulls out, I don't stand up. I don't want any more of his seed uselessly running down my legs than already is.

"Come on, guys. Who's next?" It's not exactly that I've learned to separate sex from emotion, because I have more feels than I know what to do with, but I'm on a mission.

"Is Little One getting bossy?"

"You love it. Now, drop your socks and grab your cocks." I sass them.

Dax says, "You really need to get your Little One under control, Daddy."

Mac and Finn crack up.

"The mouth on that thing is something else." Daddy's voice comes from across the room.

I'm resting my head on my arms so I don't see who steps up next. The mystery is solved when a hand rubs up and down my butt cheek.

Time to play. "The mouth on this thing happens to be your very favorite mouth in the entire world, Daddy."

The sharp smack to my rear sends jolts of excitement through me.

He says, "It very well may be, but I'll still spank you for being a brat."

"You love it. Now, why don't you put your cock to work and give me an orgasm before we run out of time."

His cock pushes into my slick lips, not the sassy ones. I'd expected another spanking, but this is perfect.

"I swear, Little One, you're going to be the death of me."

"Then you better hurry and give me one more orgasm."

He grabs my hair and pulls my head back. The final shred of control escapes me, and I can't even enjoy the laugh with Mac and Dax as my body milks his cock.

Only a few minutes passed since Dax filled me, so hopefully, I absorbed all of his seed and there's room for Daddy's.

Warm streams of his release drip down my legs. Dang it, I must be full. He loosens his grip on my hair and rubs my head as he often does when he worries he pulled too hard. Impossible. Plus, tenderness is not what I need right now.

I need dick number three because I'm ready to self-induce my labor. "The kids' movie won't last any longer just because you want to be all sweet. Mac still needs a turn."

Finn cracks up as he steps away. "Anyone else feel like we're being used?"

"Yeah, she acts like we haven't been watching the calendar too...like we don't know that the safe date just passed. It's like our cocks are tools she can use at will," Mac jokes.

"Aww, did I hurt everyone's feelings by not kissing you and telling you I love you before asking to be fucked?"

The guys bust out laughing.

"Alright, horny lady, I'm going to give it my best shot. You've been tired, your back hurts, and we're all ready to meet these babies. Cross your fingers."

"She should be crossing her legs," Dax says. It's true.

Mac slides his hand through the slickness coating my inner thigh. "I bet she'd let you catch all of this cum dripping out and feed it to her to see if it helps."

I'm about to tell him that's not a bad idea when he slides his cock in to the hilt. My body stretches around him. I gasp for breaths. I'm the luckiest woman in the world to have guys who enjoy letting me be my bratty self and are always up for giving me an orgasm.

"Mommy, when are we going to decorate the tree," Mary's voice calls from the other room.

"Just a minute," Finn replies since I'm still gathering myself. "Get your coats on. We need about ten seconds to finish up."

He's mocking Mac for his initial performance. If I could reach Finn, I'd spank him for the joke, which way underestimates Mac's stamina that first night. He made it at least a minute.

That first night holds a special place for all of us, and teasing happens for all of them. The other guys mock Finn for the way I call him Daddy. Dax is always the first to pop a boner and gets teased about whether he remembers that there's more to our relationship than sex.

As if on cue, Mac's cock swells, pushing me past the point of no return. I climax around him and he fills me with his seed in his effort to help me induce labor.

I kind of miss not being able to look into his eyes, because even six years later, I still remember our first time together.

He rubs his hands over my back. "You guys go on. I'm going to keep my cock in place—doing my part to keep all of that cum inside Roxy."

"Thanks, Mac." Finn leads Dax to the door then turns back to us. "You aren't just buying yourself time to go another round with her, are you?"

"If she wants it...she gets it."

The guys groan and head out, giving me time to keep as much labor-inducing semen in me as possible.

Mac and I have a few minutes before the decorating will start anyway. The kids have to pick a tree first, and there are a lot to choose from on his property in the Cherry Ridge Foothills.

Inside the house, we keep Mac's tiny tree—a reminder of our bodies sprawled underneath it the night we met.

"I love you, Roxy," Mac says.

"Love you too." My body tenses as the first contraction takes hold.

His hand stills on my back. "What's that?"

"I think our mission is accomplished."

"As in starting labor? It worked?" He slides his hand onto my belly. "Oh, hell yeah. That's a contraction, isn't it?"

Between breaths, I say, "Definitely so."

He pulls out, retrieves a warm washcloth, and cleans me up. He's always been tender like that. The other guys do it too, but there's something special about the way Mac does it. He rubs my back and kisses my temple until the contraction subsides.

"Can you help me get one last shower before we go to the hospital?"

He helps me wash and condition my hair, combs it out, and dresses me. I love the way my guys care for me.

Not wanting to take away from the tree decorating excitement, I say, "There's enough time between contractions, let's decorate the tree with the kids before telling anyone."

"I'd rather take you to the hospital right now."

"Not yet. But you can call your parents and have them meet us here."

It's a deal. Mac helps me cover the contractions while we decorate the tree.

When grandma and grandpa walk into the backyard, the other two guys eye me suspiciously.

"Why are they here?" Finn asks.

"Because you guys did a great job. We're going to the hospital."

"Fuck yeah. Sorry," Finn says and covers his mouth.

"You're a bad Daddy," Mary chastises him.

He wraps her in a hug. "I'll do better."

When Mary drags her little sister Joy to the grandparents, I give Finn a wink. "I think you're a very good bad Daddy."

"Watch your mouth, Little One."

Another contraction hits, preventing me from having more fun.

The guys huddle around, and when it lets up, they get me to the porch where the grandparents have corralled the kids.

Everybody joins in a group hug, we exchange I love yous, and they carry the kiddos inside.

"You ready to do this?" Dax asks as he grabs the bags.

"Nah, changed my mind."

Mac laughs, "You should have expected that."

Finn shakes his head. "Yes, you should have." Then he turns to me. "What did I do to deserve a brat like you?

"If I'm not mistaken, you bid on me, asked me to call you Daddy...and helped me believe that true love could make a bod quad work."

And we live happily ever after!

Bonus content is available for Sparkles and Spankings by signing up for my newsletter.

https://www.SylvieHaas.com

# Presents and Praise

## A Reverse Harem Romance

Sylvie Haas

# Blurb

**Just when I think things can't get any worse...my stepbrothers win me in an auction!**

When one of my best friends begs me to auction myself at the fire department fundraiser, I can't tell her no.

I also can't stop worrying that no one will bid on a plain-Jane girl like me, even for four hours of simple tasks like cleaning and gift wrapping.

Then the bidding starts, and I find out that there is something worse than not getting bid on. My three, wealthy, gorgeous stepbrothers make a spectacle and run my bid super high.

The only way I've been able to hide my attraction to them is to keep my distance. How will I do that when they win four hours of my time?

And if that's not bad enough, I find out they don't want help with chores. They want me—their untouched stepsister. I'd be a fool to turn them down, but aside from the obvious problem of our relatedness, my heart is incapable of understanding the limitations of our four-hour time block.

If you love dirty-talking men who have over-the-top ideas of how to please their woman and want to give her babies, enroll yourself in the Christmas Cherry Auction!

# *One*

# Maggie

The anticipation of putting myself onstage in front of everyone for the silent auction Roxy talked me and Izzy into has been terrifying. Luckily, as I walk toward the auctioneer without my glasses, I can't see the audience. That helps ease my nerves.

If the auction wasn't for such a good cause, there's no way I'd be able to stand in front of this many people to basically sell myself.

I probably shouldn't think of it as selling. The winner only gets four hours of my time for things like help with holiday prep or cleaning... *Rent myself?* Not much better.

The auctioneer opens the bidding at a hundred dollars and it escalates rapidly. My fear of no one wanting to bid on me is quickly put to rest.

The bidders are announced by number, and a few—thirteen, seventeen, and twenty-four continue when the others drop out. Based on the direction Jefferson, our auctioneer, is pointing and the slight turn as he addresses each bidder, they're spread out around the room, too far away for me to make out any details. They're intermingled in the mass of indistinguishable people.

With the bids approaching the four-thousand-dollar mark, we should easily be able to raise the twenty-thousand needed for the fire department's new gear since I'm one of six people who agreed to participate in this crazy auction. Maybe the fire department can get even more new gear than planned.

A tiny voice inside of me says I should ask the auctioneer to remind the bidders that I'm only offering four hours of my time. I've read plenty of romance novels about virgin auctions, and even though I would qualify, Peach Bottom Valley doesn't hold those.

A chuckle bubbles through me. Roxy and Izzy would also be candidates, and we chose skimpy Santa's helper dresses to...look enticing. My stomach knots. Have we made a serious mistake?

I walk to Jefferson and put a finger to my lips to get him to stop. He cracks a joke about needing to take a breath and leans down. I cup my hand beside my mouth and whisper, "Could you please remind the bidders that this is for four hours of general help, nothing more."

He furrows his brow. "I'm guessing your brothers understand that."

"My what?" Efforts to stay quiet falter. Thankfully Jefferson doesn't have the microphone near my mouth.

"Your brothers. They're the three bidders. Aren't you watching?"

"I took my glasses off. I had no idea. How humiliating."

His expression shifts to concern. "It's a fundraiser. Let them have a dick-measuring contest over who can donate the most money."

Tingles roll through my body at the mention of dicks and my stepbrothers. They're gorgeous—my stepbrothers, not their dicks. Well, I haven't seen their dicks, so I don't actually know. In my fantasies, those are gorgeous too, though.

Pulling myself back from familiar fantasyland, since I'm on stage in front of friends and family, I remind myself that I'm not the heroine of a romance novel, and this won't end well. My step-brothers are way older and were always annoyed by me. They probably want to torment me for four hours.

Humiliation returns. "Could you just like...speed this up so I can be put out of my misery?"

"This is going great. It's awesome that your family is so generous."

"Please, it's embarrassing being bought by my brothers."

He nods. "I have an idea."

"Thanks." As I offer him a weak smile, I turn to the audience and put on a big one. *It's awesome that my family is so generous.* Right.

As the bidding creeps over the six-thousand mark, I question if Jefferson's idea was simply to resume the bidding. Well played.

All I have to do is suck it up and let the bidding keep happening. I pull up the memory of the little boy who sat on Santa's lap and asked the big guy to bring his dad safer fire-fighting clothes. It happened when I was working a shift with Roxy, Izzy, and Jade at the Santa photo booth. That's what prompted Roxy to organize this big fundraiser.

We're helping keep fire fighters safe.

Jefferson continues rambling and pointing so I do my part and let it happen.

This was never about dating, so I push aside the silly disappointment that I'm not being bought by a billionaire. If I want to date more, I have to do it by other means than selling myself. When will I find a guy who can handle my big brain? That's not exactly what I'd like a guy to be handling but it seems to be the stumbling block for most males.

The room falls silent. Did I miss a winner being announced? I glance at Jefferson, who's blurry since I've wandered to the far side of the stage.

"You three are giving my vocal cords a workout. You gotta give a guy a break, I'm just a volunteer auctioneer."

Laughter rolls through the audience.

Jefferson resumes speaking into the microphone. "I've got an idea... You've run the bids over seven thousand and honestly, I'm tempted to see how high you'll go, but I have a proposition."

I stare at him, wondering if I should be worried. My brothers quickly express interest.

"Since you're each willing to donate more than seven thousand dollars to the fire department, and the goal is to raise twenty thousand total, what would you say about making a collective twenty-thousand-dollar donation, and you're all listed as winners?"

I'm regretting taking my glasses off since I can't discern what's happening in the flurry of activity. Based on the blurry forms I can make out, my brothers are moving closer to the stage and huddling for discussion. Otherwise, chatter has erupted.

I don't recall any rules against pooling resources, but that's even worse than one of them winning me. Anyone want my input? At least we've clarified that all I'm offering is four hours, nothing more.

"Sold," Jameson booms over the fray.

My heart stills.

I've been auctioned to my stepbrothers.

Reality sinks in. I would have preferred that no one bid than to have to commit four hours of my time to my gorgeous-as-sin, jerk stepbrothers, who spent years doing nothing other than picking on me and excluding me—their annoying little stepsister.

Jefferson clarifies the arrangement over the PA. Wonderful. Let's announce to the world that I'm a loser who got a pity bid from my brothers.

Meanwhile, I'll fake a smile, ignore the bile rising in my throat, and remember that my selflessness will benefit a worthy cause.

Wishing I could see this with my own eyes, I squint—not a becoming look according to my mother. Even without the ability to focus, they're now close enough for me to make out their thick bodies, their mannerisms, and their pure sex appeal. I swear these guys have some kind of pheromones that are designed to make me swoon.

And that's the problem...as annoying as they are, they make parts of me tingle that aren't appropriate.

Most of the girls from high school would have given a kidney to get bid on by my brothers. My siblings were hunky teenagers, then handsome young men, then the bad boys of Peach Bottom Valley. They'd been the heartbreakers. And yet, these three gorgeous men that I'm not biologically related to are completely off-limits.

If I hadn't been their little stepsister, would I have stood a chance with them? They're smart. They could handle a woman with a brain.

*They.* I scoff at myself.

My nerves rise up as Jefferson directs me to meet them at the winner's table. I question if I'm going to vomit on the stage. But in the fashion that my mother taught me to always hold my composure, I plaster a smile on my lips, wave at the crowd...then wonder why the hell I waved.

I rush off the stage. The second I step behind the thick black curtain, my smile fades, and I head to the counter where I set my glasses.

The next mission will be to find my brothers and set this straight. What that means exactly, I'm not sure. Something along the lines of clarifying that I'm required to help them, not put up with rudeness.

Roxy should be taking the stage but ignores her name being announced over the PA. It takes me a minute, but I convince her that I'll be fine, and remind her to do her part to raise money. Then on to my more difficult task.

Flinging the side door open, I set out to find my nemeses, and promptly crash into a wall of muscle—make that three walls of muscle. The scent of Axe body wash floods me with memories. I lift my gaze confirming that the three men I crashed into are the three who just bought me.

Now is not the time to go down the rabbit hole of my eternal attraction to them. Well, eternal might be a stretch, but I've looked up to them my whole life. The attraction component didn't surface until I started noticing boys as more than friends, and my hunky stepbrothers were in their prime, ranging from four to ten years older than me.

A chuckle rumbles through my chest that Bradford, who prefers to be called Ford now, still wears Axe. He's the oldest, and at thirty years old makes a gazillion bucks. They all do. Why would he still wear that? He could afford something much more elegant and sophisticated.

That is not a helpful thought. I step back, steady myself, and cross my arms. "You can't bid on me."

"We already did, and we won," Bradford says.

"Tell them you take it back."

"That's not how auctions work," Heathcliff explains. Their given names are as clunky as my Magdalena.

"There has to be some kind of family and friends clause. Isn't it wrong to buy family members?" I'm grasping at straws.

"Well, technically, buying humans is wrong so I think we've already crossed that line," Jameson says.

"Okay...so...right... We can't buy humans, which means you're not buying me. You're just donating money to the fire department, and you're not actually going to require me to give you four hours of my time to clean or cook or gift wrap or anything. You have assistants for all of that. You don't need me to do anything for you, right?" I force myself to stop rambling. If the universe is ever going to help me manifest my desires, now would be a great time.

Would it help if I drop to my knees and beg? I maintain a shred of self-respect and opt not to.

"We won you fair and square. You owe us four hours," Jameson says calmly.

"That works out to eighty minutes each. What am I going to do for you in eighty minutes? I mean, can't we just move on? I'm your annoying little stepsister. You've never wanted to hang out with me. Please don't make me do this."

My attempt at casual and flippant turns to begging. I lock my knees to keep from dropping to the ground.

"We kind of hope you want to, and it's good to see you're still fast with that mental math," Ford says.

"Yeah. Well, I don't. You teased me mercilessly, so I'd like to walk away from this and you can still make your twenty-thousand-dollar donation to the fire department. We'll call it good. And I promise I'll be nice at Christmas dinner, just like mom asked."

The adults in my life always said that when boys teased me, they liked me. The sibling component threw a wrench in that theory. Why can't I get over the fact that they don't see me as the opposite sex? Everyone knows that when it comes to gender, there are boys, girls, and siblings—who are supposed to defy sexual attraction.

If only my libido would have gotten the message.

"We won you fair and square," Heath reiterates Jameson's statement. "And you're going to give us each our eighty minutes." He winks.

My legs get a little bit weaker.

I want to shrivel up and die. It might be the only way to keep my mind from enjoying how demanding my brothers are being. It's not as if they have an ulterior motive like in my romance novels.

The Axe body wash must be getting to me. The heat level in the hallway has escalated at least ten degrees, my stomach is more fluttery than nauseous, and my girly parts are all tingly. Desperate to get away from them to give my big brain a chance to find a solution, I storm off. I stride past the seating area for the auction, and down the long hallway to the other end of the school, passing the classrooms that I attended only a couple of years ago.

Safely away from everyone, I lean against the lockers and let my head fall back with a clank on the flimsy metal. Can this really be happening? What if my brothers catch me looking at them too long or what if I say something embarrassing about how attractive they are? I made that slip once in front of them and their friends. Never experiencing that level of humiliation again would be just fine. Ford promptly explained in no uncertain terms that he's not into incest.

Before I could stop my mouth from letting my brain point out that stepsiblings don't share a blood relation, thus there was no incest, I made the situation worse.

Speaking of friends, Roxy should be on stage and I'm not there to see how her bidding's going. I trudge back, squeezing past the double doors at the end of the hallway, then hover at the back of the auction room where I hope no one will notice me.

I can barely see over the shoulder of the guy in front of me. It's Mammoth, the bartender at the biker bar in the Cherry Ridge foothills. When he offers to let me stand in front of him, I grab his arm and let him know that I'd rather stay hidden. Makes no difference to him.

The bidding is halted for some kind of negotiation, and Roxy ends up getting won by three billionaire-looking guys. They also settled on the full twenty thousand. Wow! Lucky her...at least in my fantasy brain.

In reality, there's only a smidge more likelihood that anything *fun* will come of her situation than mine.

Then Isadora takes the stage, and the bids on her skyrocket too. I'm truly thrilled that the auction is such a massive success.

While the bids on Izzy are coming from several tables around the room, one table, in particular, seems dead set on not letting anyone else win. Their bidder's paddle is in the air constantly. The trio doesn't even bring it down once they've been acknowledged.

Izzy has a thing for the broody, rugged type. It's way past time to get my fantasy brain in check. This isn't a virgin auction.

I'm also curious if Sasha is going to make good on the rumor that she's going to buy all three firefighters. She just got over a nasty breakup, and while she says she'd just like to have a little man candy around the house, we all think she has ulterior motives.

The three firefighters are also part of the local MC that Mammoth is in. He must want a front-row seat to watch his friends get bid on because he leaves our post at the back wall and chooses a spot much closer to the stage when the first guy takes the stage.

I glance around the room, wondering where our other friend, Jade went. I'd seen her talking to the high school principal right before the bidding started. Haven't seen her since. Or him for that matter.

She's only nineteen, just a year younger than the rest of us, but was too nervous to let people bid on her, so she's supposed to be helping with the soup pot luck.

Dang it. I'm exposed. James sees me, and with a quick "Hey," he and his brothers head toward me from three directions. I tug the top of my strapless dress up. That only reveals more of my legs. Oops.

"Let's go," James says, reaching for my hand.

"I don't have to do my hours right now."

"Might as well get them over with."

"I'll call you tomorrow."

"No, you won't. You're stalling." Heath calls my bluff.

"I'll do it. I promise."

"Are you busy tonight?" Ford asks.

Since I planned on being at the auction, they know I'm not busy.

"Exactly. Let's go." Ford leans down, grabs my hand, and tosses me over his shoulder.

I pound on his back to put me down, but quickly realize my short skirt has ridden up. Reaching behind myself, I fail to tug it down. Thankfully, James comes up with a solution. He gathers all three bidder paddles and holds them up behind my butt.

My worry about not getting bid on is long forgotten. My brothers have found new heights of embarrassment for me.

# Two

# Maggie

After a lot of grumbling, I convince Ford to drive to my house so we can sort this out. It's the only strand of control I have. And I'm barely hanging onto it.

The thing that most unsettles me is that I want to let go.

I liked being over Ford's shoulder. I liked James paying attention to my butt. I liked the way Heath helped me to the ground so gently when we got to the car.

Sitting in the backseat next to Heath, I saw him reply to a text from his dad saying that they couldn't hang out with him because they have other plans.

Me. I am the plan. My heart flutters at the potential.

My plan for the evening had been to swap my skimpy Santa dress for sweatpants and a baggy t-shirt that Jameson doesn't know I stole from him a couple of years ago. His scent is long gone, but I love being surrounded by...him.

I also planned on putting a scoop of mulling spices into the diffuser, simmering it in apple juice, then popping my fuzzy-sock-covered feet up while I enjoy the hot apple cider from my favorite mug while watching the Hallmark Channel.

My Plan A cautiously gives way to Plan B as I lead the three of them up the stairs to my apartment. If only I understood what Plan B entailed.

The ringtone for my mom ripples through the night air as I step onto my private balcony. Does she have some kind of mom radar for reminding us to be nice to each other?

I click the screen to ignore the call.

Before unlocking my door, I turn to the guys and say, "My house, my rules. No picking on the little sister. No ganging up on me. No—"

"We're not your idiotic teenage brothers anymore. We've matured. I promise. We know how to treat a woman." James caresses the back of his hand over my cheek.

Wooziness washes over me as I imagine a flicker of interest. Will I really get what I wanted all these years? Can I forgive them for all the big brother taunts? Every cell of my being wants to believe him.

Turning to the door, I hold the knob as much for stability as to unlock and open it. I step into the entry nook, and motion for the guys to go to the right, which leads to the living room and kitchen. The opposite way opens to a small hallway with a bathroom and bedroom. I guess the designer thought an official entry would make the apartment feel nicer.

Heath and Ford make themselves comfortable on my couch, but James waits in the entry while I lock the door.

"Go ahead. Make yourself at home."

The flicker of interest I'd seen is no longer a flicker and has become more mischievous. Is he holding back a taunt? I study him, noting that he hasn't changed his bad boy haircut that parts on one side and the long bangs hang down, grazing his eyes.

I shake off the way-too-familiar attraction my body betrays me by harboring. My defensive walls seem like a better option.

"Not changing your haircut in seven years isn't exactly a sign that you've matured, but whatever."

Those damn bangs still make my sex tingle, still cause me to have trouble breathing, and I still want to be the woman he gives a smoldering gaze to as he looks through them.

But alas, I'm his stepsister who he just bought at a charity auction so we might as well get to making amends. At least mom will be happy.

I sidestep to leave him alone in the confined space. He can stay there if he wants.

My next footfall should take me around him, but he grabs my wrist—gently. Electricity shoots through me. God, what my body does at his touch. It's ridiculous. He tightens his grip, pulling me back.

"What?" I ask, keeping my gaze averted.

"Hey." How can a single word, spoken in a soft, deep tone bust through my defenses?

I lift my gaze. James's eyes meet mine. Not quite the smoldering gaze, but it's intense. Then lifts his eyes upward and tips his head slightly before he looks back down at me. A wicked grin breaks over his lips.

I don't have to look up to know what he looked at. The question in my brain... Why is James, of all people, pointing out that we're standing under the mistletoe?

"No thanks." I dismiss his offer.

"But you love mistletoe."

"I do. But you made it painfully clear on the Christmas after my eighteenth birthday that you would rather kiss a cactus than kiss me under the mistletoe."

"Yeah... well, I was wrong. And even if it was true, I was an ass to say that. Let me prove that I've matured." The pitch of his voice is laced with secret panty-melting ingredients.

I have no idea what Heath and Ford are doing, but I presume they're watching since I detect their eyes boring into me.

Then the world fades and all I can think about is how much I want to kiss James. Am I so easily forgetting how I'd wanted a little peck at that ill-fated Christmas party when he turned me away in front of friends and family? Has my insane imagination learned nothing?

I surrender to his efforts, allowing him to pull me closer until the lengths of our bodies are touching. My neck instinctively cranes to meet his deep brown eyes.

There's nothing brotherly there. This has to be a prank. If I'm going to revert to Plan E, for Escape, I better do it fast.

I snap out of the mental trance but continue to enjoy the way he holds me. "Are you about to lecture me on how stupid it is to kiss under poisonous plants? Isn't that how you phrased it when you stormed away from me?"

"Like I said, I was an idiot."

"Yeah, so, apology accepted." Now I feel like an idiot. He didn't apologize. Okay. I clearly can't think when I'm close enough to see the tiny flex of gold in the brown of his irises. This is not good.

"You got it all wrong, Maggie. Not that there was any other way for you to get it. I was hiding. I was frustrated by my attraction to you. I felt guilty like I was betraying the family by how badly I wanted you."

"Oh, right. I'm supposed to believe that you refused to give me a peck on the cheek and embarrassed me because you liked me. You have no idea how hard it is to be the shy, nerdy, plain girl who never gets asked out."

He raises an eyebrow, causing me to realize my slip.

I scramble. "Not that I wanted you to ask me out. I just wanted to have fun with a simple sprig of mistletoe at a silly Christmas party where everybody else had been willing to humor me with a peck on the cheek. But no... you freaked and ran out of the room."

"I'm sorry about that."

"I guess you didn't get to hear the musings that maybe you had to vomit. Wasn't that what you said, Heath?" In the split second when I spin around to face our other two brothers, indeed, Heath and Ford are staring at me. But it's not humor in their eyes. It's not revolt or confusion. I swear, it's lust. Yeah, I'm going to call it lust because attraction is too much for my brain to process.

Heath stammers. "I...well... I'm sorry, Maggie. It was a bad joke."

James spins me back to face him and cups my neck in his hands. The smolder. Oh my god, it's in his eyes—the look I've always wanted. In slow motion, he leans down. I'm faintly aware that his lips have parted and I'm licking mine.

Am I going to let this happen? He pauses, mere inches from my lips. I try to anticipate the punchline, to be ready for the reveal, but even as I try to steel myself, I'm putty in his arms. I'm weak against his gaze.

He drops his lips to my ear. "I've wanted you for too long, Maggie. I know it's wrong. I ran because I couldn't hold back the erection I was getting for my little sister, who had finally turned eighteen. I'd played out too many fantasies of what I would say to you. And when you pulled me under the mistletoe for a kiss, it didn't matter that I'd watched you do the same with our grandfather, with the neighbor, with your friends, even your girlfriends. None of it mattered. I was under the mistletoe with you and I couldn't control myself."

His lips trail over my cheek and crash into mine, obliterating my world. The kiss is chaste in a way. There's no tongue. But there's nothing innocent about it. It's not a peck on the cheek. It's not a simple kiss. It's a promise of everything he's repressed. He's waiting for permission.

Or is that me? Is that my side of what's happening? I'm so confused.

He pulls back. My eyes are closed, and my lungs struggle to sustain me. He says, "Please tell me you feel the same way."

This isn't how the stepbrother porn I shamelessly watch works out. I pray that James doesn't remember the time he caught me watching it. On the videos, there's always some silly setup that's all about sex. I have too many feelings.

I have to figure out how to handle this. How to move forward. Escape...that's a nice option. "I tell you what, go sit down, and I'll grab drinks. And by drinks, I mean water."

Rushing to the kitchen, I keep my eyes on the ground and hurry past Heath and Ford. I can't deal with all of the confusing emotions bubbling inside of me like a witch's cauldron.

I pull cups out of the cabinet then realize I could offer the hot apple cider I planned for myself, but when I turn, Ford is right behind me.

"I'll get it. Why don't you have a seat at the bar," he says.

The bar. That's a nice way to put the counter that divides the living room from the kitchen. Since my legs are about to give out, I accept his offer. I add the option of mulling spices and apple juice, which everyone agrees to, and he gets to work.

Perhaps Heath doesn't want to be outdone because he rushes into the kitchen to help.

James walks up behind me, rests his hands on my shoulders, then whispers in my ear. "Remember that time I caught you watching porn?"

So, he does remember.

"It was just—"

"I know your kink." He puts a finger to my lips to shush me. "I can give you that fantasy."

Breathe. Stay upright. Refrain from telling him I still shamelessly watch it...and think of the three of them. I'm doing all of the normal life-sustaining things as he spins me sideways on the stool and kneels in front of me.

If I doubt what he's proposing, his hands resting on top of my knees, his fingers begging for space between my legs, makes it undeniable.

I glance at my brothers across the kitchen. Their backs are to us.

After a single breath of consideration, I decide to believe that we've all matured and that I'd be a fool not to go after what I want.

I part my knees.

# Three

# Jameson

I gambled, and I won. During the kiss, when Maggie's lips gave in to me, it became clear the desire wasn't mine alone. She shares it. The question is if she shares it with all of us, or just me.

The guys and I talked before the auction and decided we'd be willing to have a group thing instead of making her choose. Not exactly magnanimous.

Honestly, it makes sense so that we can be sure she's taken care of at all times because this isn't a one-and-done scenario for us. We're leaving it up to her if she wants one, two, or three of us.

She deserves more than one man can give her. And here I am, crouched under her kitchen counter, hidden from my brothers, about to make my bid for her affection.

They're asking her questions about where she keeps her spices, and when I look up, her eyes are focused on them. Listening to cabinets opening and closing, and mugs being set down, I wait for her to meet my gaze. My fingers are already tucked into the waistband of her panties.

She gives me a nod and then lifts so I can pull them off. I can barely believe that I'm going to give my stepsister an orgasm. After her comment about being the shy, nerdy, plain girl who never gets asked out, I'm stoked that I could be her first. But I'm troubled that she thinks of herself as shy and plain. She's anything but.

I'll give her credit for nerdy though. Those damn glasses, which she's pushing up her nose as we speak, are part of her hot nerd vibe. How does she not understand that?

I can't wait to rock this nerdy girl's world.

Is she focusing on our brothers because they're looking at her or is she nervous about taking the next step? I rub her outer thighs first. Her skin is so silky smooth I don't even deserve to be touching someone as perfect as her. I work my way onto the tops of her thighs with several slow strokes and then to her inner thighs. Back and forth, caressing from her knees to her sweet curls.

The scent of her sex already has my mouth watering and my cock hard, but her legs are too close together to get my mouth where it can do its best work.

My thumbs hook between her knees and tug ever so slightly.

She gives me an inch, but I need more. I need to taste her sweet pussy. I plant kisses on her knee, on the top of her thigh, inside her thigh, and then I wrap my hands behind her butt so

I can scoot her forward. I've gotta get that sweet sex as close to the edge of the stool as possible.

She shifts—more eagerly than I anticipated. I almost nut on the spot. My athletic pants are no match for my erection. And as much as I can't wait to lick her into euphoria, I want to bend her over this counter and fuck her right here. Make her orgasm on my cock. Have her scream my name while my brothers make cider.

That's how it should be. One of us takes care of her sexually while the other two tend to any other needs. They could cook, clean, tell her a funny story. I don't fucking care. Anything that makes her happy while my dick stretches her virgin walls while I fill her with my seed.

I pull myself back from the raging fantasy I've held onto since the day she turned eighteen.

Knowing my brothers are bound to catch on soon, I kiss my way to her sex. I don't make any bones about what I'm going to do. She doesn't push back. In fact, one of her hands rakes through my hair while I nuzzle my lips and nose against her curls.

My sweet stepsister is so wet. So wantonly wet. I'm coating myself in her scent. We belong together, and I don't want this moment to end.

I think of the saying, 'A watched pot never boils', and I hope that somebody in this room is watching that pot of apple cider. I don't ever want it to boil. I don't want anything to change what

I have with Maggie at this moment...before I have to share her with our brothers.

Is it rational to think I would stay on my knees between her legs the rest of my life if she'd let me? I would if it would make up for me being a jackass.

I would ruin her with orgasms. And so I start.

Teasing my tongue into her curls, I slide it between her plump pussy lips. I rub a hand over my cock to relieve some strain then quickly return it to her ass cheek so I can hold her face against me. Several passes over her clit, with varying licks, sucks, and circles, reveal what she likes best.

When I settle into her favorite combination of sucking and licking, her breaths become noticeable.

"Hey, anybody see where James went?" Heath says.

"No," Maggie answers too quickly. Her fingers tighten in my hair.

"He must have..." Maggie tries to answer but a gasp intertwines with a moan—an unmistakably divine sound coming from a woman.

Our secret's out.

Heath surprises me by being the first to comment, "Wait...is James..."

"Stay over there." Maggie's swollen clit is my playground. She can't contain her arousal from any of us.

Ford laughs out loud. "Damn. He's eating your pussy."

"Nothing's happening." The pitch of Maggie's voice humors me.

"Don't be silly, Ford. Of course, James isn't eating her pussy. She's sitting right here where we could catch them. That only happens in porn." His overly done, matter-of-fact-tone is almost enough to crack me up.

"Let's not discuss this." Her fingers tighten.

"You won't mind if I take a look, then?" Ford says.

Working her into a frenzy, I barely give her breathing room to answer.

"No. Stay there," she says.

"What will you give me to stay over here?"

"What do you want?" She moans the second the question is out of her mouth.

"Maybe we could swap presents later?"

"Fine." She can't hold her moans back anymore. The only sad thing about giving her an orgasm is that our little ruse will come to an end. Having taken her to the edge, I let up.

Ford says, "But I didn't wrap your gift yet. Do you happen to have a box and paper?"

"In the living room, but the only present I have for you is for the swap at Mom and Dad's house."

"We can improvise." The tone of Ford's voice overflows with enjoyment. I don't know what he's planning, but knowing him, it will be fun.

My brothers and I have never done anything like this in front of each other, and definitely not with our stepsister. And for the moment, I'm the only one of us who's grabbed her ass, stared into her eyes, and slid my tongue between her lips. I'm living the best life.

Except compared to Maggie. She's a step ahead of me, and this orgasm is building hard.

"Impro...um..." Maggie's breaths are too heavy to allow coherent words. Her eyes keep trying to flutter shut best I can tell.

"Aw, Maggie, you said you didn't get me a present, but it looks like you're about to come. I'll take that as a present," Ford says and Heath voices agreement.

She thrusts her hands between her sex and my mouth. Damn. She was so close. Is she nervous about having an orgasm with spectators, especially if it's her first? Must be a trip.

Teasing my tongue between her fingers, I test her.

She addresses Ford. "No, I'm not. Mind your own business."

"If we're in the same room as you, and you're about to come, it's our business.

Maggie could push me away. She could tell me to stop. She could walk away. But she doesn't. She's as turned on by this as we are. And the proof is in her creamy cocktail that's all over my face.

I nudge her hand from between us and she returns it to my hair.

"You could at least be gentlemen and turn around," she says to our brothers.

"Babygirl, what part of me carrying you out of that auction over my shoulder makes you think I'm a gentleman?" The tone of Ford's voice is growing more deliberate and needy.

"Please...I've never..." Her gasps and the way her body lurches won't convince anyone to stop watching.

"Never what, Babygirl? Come while someone's watching you? Come while you're thinking of your stepbrothers? I sure as hell can assure you that I've come while thinking about you. No chance I'm going to look away and miss your orgasm face."

The quiver in her legs betrays how close she is. I pull back the slightest bit. "Let go, Angel."

Her hands tangle in my hair. Her cries fill the air. I'm looking up, watching the best I can as she loses the battle for control. My brothers must have quite a show because her head is thrown back.

"James...right there...keep going."

I fucking own her. She falls apart on my face, drenching me in her cream, and I'm in it for everything she has to give.

Slowly easing her down as her fingers relax and her breaths calm, I offer a teasing glance of my tongue over her clit. Her fingers flinch. Her body lurches forward.

Our brothers alternate between groans and uttering words I can't make out. I hope they're stroking their cocks for her.

"Here's your cider when you're ready," Heath says, and I hear two mugs being placed on the counter. Leave it to Heath to act as if nothing happened. He's more reserved.

I'll pass on the cider. The only thing I ever want to drink again is her cum cocktail.

"Better drink up, Babygirl. You're going to need to stay hydrated for tonight." Ford finds a respectable way to address the wild night we envision with her.

Maggie's head falls forward as she looks down at me. "Thank you."

Her statement is so soft, I don't know if our brothers can hear it.

Kissing my way over her thigh, I uncurl my body from my hiding spot. It's time to openly claim her. Cupping her head in my hands, I lower my face to hers. She doesn't balk at her wetness slicking my face.

Trailing kisses across her cheek, I keep my comment between us. "Was that your first time with a guy?"

She nods.

"There's a lot more where that came from." I claim her with my mouth, taking what I can. Heath and Ford close in.

Cider is no longer the most tempting thing in the room.

# *Four*

## Ford

If I had to name the top ten moments of my life... I'd have to admit that I can't remember a single one after watching Maggie come.

It's like watching my life flash before my eyes. All I ever want to do is give her orgasms. All I ever want to see is that total surrender on her face. All I ever want to feel is how she'll tighten around my cock.

Heath navigates around me, takes Maggie by the hand, and leads her to the living room. Probably a polite move to give her a minute to regroup.

James gives me a sly grin before joining them.

Maggie excuses herself to change, and I'm bummed I won't get to fuck her in that super hot Santa's helper costume, but her wardrobe won't be a deal-breaker.

"Is she as good as I've imagined?" I ask James.

"Your wildest dreams won't even touch this." He drags a hand over his jaw.

Doing our best to keep our conversation sane and quiet, while we discuss that this is all new for her, I start preparing my present.

By the time she returns, the box is on the paper, and she has no idea it's empty or that I cut a hole in the backside. And while her sweatpants look comfy, she'll be even more comfortable when they're on the floor and she's riding my dick. The threadbare Batman t-shirt can stay since it's so thin I can see the darkness of her nipples, but by the time I'm done with her, she'll have a new favorite superhero.

Where I conjure enough restraint to go through with my present wrapping idea is beyond me, but I stay on the living room floor while she joins James and Heath on the couch. Surely it occurs to her that I didn't have anything that required this big of a box with me when I arrived. Maybe she's already on to my plan. As long as she plays along, that's fine.

"Hey," James is staring at her. "Is that my shirt?"

She grips the hem and looks down as she holds it out. "This old thing? I don't remember where I got it?"

"I should have known you were the reason I couldn't find it. Looks better on you anyway."

Heath grumbles, decidedly uncomfortable about something. Why does his hand go to his pants pocket? I watch for a second but he regroups as if nothing happened.

Talking and laughing with the three of them takes me back to so many happy memories when we weren't telling her to buzz off. It only highlights how wrong it was for us to buy her and set this evening in motion.

Her smile, her laughter, and the ease of how we get along give me a microsecond of pause that our ten-year age gap is too much. As the oldest, should I know better? Should I do better? Fuck no. I'm not backing out and leaving her to James and Heath.

Maggie's always been smart. She's more than capable of making her own decisions, but how did our little sister grow up to be such a bombshell, and not even realize it? When we took notice of her, we each kept a respectful distance. It was the only sane thing to do. I was twenty-eight when she turned eighteen, that's worlds apart. But here I am at thirty, ready to play out a porn scenario and have my stepsister unwrap my cock.

Immaturity on my part would be an easy summation, but it's more about me not being able to think of anything but her the last two years.

I angle my head up from my special wrapping job. James is pulling Maggie onto his lap. If he'd done that with any other girl I had my eye on, I would have lost my shit. Then again, none of those relationships lasted.

Instead, there's something comforting about the gesture.

Actually, I'd have lost my shit when he had his head between her legs or when he kissed her under the mistletoe. Something about this works.

Poking the scissors through the wrapping paper that's covering the hole, I'm ready to give Maggie my gift—the classic stepbrother dick-in-the-box. Not exactly clever, but it's fun, just like James eating her out under the bar.

I shove the warm, mushy feelings I have for her down deep. Right now, it's important to keep it light. We have a lot of time to make up for.

A flicker of hesitation worms through my mind when I realize she could think I just want her to jack me off. I'll be sure to please her too since she's a good little stepsister. The question will be how I go about that.

I'd love to squeeze my cock into her tight virgin pussy but that may be a fantasy from viewing her with my 'innocent sister' glasses on. I only see her the way I want to. Technically, all she indicated to James was that she'd never had her pussy licked by a guy, but we all suspect that won't be her only first tonight.

Winking at Heath, who's stroking his hand through her hair, I say, "Keep her busy for a second."

"Yes sir, Ford."

I carry the wrapped box into her bedroom so I can get my pants shucked down. Thankfully my athletic wear has an elastic waistband that allows me to ease them to the tops of my thighs. They stay in place.

I look around her room. I'm in her space. The blues and greens of her beloved ocean, which she never gets to see here in Peach Bottom Valley, give me an idea to take her on a vacation. I'll rent a boat and take her out to sea. I'll get a fucking two-seater jet ski so she has to wrap her arms around me. I'll fuck her on the jet ski. So many ideas...goals. But first, we have to pull off tonight.

My cock is already hard, so the stroke I make over my length is simply to take the edge off. I use the tall mirror on the back of her bedroom door to position the box where she won't be able to tell that my pants are down. The box isn't too tall, so she'll be able to reach in easily.

"Okay, time to unwrap your present, Babygirl," I call out loudly.

She has a nervous smile as she enters the room. My cock twitches and I'm pretty sure pre-cum drips into the box. This won't be a box to reuse.

"Okay Ford. I don't know what's going on, but shouldn't we wait until we're at mom and dad's house." She shrugs and tips her head a little.

"This can't wait."

She screws up her lips, pushes her glasses up a little, and shakes her head. "You know how mom is. We don't open Christmas presents early."

"Well, trust me, you don't want to open this in front of our parents."

Her eyes light up. "Is this a *special* present?"

"It's special all right, and it's only for you since you're such a good sister."

"Only for me? You've never given it to anyone else?"

Damn. That's the difficult thing about trying to talk dirty, it can go wrong. She knows I've had sex, or I would presume she does. What's her game? Does she want me to lie? No, she's too truthful. It's a test. Got it.

"Not in a couple years, Babygirl."

"Why?"

"Because I realized it belonged to you." I've craved this moment. My body is supercharged with the need to get my hands on her, pull her close, and make sweet love to her, but the box must stay in place.

She sets her hands on top of it and trails them over the side. "It's so big."

"You have no idea." My cock is so swollen it hurts.

She takes her time removing the bow and peeling the paper down the sides. My fingers flex against the box. I'm about to snap and blow my load on the cold, thankless interior of this cardboard. They never explain that part in the damn videos.

Maggie toys with an edge of the wrapping paper. "I've never gotten a present like this before."

Oh holy night, is that her confession that she's a virgin? The stars are shining on me. Before I get excited about providing her first Noel, I test the waters. If I don't need to be slow and careful, I won't, but that leaves me pretty torn because I want to be her first.

"You've never gotten a present...this big or from a stepbrother or ever? What part of this is new?"

"The whole package...well except for the...you know...James's gift."

A growl rises through my chest. Her eyes widen. Hell, if that surprises her, she'll get an earful when I fill her womb with my seed. It's killing me to keep the box in place. *Fuck the ruse.* No, she likes it.

I grip one hand around the front of the box and lift the other, cupping my fingers under her chin, and brushing my thumb over her cheek. She's so soft, so delicate, so virginal. I'll take it all.

Maggie lifts her eyes to mine, looking up at me from under her bangs. She nibbles on her lower lip. My body tenses. My legs are all but shaking. With a mere foot and a half between us, her hand brushes over mine as she slowly removes another strip of paper. Is she tearing it like that to stall? To torture me? Tease me? Decide if she'll go through with it?

"Does it come with instructions?" she asks hesitantly.

All that's left are the top flaps of the box, which I've loosely taped. In seconds her hands can be on my cock. I long to see those delicate fingers wrapped around my shaft. But even more so, I've waited for the day I could show her how beautiful she is.

"I can talk you through it if you're nervous." Don't I feel like a fucking idiot now, standing here with my penis in a box?

"That would help." She nibbles on a fingernail, but I catch her hand in mine.

"I'll take care of you, always. You don't have anything to be afraid of."

Bending the flaps out, she gasps and stumbles backward into the door and slams it shut.

I toss the box. Thankfully the cardboard doesn't paper cut me as I bump it on the side of my cock. Note to self, *that never happens in porn videos.*

I faintly hear our brothers asking if everything's okay. Assessing her reaction, now that she's had a second, I determine from the slack-jawed stare at my cock that we're fine.

"All good," I reply so they don't come to her rescue. Then softer, I ask her, "We are, aren't we?"

She nods and says, "Oh my gosh, I was not expecting that!"

"You seriously didn't know?"

"I caught on to what you were doing, but..." She swallows and timidly extends a hand toward my shaft. I catch her fingers and guide them over my slick tip, then down my shaft and back up, before letting her take over.

"I've never seen one in person. It's gorgeous!"

*Gorgeous.* I toy with the term. Not the obvious ego boost like, 'wow, put that monster cock in me', but gorgeous is good. I rock my hips to slide against her fingers.

"Not as gorgeous as you, Babygirl. Nothing compares to you."

"You're just saying that." She dips her head and pulls her hand away.

Pressing my hands on either side of her shoulders, I trap her between my body and the door. The steel rod of my erection presses into the softness of her body and I lean into her. My pre-cum spills onto her shirt, the first step in me claiming her from James.

"Look at me." My voice is so low, I barely recognize it. Maggie transforms me into this beast that can't survive without her, leaving me unsettled at how badly I need her.

She hesitates a beat before complying.

"Good girl." I graze my lips over her forehead. "I want you to remember something." I want to give her every present she's ever wanted, from the designer jeans she asked for several years back but our parents said were too expensive, to the prettiest jewelry, a fancy new car, a luxury home... everything. But that's not what she needs.

"What?"

"You're perfect." I slip her glasses off and set them on the dresser beside us. "I don't want you doubting yourself ever again."

"You don't understand."

"You're right, and it's now my life mission to help you see yourself the way I see you."

"How do you see me?"

Resting my forehead on the door beside hers, I say, "There aren't words for it, Maggie, but you felt how hard my cock was..."

"And thick. Will it fit?"

My jaw clenches at her admission that she wants to have sex. I assure her, "You're made for my cock, but I'll go slow."

I slide a hand down her arm, entangle my fingers with hers, and bring them back up beside us so I can kiss them.

"Can I tell you something?"

"Don't ever hold back from telling me anything, Babygirl. It may have taken me a while to figure it out, but I was put on this planet to make you happy and protect you." I breathe in the scent of her floral shampoo. I've been so consumed by being this close, this intimate with her, that it hadn't registered.

"I watched all that stepbrother porn because I've wanted this for a long time. I thought something was wrong with me, and that because I was messed up, that's why no guys asked me out."

"You've wanted to stroke my cock."

"And suck on it too. Is that wrong?"

"The only time I'd turn you down for sucking on my cock is when I need to be inside your pussy." I guide our joined hands down and loop her fingers around my cock then slide my hand between her legs, over her sweatpants.

I ask, "Can I unwrap this present?"

She looks up, meeting my gaze, so fucking sweet and innocent. "Yes, please, but I can't promise that it's only for you."

My chest tightens. My blood boils.

"It might be for James and Heath too. That's okay, isn't it? I don't know how this works." Her explanation comes in the nick of time. I can breathe again. How easily I forgot about them?

"Babygirl, none of us know how this works. We'll figure it out together."

"Since you said I shouldn't hold back... I want to do this first with just you, then do you think we can all have sex together?"

My throbbing cock elicits a giggle from her. I can't help but smile when she smiles. But damn! I don't think she understands the fire she lights in my soul when I think of her being taken by the three of us. I'll fill her with a baby tonight, but it doesn't mean we can't keep her loaded with our cum, marking her as ours, satisfying her every fantasy.

"We talked about it earlier. That's why we went to the auction. We want this, and there was no way we could handle any other guy buying you for any reason." Lifting my hand to the top of her pants, I use my fingers to push them down. She lifts her butt from the door, but since I'm not ready, her hips press into me, causing my shaft to strain even harder in her sweet, delicate hand.

"This, sex with all of us? You talked about it?"

Her pants fall to her feet and I use a foot to hold them down while she steps out. My thigh between hers is enough of a signal, she spreads herself wide for me.

"Not just sex. A relationship."

"Wouldn't that be hard to make work?"

"I told you never to doubt yourself. If you want us, you get us." I cup her sex. This time, my middle finger dips into her sweet pussy. She's swollen. She's wet. And holy mother of vice grips. Even though I know I'll fit, I'll have to be gentle. My hips flex, desperate to ignore caution and seat myself inside of her.

I'll be lucky if I can get more than my tip in without blowing, she's so tight. That'll happen soon enough. Right now, my focus is on getting her off.

Her fingers tighten around my cock. Dangerous territory for me. Her other hand grips my shoulder and her nails dig in. She's going to be fun when she rides me. And since I already got an earful of how she orgasms, I can't wait for her to drive my brothers insane when they hear her have her first orgasm on a cock.

"I can't believe I thought you guys hated me." Her words pain me. I can't believe I was a jerk.

"If I could change the past, I would. If I promise to give you the brightest future, can we leave the past behind us?"

"Well, you haven't left your Axe body wash in the past."

I'm not sure if I should be ecstatic or embarrassed that she noticed.

I laugh. "You know why I did that, right?" I tease my finger in and out of her.

Her hips flex. She gasps and gives up on trying to answer. Her head falls to the side and her eyes close as she gives into my ministrations. Her fingers slide up and down my cock. The pre-cum leaking out is enough to keep the glide smooth.

The package deal of me inside of her, and her fingers wrapped around me takes me close to the point of no return. I barely stay ahead of the climax. With the fingers of my other hand, I tip her head back to face me and kiss her sweet lips.

"You're so beautiful, Maggie. You're so amazing. I can't believe you're giving me a chance to be with you. A chance to prove that I'm worthy of your future."

We fall into a heavy kiss. My admission heightens her passion. Our tongues dance, my cock strains, and I'm torn between fully immersing myself in the moment, memorizing every move of her tongue, the press of her lips, the softness of her body against mine, and thinking of anything except her so I can last longer.

I'm captivated by the way she timidly strokes me, which causes a mental scramble for distraction so I don't come before she does.

Her hips start a tiny series of bucks against me. I have her. Her tongue can no longer keep pace and her mouth falls slack. I move my kisses to her cheek, down her neck, and into the crook of her collarbone. "That's right sweet Maggie, come undone for me. Come on my hand."

And she does. She falls apart, her legs buckling. I have to lean in to support her. My free hand barely catches her arm as her cries break free. Her strokes over my cock falter, but the wrap of her fingers makes me blow my load, coating both of us in my cum while her release drips over my fingers.

When sanity returns and the reality of what happened sinks in, I say, "Holy fuck, Maggie. That's even better than I dreamed of."

"You dreamed of this?" she says, breathlessly, through the tail end of her orgasmic bliss.

"And so much more. When I said I wanted you to see yourself the way I do, I don't know how to convince you that you're my everything. You're the reason I never quit using Axe body wash."

She chuckles. "I'm the reason?"

"You came in one time after I'd just put it on and said that it smelled really good."

"I remember that day. You told me to go away."

"I felt so guilty."

"Because I was too young?"

"I was already fighting my attraction to you. I'd tried to keep you at a distance but my heart was wrapped around your little finger."

"Wait. You kept wearing Axe because I liked it?"

"I knew that one day I was going to hold you in my arms, and when I did, I wanted us both to be able to remember that this isn't new. We may be trying something new. We may be in uncharted territory. But the feelings we've had for each other aren't new. Let me make love to you."

# Five

## Maggie

*Make love?* That's not how porn videos work out. Why did he have to say it like that?

Ford's heartbeat thumps from his chest to mine. He's not wrong about the feelings, they've been there forever.

The scent of the body wash that he wears for me, keeps a whirlwind of emotions whipping around my chest. The fun and games of playing out stepbrother porn is replaced by something intense. His talk of relationships and dreams and futures... am I so used to being overlooked that I can't accept the clear meaning of his words.

All of the old sibling nonsense is gone. The sincerity in his words and James's under the mistletoe make me want to give in. That's where it gets too crazy. They're acting like we can *all* be together.

My eyes can't focus. The room sways.

"I can't breathe."

He leans away, gripping me with both hands—one messier than the other. That makes the room sway more. We just gave each other orgasms, and before that, he and Heath watched while James ate me out.

I must be dreaming.

"Are you okay? Do you need to lie down?"

"I need to step outside."

Sliding from between Ford and the door, I hope the cool evening air will wake me up. Isn't that silly. Why wake up from a dream this incredible?

He catches my arm. "Your pants."

Glancing down, my need for air supersedes my need to cover up. It's nighttime and my balcony has a privacy wall anyway. Not that I've ever used it for privacy. Tonight's going to be the first time for a lot of things.

Relieved that I don't have to pass through the living room to get outside, I soak in the crisp air and the moonlight glinting off snowflakes. The peace and serenity of the night help take my nerves down a notch. A trail of steam from the train in the distance gives me something to focus on.

I never gave myself a real chance of getting all three guys. It's a lot to take in, but I've never felt so loved. That's the scary part. In my fantasies and on the porn, that heavy love vibe stays out of the way.

Hearing it come from Ford's mouth only amplified the awkwardness. Can we make this work?

# Six

# Heath

I'm officially the only brother who hasn't given Maggie an orgasm—if I can trust what I heard coming from Maggie and Ford. Jesus, that woman gets into it.

I stare at the multi-colored, great-at-hiding-stains, low-pile carpet. "Do you think he fucked her?"

James assesses the situation. "They were bumping the door, but not hard enough to be a good fuck. I'm pretty sure Ford would have plowed that door down."

I huff at the visual, but my balls tighten at the possibility that I can be her first. "Do you think she didn't want to, or they're just gearing up?"

The bedroom door opens, and in a flash, a pants-free Maggie steps into the transitional entry area then fumbles with the front door lock before flinging it open, and disappearing into the darkness.

Without a word, she pulls the door shut.

Ford's slower, and I'm already across the room, grabbing the door knob, as he steps into the entry.

"Is she okay?" I ask, glancing through the peep hole. She seems fine. She's standing on her balcony, which has a solid enclosure about four-feet high. Nice for privacy while leaving an open feel.

"Yeah. She's incredible." He rubs his lips and the deep inhale gives me a hint that he's breathing in her scent. Lucky bastard. He better not have fucked this up for me.

"I mean, why did she go outside?"

"Oh, she needed some air." His grin is a clear boast.

"And couldn't stop to put pants on first?"

"Now *that* I can't explain." Ford steps back into her bedroom, grabs her clothes, then hands them to me when I make no concession of giving him access to the door handle.

"Give me a minute with her."

My brothers agree. They can commiserate over how incredible it is to give her orgasms, something I'm desperately in need of doing.

Joining her on the porch, I make note of her fuzzy socks keeping her feet warm, then step behind her, looping my arm around her to offer the sweats. "Want me to keep you warm, or would you rather stick these on?"

Her giggle sets a relaxed tone. Thank god.

"You're not going to try to talk me into going inside so you can try to top your brothers?" She wiggles her ass into me. That's an even better tone.

My cock's hard as steel, ready for me to join her in being naked from the waist down, socks excluded. The light scent of flowers in her hair, like freshness and springtime, is a stark contrast to the thin layer of snow collecting on the ground.

She lets the gently falling snow collect on her palms—something I've seen her do a million times. How can that make me want her even more?

"Why bother going inside when we have such a beautiful view? And even though your ass is incredible, that's not what I'm talking about."

She angles her head to the side. "What are you proposing?"

Stroking my free hand down her arm, I lean in to kiss her forehead. How did our nerdy little stepsister become so adventurous? And how did no guy her age not tap into this side of her?

"I'm proposing to do anything you want."

"Anything?"

"If it makes you happy, I'll do it."

"That's a dangerous claim."

"Try me." My brothers and I got into a few Truth or Dare games that posed some pretty messed up challenges, like running down the middle of the street naked, but I doubt Maggie's interested in pushing that type of limit.

"Would you get naked out here?"

Don't have to ask me twice. I step backward and strip my pants and underwear. Maggie's hands fly over her mouth.

I shrug it off. "You asked."

"Sure, but wow, your..." She waves a finger up and down, pointing at my erection. "It's standing straight up."

The curve of her hips and the dark tuft of hair between her legs has me salivating. I can't believe I'm half-naked outside with her. I'm even more surprised by her statement.

"Please tell me you know what an erection is."

"Oh, I do. I just haven't seen a lot of them."

"How many?"

"In person?"

I nod.

She worries her lower lip. "One."

"Ford's?"

"Yes."

I pull her close, trapping my cock between us. Her shirt is wet, and I cringe at the thought of why. Adjusting my positioning, I settle into a dry spot. "What did you and Ford do?"

"I'm still a virgin if that's what you're asking. Just fingers."

I swallow hard. "I want to change that."

"Ford was going to, but we both had orgasms and I got overwhelmed and ended up out here."

His missed chance becomes my opportunity. "Are you okay or is something wrong?"

She wraps her arms around me. "I've never been better."

"So why rush outside?" I stroke my fingers through her hair.

"I don't understand what we're doing—I mean, I understand what we're doing physically, I just don't understand what this means. Are we friends now? Friends with benefits?"

"Sweetness, we're a lot more than friends."

"Duh, family, but that's why I'm having trouble wrapping my brain around this."

"First of all, we're not blood relatives even though we grew up together. Think of it this way... If our parents weren't married, the weirdest thing about tonight would be that you got bought by three guys who worship you."

"But our parents are married."

"Are you saying you want me to put my pants back on?"

"No." She bucks her hips into me.

"Good answer. So, can I fuck you on your front porch?"

She cranes her neck. "I like it when you put it like that."

"Like what?" I'm not sure which part of my phrasing worked for her. Using *the F word*? My heart lightens at my sweet, innocent sister.

"Nothing...um...we're going to do this right now?"

"Right now, tomorrow, every Wednesday...like I said...whatever you want."

"What if someone sees us?"

I drag a thumb over her plump lips. Are they extra plump from Ford kissing her? Possessiveness rolls through me, but in a non-competitive way. I'm mostly bummed that I didn't get to watch.

Keeping in mind that this is her apartment, I acknowledge that her friends and neighbors could potentially see her, even though no one and nothing is stirring out here, not even a mouse. I chuckle at my Christmas joke, but keep it to myself.

"The only thing anyone could see is me kissing you, so I won't, but trust me, I want to."

Her shoulders pull up. "Thank you."

"But I will fuck you."

Her body stiffens.

"Are you okay with that?"

"I definitely want to have sex with you and Ford and James, but out here?" She screws up her mouth.

I spin her around. The ambient light from the parking lot isn't exactly the romantic glow from candles, but the rest of the scene works. "What better place for your first time? And since you're playing out porn scenarios, you might as well check off balcony sex."

"And end up as one of those public sex videos?" She swivels her head left and right, presumably deciding if any neighbors are likely to be filming.

"It's dark. No one would get a good shot."

She laughs. "That's comforting."

"With the parking lot in front of us, any possible vantage point is pretty far away. You feeling frisky?"

# Seven

# Maggie

*Frisky?* More like horny. How can I be so sure I need a dick inside of me when I've never experienced it. Must be instinct kicking in. I can't believe I'm considering this.

I study the other apartments. Some have lights on. A couple are vacant. A few neighbors have gone out of town. I'm on the second story so no one can see from above. With the privacy wall, our naughty bits truly are protected.

There's one thing I wanted to do before having sex though. Before losing my courage, I turn around and drop to my knees. Wrapping my hands around Heath's shaft, I kiss the tip. The musky bead catches on my lips, leaving a little string between us as I pull away.

My tongue darts out, savoring the salty treat. Are women genetically programmed to crave this? My intent was one little kiss, but now I'm torn between wanting his dick in my lady parts or my mouth.

"I wasn't expecting that, Sweetness." His fingers tangle in my hair.

I thought guys just did that in porn videos so the camera could get a better shot. Geez, it's hot. It's making my sex tingle and ache even worse. Diving in for another kiss, I add tongue. His tip is so smooth.

I love it. I love each of their nicknames for me... I need to quit saying that word.

He groans and his fingers maneuver my head, holding me close to his body. "Sweetness, if you make me come like this, I'll expect you to swallow like a good girl."

Swallowing it is. A shiver runs through me but has nothing to do with the temperature. Fully opening my mouth, I let my tongue lead the way as I slowly take his cock into me. Why does this feel so incredible? I snake a hand between my thighs to ease some of my own pressure.

A choking sound comes from Heath as he drops forward and one of his hands catches on the top of the wall.

I pop off of him. "Am I doing it wrong?"

"The better question is if you lied to me, Sweetness."

"Lied about what?"

"Only having seen one cock. You're way too good at this."

A sense of pride flows through me. I stare up at him from my knees and dip my finger into my sex. It's insane how wet and swollen I am. "Beginner's luck?"

"I'm the one who's lucky here, and I can't believe I'm saying this, but get up."

My stomach tumbles, and I stay in place to make my point. For added effect, I stroke my hand along his shaft and kiss him again. "If I did it right, why can't I keep going?"

"Because I've got a giant load of cum I need to put in your pussy. You can suck my cock later."

"You afraid I'll choke on your huge load?" I'm proud of myself for that comeback and increase the pressure on my clit.

"You'll choke, but that will be because my cock is in your throat. I can already tell you're the kind of girl who can take it deep."

Swirling my tongue around his tip, I ask, "So, I rephrase my question. Why stop when I could prove you right?"

"Because this giant load of seed is my best bet for getting my virgin sister pregnant."

"Step," I blurt out—not that it changes anything, or addresses the bigger bomb he just dropped. A bomb that has me exploding with unexpected excitement.

He loops his fingers around my upper arms and pulls me to standing. The resistance of my hand that's busy between my legs catches his attention. I'm so busted. Will he still consider me a good girl?

His eyes shift from mine to my hand then back to my eyes, but now there's a hunger. The same switch flips in me too.

Inhibitions are gone. Primal urges take over. I'm consumed by the need to have a cock inside of me.

"Sweetness, were you going to have an orgasm without me?"

"I was sucking your cock. I'm pretty sure that meant we'd do it together." Where does my sultry voice come from?

His lips crash onto mine and my hands fall limp as the command in his kiss melts me. If the universe plans on sending any signal to tell me to stop, it better hurry. I'm—

Heath pulls away. "I'd apologize for risking your neighbors seeing us, but I'm not sorry. Hold on a second."

I'm stunned when he bends down and seems to be getting something out of his pants pocket. A condom? I can't tell. That would mean the pregnant comment must have just been sexy foreplay.

He gathers my hands in one of his and brings them between us, while he presses his hips into mine. I appreciate the body heat.

"This is for you."

Slipping the object into my hands, he cups my shoulders while I inspect the Batman flashlight keychain. Memories come flooding back.

"Is this..." I feel silly trudging up a sibling argument from a few years ago but I'm stunned.

He looks somber as he nods.

"You swore you didn't steal it." My obsession with the Dark Knight goes way back. I'd been so excited when a friend gave me a keychain flashlight that sent out the bat signal when squeezed.

"Not a proud moment." He works his fingers over mine, angles the flashlight, and presses. The signal lights up the divider wall between my apartment and the neighbor's.

"Why did you steal it? And how can it still work?" Confusion clouds everything, especially about why he's giving it back after all of these years.

"New batteries. And I stole it because I was jealous. I didn't want you imagining anyone coming to your rescue but me."

That's a lot for me to process. "But you were like twenty—"

"Ridiculously in love with you even then. Let's not bother with the math."

I squeeze the light again and say playfully, "You're okay with me summoning other men now?"

"As long as you understand that I'm about to fuck you."

His gaze lingers on my eyes but the weight of his lips on mine has me trapped in a phantom remnant of his kiss from moments before. He spins me around, slides his hand between my legs from behind, and eases his fingers into my sex.

This has to happen. I'm barreling closer to release under his touch.

My sweatpants are draped over the ledge. I'd forgotten all about them, and they quickly leave my brain again as I back into him, wanting more.

His words are soft and low, ensuring that they're only for me, even though no one's around. "I won't be proud of how fast your sweet pussy makes me come, but I'll get my cum so deep inside of you, you'll be pregnant before we ever leave this porch. Understand?"

There he is with that pregnant thing again. Why am I nodding?

"Say it out loud, Sweetness. Tell me you want it." He pulls his finger out and positions his cock between my legs. "And not just one...I want to put at least two babies in you tonight."

The closeness I always felt toward my brothers, despite being held at arm's length, makes sense all of the sudden. We're meant to be. The time and place just had to be right.

"I want it."

"What a fucking good girl you are. Hold onto the rail and go up on your tiptoes."

My body becomes a jolt of electricity as I comply. I'm about to orgasm listening to the gravelly tone of his voice.

He pushes against my entrance, easing himself inside. The cool air infiltrates everywhere possible, but his cock is hot. He's stretching me as he slowly inches in. My fingernails dig into the wooden rail. Breaths only come as I force them. And Heath's groans assure me that he's in as wild of a state of existence as I am.

High-pitched whines escape me, causing him to remind me to keep quiet. "Grab your sweatpants. Bite down on them if you're worried about the neighbors hearing."

I don't care anymore. "Don't hold back."

"You don't know what you're asking for."

"I want to be good for you. I want to know how to make you happy. The only way I'll find out is if you show me. I'm not fragile. I'm made for you."

Light washes over us from behind as someone opens the door to my apartment.

"Close the door," Heath hisses.

"Better hurry up, James," Ford says. There's shuffling, the door closes, and Ford and James appear on either side of us.

Ford leans in for a kiss but I keep it brief and tell him, "I don't want the neighbors to see."

There's a pause before he laughs. "Heath literally has his dick inside of you and you're worried about a kiss?"

"My house, my rules."

"Fuck." Heath's fingers dig into my waist as he shoves his cock the rest of the way in.

I cry out, only my brothers, the snow, and the celestial bodies bear witness to this intimate moment. Heath pauses and confirms that I'm fine before thrusting slowly then speeding up. The prying eyes, lips, and hands of our brothers don't bother me. It's amazing how right this is.

My orgasm is too big, too tempting, I don't resist. I splinter apart, shattering in my own beautiful avalanche. My walls clamp on his cock over and over again as he drags in and out of me. The stretch, the tightness, and the soul-obliterating fullness are more than I ever expected.

Porn can suck my figurative cock, because this is better than hours of in-and-out.

Then Heath's rhythm changes, his fingers flex and regrip me, and his growls fill the air as headlights turn into the parking lot.

Adrenaline and the need to stop spike inside of me even though I'm pretty sure Heath will be done growling before the car is parked and anyone gets out.

The warmth of his seed fills me, as promised. The car continues toward us. Heath's head drops into the back of mine. The car pulls into the spot closest to my apartment.

I'm not a car person, but the shape of the vehicle gives me a reality check as my blissful state fades.

It's my mom. And when the passenger door swings open, I note that she brought my stepdad.

My brothers mutter various curses. Somebody swipes my sweatpants from the ledge then James kneels and holds one of the legs open, helping me partially dress, while Heath is still inside of me.

"My cock stays where it is. I'm not risking letting my cum spill out just yet." Heath drives his point home by pushing in a little bit further.

James does his best to pull my sweats up to mid-thigh then stands up as if life is normal. "Hey Mom, Dad. Why are you guys here?"

Our parents draw closer to the bottom of my stairs as all of us exchange greetings. My heart bangs so hard it might break a rib. I try to wiggle free but Heath tightens his grip. What is he thinking?

Mom says, "I was worried. We heard about the auction then none of you were answering your phones."

Dad adds, "Throwing your sister over your shoulder...what were you thinking? That's not how you should treat your sister."

Mom reaches for the handrail.

"Stop!" My panic is bound to be evident, no matter how much she taught me to use composure.

Our parents halt, look up, and wait. Now what?

Ford steps to the top of the stairs, and says, "Sorry about my lapse in judgment at the auction. We've worked it out, right, Bab—sis?"

This is like watching a trainwreck.

"Yeah, we're better than ever." I can't believe we're chatting with our parents while Heath's cock is plugging me so his cum won't leak out. And in an insane way, I'm okay with that. What has my world become?

Heath pumps his hips. "You could say we've taken our relationship to a whole new level."

James busts out with laughter then agrees.

Mom asks, "Then why don't we come up for a family—"

Heath cuts her off. "You can't come up because we're doing this great sibling bonding and we're working on a present for you."

Then he puts his lips next to my ear and quietly says, "Their first grandbaby."

A shudder washes over me at how much I hope it's true. It also occurs to me that I thought cocks were supposed to get soft after ejaculation. How is Heath keeping his hard?

"No peeking at your gifts early. We'll see you tomorrow for the family party." He waves confidently.

There's obvious surprise that we won't let them come up, but our parents retreat to their car and leave.

Relief holds itself back until their car is out of the lot, then I slump onto the rail. "Now we have to come up with a group gift."

"Other than the baby?"

"We have a lot of explaining before that will make sense. How about we do a bunch of group photos and promise to send them a photo each day for the next month," Ford says.

James adds, "Good idea, and we can make a bunch of those coupons mom used to make for us when we were kids like a family dinner and movie night with the parents and whatever else."

"Sounds like a plan. I've got paper and markers. Shall we get to work," I presume Heath will take the hint but he just pumps again.

Ford glares at Heath. "The first thing I'm working on is getting his dick out of you so I can get mine in."

"Things never change, do they?" I say.

Ford eyes me questioningly.

"You always were the one who wanted to stay up and play all night instead of getting your work done. If you don't watch out, you'll be getting nuttin' for Christmas." I crack myself up with the lyric from the old song.

"I'm pretty sure you're the one who's getting nuttin' for Christmas!"

Touché. My heart is as warm and happy as my womb. We really are perfect for each other.

"A whole lot of nuttin'," James adds, then we make our way inside.

"Wait," James pauses. "Do we owe you an apology?"

"I don't think so."

"When we first got here, you said, this was your house and your rules, and we weren't allowed to gang up on you."

"That was before I learned there are ways I like being ganged up on."

Then they spend the rest of the night ganging up on me in all the best ways.

# *Eight*

# Maggie

My stomach tightens a split second before the unmistakable growl fills the room. The Pop-Tart snack we ate in the wee hours of the morning has worn off.

"Our Angel isn't immortal...she needs food," James teases.

The guys reluctantly peel themselves away from me. Surely, they're hungry too.

Finding my glasses and trudging on wobbly legs to the kitchen, I glance at the clock on the microwave then out the window at the road. "Crap, guys. We have to be at Mom and Dad's in two hours, and it'll be a thirty-minute drive in this snow, and we definitely need to shower."

I rip the foil open on another Pop-Tart pack and pull one out. Ford takes the other pastry. Bypassing the toaster, I nibble the outer edge before downing the yummy, frosted, chocolate-filled center.

My brothers don't see what the hurry is, but they follow my lead. It's almost like they're lovesick puppies afraid to let me get more than a foot away. Their adoration empowers me and makes me feel special—the polar opposite of what I thought of myself before last night. I've learned a lot about myself, and that's what causes the spring in my step and the confident outlook.

It's entirely possible our parents will freak out about us getting together—if not for the stepsibling thing, then for the abnormal relationship.

After gulping the water that's left in someone's cup on the counter, I head to the bathroom. The guys are hot on my heels. I'd never thought about how good my ass looked, but after all of their praise, I'm fine with them trailing behind me.

I adjust the shower water and turn around just in time to see Ford grab my toothbrush.

"Whoa! Put that down."

"Why? What's wrong?" He holds the toothbrush up and inspects it. "Is this what you use to clean your fishbowl or something?"

"No, that's what I use to clean my teeth."

"Excellent decision for a toothbrush. Those nerdy glasses aren't just for show." Ford cracks himself up. "I was going to brush my teeth."

"You can't use my toothbrush."

Heath and James are leaning against the counter, watching, but I can't tell where they stand on the shared toothbrush thing. No one comes to my defense. It could just be a matter of enjoying seeing their brother get told no.

"Why not?" Ford asks.

"It's gross."

"Do I have to remind you where your mouth has been? Or that you just drank out of my water cup?"

I shake a finger at him.

He stares at me in stunned silence. Steam starts to escape the shower, and in the brief second that it catches his attention, I snag the toothbrush from his hand.

"Alright, guess I'll use my finger." Ford pulls the top drawer open, grabs the tube of toothpaste, and flips the cap.

Anxiety rises in me as his fingers wrap around the squishable container. *Oh no!* He's a tube crusher. This drove me crazy when we were growing up.

"Wait!" I reach for the toothpaste, but it's too late. The ridiculously long strip of paste on his finger is proof that the damage is done.

They all look at me as I throw my hands up and exhale my frustration.

"You don't share toothpaste either?" Heath asks, with intense confusion.

Clenching my teeth, I snag the tube from Ford's hand. "I forgot you're a tube crusher. Look at this."

They're still staring, but the slight shifts in their expressions are to disbelief.

I hold the mangled container up. "You made a mess of it."

"What does it matter?"

"Tossing my head back, I mutter, "This will never work."

"That's what you said before I proved my cock would indeed fit inside of you." Ford keeps the mood light.

I shake my head. "Does male humor never change?"

"Not really," James clarifies.

I catch Heath's eye, but he smirks and shrugs. "It was funny."

Ford calms himself. "Okay, seriously, why does it matter if we squeeze from the middle or the bottom."

"Squeeze from the bottom." Heath chuckles and nudges Ford with his elbow.

Ignoring their silliness, I state the obvious. "It's prettier when not mangled. It lays in the drawer better. And how will you ever get all of the toothpaste out when it's gnarled like this?" I squeeze from the bottom of the tube, then press the end against the edge of the counter and re-flatten the empty portion.

My audience is so captive, you'd think I'm doing a striptease. Nodding at his toothpaste-covered finger, I say, "I guess that when you use that much extra toothpaste, you don't care about getting the most out of your purchase."

"I never put that much thought into it. I'll be happy to buy you a new tube." Ford's voice has a hint of remorse.

Holding the nearly pristine tube up, I say, "There. It'll be fine, besides after last night you need extra to clean your dirty mouth."

I wink then pull the shower curtain back, with my toothbrush still in my hand, and let the warm water cascade over my body. When I'm settled, I set my toothbrush in the shower caddy.

Heath steps in behind me and when I reach for my toothbrush, he assures me. "Don't worry. I'm not interested in that. I just want to pamper you."

He squirts shampoo in his palm then works it through my hair, giving an even better head massage than my hairdresser. The erection prodding at my backside is an added bonus.

Ford peeks around the edge of the curtain, the paste still on his finger. "You're serious? I've had my cock in your mouth and my tongue down your throat. Well...my cock went there also because you are an absolute angel. We've swapped spit and I've come all over you, inside and out, and you're worried about a toothbrush?"

"A girl's gotta have her limits. Be glad that seems to be my only one."

He shakes his head and my eyes fall shut as Heath uses the shower wand to rinse my hair. I'll never underestimate the gift of pampering again. When he lifts his arm to return the showerhead to the hook, Ford takes it.

"Here." He sucks the paste from his finger then grabs the showerhead, trails it down my body, pauses on my curls, and turns the spray nozzle to massage mode. My sex tingles. Out of all of the new experiences I've had with them, I'm very familiar with this maneuver.

Meanwhile, Ford swishes the toothpaste then spits it down the drain as he lowers the magic wand.

I'm surrendering to Heath's fingers spreading conditioner through my hair, his steel rod of an erection ready for shower sex, and Ford's addition, when I catch Ford's eyes flit to the shower caddy.

Pulling myself from the sexy promise, I grab my toothbrush and cup it to my chest.

Ford shakes his head and deprives me of the massaging spray as he positions the shower head in the cradle and trails a finger back and forth across my breasts. "Come on, Babygirl. Have you ever shared a toothbrush? You might like it."

I love how playful he is, but this is a hard no for me, no matter that it's completely illogical. I'm one hundred percent on Team Don't-Share-The-Toothbrush.

"Nope. My house. My rules." I tip my head back for Heath to rinse the conditioner out.

Wiggling his fingers into my toothbrush-clenching fist, Ford says, "Come on. Try it once with me. I'll be gentle."

James's laugh carries over the water. "Just use mouthwash, dude."

"I want to be her first."

We're all laughing. My heart is full. Ford pries a little harder as Heath caresses my body with my pearly soap on my bath pouf.

Ford almost has my toothbrush loose.

"Red," I blurt out, firming my grip.

Heath stops washing me and Ford furrows his brow. "Red?"

"It's the safe word, right? It's what everyone uses in the novels I read."

Ford smiles and huffs. "After everything we did, you're using a safe word on a toothbrush?"

"Yep. And you have to stop."

"I will, even though we didn't set the word up." Ford steps into the shower, sandwiching me between himself and Heath.

"I'm feeling a little left out here. How big is that shower?" James peeks in, but the space is clearly full. "At least I can watch."

He winks and I'm shocked at how the subtle gesture sends shivers through me. Am I more turned on by the prospect of being taken by two of my brothers in the shower, or by being watched?

Ford slides his hand to my sex while Heath peppers kisses down my neck. I wrap my hand around Ford's cock but he intertwines his fingers with mine and lifts them to his shoulder.

Whatever his plan is, I'm game...unless it's to wear me down and make me beg him to finish me in exchange for using my toothbrush. Not going to happen.

He kisses my forehead but I'm already too far gone to appreciate it. My head drops against his chest. I'm practically panting from the water's heat cloaking me, the heat of both of their bodies encircling me, and the heat of my next orgasm firing inside of me while James watches us.

Ford's voice is low and intimate. "Maggie, when I said you were mine, I meant it."

Sanity washes away. I lose track of his words. I don't know whose hands are whose anymore. Release is so close.

Then it's gone. His hand is tipping my chin up.

"Tell me you understand that you're mine."

Fucking hell. I'm criminally insane I'm so close to climax. But I grasp just enough of a thought to have fun.

"I understand. I'm yours...but my toothbrush is not."

# *Epilogue*

## Maggie

### Next Christmas

James grabs my arm as I head to the front door of our new home. It's a special night for us since we're headed to the second annual Christmas Cherry Auction.

"Did I forget something?" I whip around then look down and make sure I'm fully dressed, including shoes. With my pregnancy brain turned mommy brain, I've been known to do things like leave the house without pants or shoes. It's pretty bad, but thankfully I tend to remember when I get to the car.

He looks up and I follow his gaze.

"Oh my gosh, who put the mistletoe up? I can't believe I forgot about it." More proof that my brain has turned to mush. Thankfully our parents help out with our baby boy quite a bit, which is where he is now.

Mom and Dad were embarrassed by our relationship at first, but they love us and our child, so they accept our decisions. It is also bound to help that we're exposed to all of the crazy relationships in Eggplant Canyon, Peach Bottom Valley, and the Cherry Ridge Foothills.

Heath wraps his arms around me from behind and whispers, "It sure as hell wasn't Batman. He's not good enough for you."

"You're still jealous?"

"Light that bat signal all you want. You know who you belong to." He inches my skirt up but not high enough to expose the new panties I treated myself to.

I lean back, flopping my head into his shoulder, my eyes falling shut a split second after noticing James kneel in front of me.

My brain isn't too jumbled to understand what a lucky girl I am.

"And just in case you forgot who you belong to, I'll give you a special kiss under the mistletoe to remind you." James caresses my legs before pushing my skirt into Heath's waiting hands.

It's torture to suppress my laugh, but I only have to hold it for a second. I know the exact moment James sees my new panties.

"What the fuck?" James's laugh is low and satisfied.

Ford must enter the room because his deep laugh joins in as I'm no longer able to contain mine.

"What's so funny?" Heath asks.

"We might have to keep a tighter leash on Maggie. Seems her boyfriend might have bought her new underwear."

"She doesn't have a boyfriend." Heath steadies me, steps back, and lifts the backside of my skirt. "Sweetness, since when do you have Batman underwear?"

"Since I bought them at the store." That will get him riled for sure.

The possessive growl that rips through his chest is one that's always accompanied by a harder-than-normal erection—the kind that's extra satisfying to ride.

"Aren't you a little old for Batman underwear?"

"A girl's never too old to have a fantasy."

He growls again but this time, it's accompanied by the sound of a zipper being undone and clothes being discarded. James strips my panties, and Ford steps closer, claiming my mouth in a kiss. The first one under the mistletoe this year. Thank goodness they didn't let me forget my favorite tradition.

Warm breath eases over my sex moments before James's lips move in. Kisses and his tongue escalate the knot low in my belly. Without warning, Heath lodges his cock between my legs, sending James scurrying backward.

"What the hell, dude. My mouth was right there."

Ford pulls away to see what happened, and James wipes his face with a level of disgust only a brother could muster.

Heath unzips my dress and slips it over my head. "You had your turn to kiss her under the mistletoe, now she's getting fucked under the mistletoe, and not by Batman."

The funny thing is that my fascination with Batman wasn't sexual until a year ago when I realized how stirred up it got Heath. But my fantasy remains the same...to be claimed by my stepbrothers.

In seconds, I'm turned and hoisted to straddle Heath's waist as he sinks me onto his cock. The other two join in and once again, I'm living my fantasy.

Except in those moments when they forget how to properly squeeze the toothpaste, or think they're being sly and use my toothbrush.

They can still be annoying as hell, but I've learned that some of the teasing and tormenting really is because they're head-over-heels in love with me.

And we live happily ever after!

A bonus scene for this story is available exclusively to newsletter subscribers if you need a little more of these naughty siblings and want to know how the jet ski works out.

https://SylvieHaas.com

# Tinsel and Teasing

## A Reverse Harem Romance

Sylvie Haas

# Blurb

**When at first you don't succeed...tease them again!**

In a fantasy world, getting won by three mountain men in a charity auction would be a dream come true.

In reality, I've been auctioned off to three burly men who boast that their flannels need washing and their bellies are growling for a home-cooked meal.

Will I be able to tease my reality into a fantasy, or will I make a fool of myself in front of three very generous mountain men?

If you love dirty-talking men who have over-the-top ideas of how to please their woman and want to give her babies, sign up for the Christmas Cherry Auction!

# One

## Isadora

Rushing to the seat my friends saved for me, I plan on watching the auction from the audience until it's my turn to take the stage. Maggie and Roxy are up first.

As I weave through the maze of tables and chairs, my heart skips a beat that the table behind ours is occupied by three burly mountain men. Our town isn't that big, so I'm aware of them—good and respectable, but reclusive men. They live off-grid way up in the Cherry Ridge mountains and one of them has created quite the stir on social media by doing lumberjack things under the social media handle 'Hardwood'.

Yes, I'm one of his followers.

I'd secretly hoped one of them would come to the auction to bid on me. Can I tease them into it? I'll give it my best shot.

I stare at them—too long—and lock eyes with the thickest, bearded one. All I have to do is look away and navigate past a couple more people to get to my seat, but I don't.

Lost in his eyes, I wonder how good he would look between my—

A miscue catches my foot on the chair I'm passing, and I flail toward the lumberjacks. It's possible that I shriek too, but that's drowned out by the slap of my body onto their table.

All three of them have their attention on me, although the mounds of my boobs that are amplified as they're squished against the table are garnering the most attention.

A glance at my cleavage before I right myself assures me that my breasts didn't pop out of my dress in the accident.

"Are you okay?" they ask simultaneously, rising to their feet.

"Yeah, all good." I pat the table as I push up and away, noticing the bidder's paddle in the center of their table. "Show's over, you can return your attention to the stage."

That isn't what I had in mind for teasing them. Can I swallow my pride and try again?

They're exactly the kind of guys that bid on me in my dreams about the auction. Rugged, handsome, capable men who would take my cherry then keep me for their own while we live off the land and have a brood of kids.

That's the dream—one that probably has my grandma rolling over in her grave. I run my hands through my hair as I turn to my seat.

The reality is that if I can't even walk between tables and chairs, how could I expect them to trust me to live in the wilderness with them? The other reality is that getting to my job, my internship, and my college classes would be extra difficult from way up in the mountains.

But seriously, the auction is just for four hours of my time to assist with basic chores. I'd rather do that for them than anyone else in this room.

With nothing to lose, I look over my shoulder. "If you want to see more of me, keep that bidder number handy."

I toss in a wink for good measure then sink into my seat before their slack-jawed expressions have a chance to change.

Daisy and Nikita quietly fuss over me, and I assure them I'm fine.

Shuffling from immediately behind me catches my attention, and Daisy's eyes go wide. Glancing over my shoulder, I'm shocked that one of the guys, not the social media one, moved to the seat right behind me, and inched it closer than would be considered normal.

His two friends remain on the other side of the table, watching intently.

Unsure how to cope with this lumberjack's proximity, I return my attention to the stage. Is the universe giving me a chance to toss a little non-awkward teasing their way?

I need a second to think up something better than what I used in my dreams. *Hey, now that you won me, would you like to pop my cherry?*

A tap on my shoulder tells me that my time is up.

"Isadora."

He knows my name? How the hell can his voice sound like sexy, swirling heaven?

My throat feels dry. My body must be sending all hydration to my sex because the sound of my name on his lips has wet heat pooling between my legs. Slowly turning my head, I keep my voice down. "Yes, do I know you?"

"You're going to." His chiseled jaw, iceberg-blue eyes, and broad flannel-covered shoulders add to the confidence in his statement. The rich scent of his cedar cologne fills me with a torturous combination of Christmas coziness and wild sex—or what I presume wild sex would feel like.

Increasingly unsure of how to cope with his closeness, I decide to be playful. "Your confidence is almost as big as your..." I glance at his lap. "Shoulders."

He chuckles. "You like big shoulders?"

I choke on how easily he plays along. This is good. "Before I reveal such intimacies, what makes you so certain I want to get to know you?"

"You already fell for me. Then I caught you checking out my...shoulders, was it? Trust me, Sweetheart, when we win you tonight, you'll get to know all of us."

"We?" I tear my gaze from his blue eyes and take a deep breath while casually looking past him to his two friends. "You're bidding together?"

"Not just bidding... We're going to make sure we win."

Have my dreams taken over? Am I imagining the sexual undertones? I need to get a grip. It's not the Christmas Cherry Auction, it's Christmas Cheer, and we're raising money for the fire department.

For crying out loud, I was working as Santa's helper when that sweet little boy climbed onto Santa's lap and asked for better safety gear for his dad. Making his Christmas wish come true is what prompted the auction in the first place.

We have a serious mission so I attempt to distract myself from the naughty thoughts. "Let me guess, the three of you are bachelors who don't know how to properly cook or clean and you need a woman to come work her magic."

Yes, I'm a woman, and I volunteer as tribute because my distraction has already gotten distracted.

"Guess you'll find out when we win you."

"We'll see if you have what it takes." I'm too flustered to banter, so it's a cop-out. Plus, I wanted to get a feel for the auction. I force a smile through my nervousness and return my focus to the auction only to realize Maggie's stepbrothers are bidding on her. Crap. I'm not sure she realizes what's happening since she doesn't have her glasses on.

She's going to freak out. If I didn't have my heart set on being won by the mountain men, I'd beg them to bid on her to keep the stepbrothers from winning.

There are limits to friendship. It's healthy to put boundaries, right? So, it's okay to keep these guys for myself?

Thinking of boundaries, I haven't seen Jade in a while. I heard that she pissed off the principal and he'd ordered her to go to his office. Is my over-the-top thinking out of control that I imagined him ordering her there as part of...no. Surely, she's not hooking up with the principal while half the town is out here. She's always been the puppy-love kind of girl, fantasizing about so many guys.

Fantasies...while my dream guys are sitting at the table behind me, Maggie is living out a nightmare.

I let Daisy and Nikita know I'm going to comfort Maggie.

I stand, smile at the sexy lumberjacks, and wink. "Keep that paddle ready."

Their eyes barely have a chance to go wide before I spin around and carefully weave my way through the tables to get backstage. Maggie's going to need support.

# Two

# Luke

"Are you going to bid on her?" One of Isadora's friends asks when she's out of earshot.

"I'm going to win her." I don't bother to explain that I'm in this with my two buddies.

That elicits a big smile, followed by giggles the second she eyes the other friend, and says, "That would make her day."

The comment is simple but swells my chest. She wants me? That must mean she's mentioned me. The truth is that she's probably interested in Hardwood, or as we know him in real life, Clyde. I cannot understand how he makes money filming himself doing normal shit like carrying logs and chopping wood...shirtless.

Everyone knows you don't do crap like that without proper clothing.

My heart sinks when Roxy takes the stage. I'm ready for Isadora. Patience isn't my strong suit. I like to get shit done.

Clyde says, "Damn, these bids are high. The goal for the entire auction was twenty thousand, but the first winner covered that and this chick is going for a pretty penny too. You don't think we'll be outbid, do you?"

I crane my neck over my shoulder since I'm still sitting at the front edge of the table. "Nobody's going to outbid me."

"Us," Knox grumbles.

"I'll bid on my own if I have to."

"Chill man, I'm in for whatever it takes."

"Feel free to back out. I'll be happy to keep her for myself." A possessive streak burns inside of me, but the three of us are as close as brothers. I would never go back on my word with them.

I'd just like to figure out how to get her alone for our first time. For *my* first time. I'm way too old to be a virgin. It's the only secret I've kept from my Clyde and Knox.

But I'm getting ahead of myself. The winner gets four hours of basic help from the person they win, not four hours of sex. So why can't I get that idea out of my head?

The memory of her bent over our table, her tits spilling out of the top of her dress, and the blush on her cheeks has my dick hard. I'd take that sight again any day. I'd also appreciate the view from the other end, my hands taking in the curves of her hips, my cock prodding for entrance to her sweet pussy.

Her scent enchanted me. I inhale deeply but only a hint of it is left. I've got it bad for her. All of us do. From the moment

171

Clyde showed us posts about this auction in the social media gossip group SmorgasSmut, we were all obsessed with her.

I haven't been paying attention, and suddenly the auctioneer is taking a break, calling some people up front for a discussion. Does the rich dude from Eggplant Canyon who volunteered to be the auctioneer not understand that auctions don't have secret deals?

Nervousness weighs in my stomach. Is he trying to control who wins? I'll come unhinged if he interferes with me winning Isadora.

A few moments later, a consensus has been reached, and three guys are declared joint winners, just like with the first woman. I'm bidding with Clyde and Knox. By my count, that makes three. Let's keep the pattern going.

The blonde leaves the stage, seemingly pleased with raising the full twenty thousand, and undaunted by three strangers winning her. Will Isadora be as willing?

I lean forward, resting my elbows on my knees, my hands balled in front of my mouth.

My leg starts to twitch, forcing me to reposition. I sit back and rest a hand on our table, tapping anxiously with my knuckles.

Then Isadora takes the stage. I can't make out any of the auctioneer's comments because I'm consumed by the desire to rush up there, scoop her up in my arms, and steal her away.

Comments from men at the tables around us make me angry. They're going to bid on her. It's not that I consider them competition because we *will* win but I don't want them looking at her, talking about her, or even thinking about her.

Barely able to stop myself from causing a scene, a shred of logic tells me that confrontation would run too much risk of worrying her.

I grab the bidder's paddle from the table and extend it in the air. I don't know what the bid amount is, but I keep accepting whatever numbers the auctioneer rambles through the PA system .

Knox must not want to feel left out because he rips the paddle from my hand and holds it as high as he fucking can, not bringing it down when the bid is acknowledged, simply flicking it with his wrist every time someone else gets acknowledged.

Finally, the auctioneer declares us winners of sweet Isadora.

Now for the hard part—convincing her to go home with us. Although, after the scene with the first woman auctioned to her stepbrothers, and the second woman won by strangers, I don't suppose it'll be that weird.

After the way she was flirting with us and teasing us, all I can hope is that I don't fucking embarrass myself when they figure out I'm a virgin.

# *Three*

# Knox

Since I was holding the bidder's paddle when the winner was declared, I like to think that I have a claim to Isadora, but the deal with Luke and Clyde is that we're equals.

Our time in the military together took us through some rough shit. We have each other's backs.

And when we saw Isadora's picture in the auction information, the only solution to how much each of us wanted her was to share. With her permission of course. Any tasks beyond cooking, cleaning, and gift wrapping are a long shot, but those domestic tasks aren't what we want.

This is the woman I want to give my virginity to—one of the few things I haven't revealed to my brothers. I'm at least ten years overdue to have sex but until seeing Isadora's picture, I hadn't found the right woman.

Then she ended up at the table right in front of us. I'm willing to accept fate. And even if her falling on our table was pure coincidence, she teased us on purpose as if she wants us to win her. I recognize a win-win situation when I see it.

The bigger problem is that she might know about Clyde's social media persona where he's a lumberjack sex symbol or something.

Jealousy courses through me that she could have ulterior motives and might not be game for all three of us.

We head to the winner's table, not wasting a second, and the sweet lady sitting at the table makes a joke about three guys winning each of the women up for bid. This isn't funny to me, none of it's funny. I won't be relieved until we get Isadora home.

Clyde keeps the tone light. "I guess people realize that four hours of a good woman's time is pretty damn invaluable. I'm just trying to figure out how many casseroles she can put in the freezer so my belly stays full for a good long time."

I look at him, surprised, then see the playful look in his eye.

Luke adds, "Yeah, we've got piles of flannels that need washing. I guess she can work on those casseroles while she's running all our laundry through our washing machines."

A few people watched us at first, but more have turned our way, particularly in Clyde's direction.

One man says, "It's got to be a gimmick for his social media. He probably has fake followers and needs to pay a woman to pretend that she's obsessed with him."

The bitterness in the statement doesn't sit well with me. Even though I question Isadora's motive, I don't like other people talking shit about my brother. Punching a stranger could get me arrested and nix the chance of taking Isadora home, though.

"I bet he'll put her name on a piece of wood," a woman says, clearly familiar with Clyde, or rather, Hardwood's weekly drawing.

I turn to see who said it, but as my eyes land on the cougar-style women who are ogling Clyde, Isadora walks up.

She had to have heard the comment. Does she understand the 'name on the wood' reference? I study her expression, detecting no hints of recognition. My eyes dart back to the cougars.

Isadora laughs. "I guess they're jealous that you big, burly men didn't win them."

"We got exactly who we wanted." I wrap an arm around her and pull her close, my protective instinct taking over before I realize what I'm doing. I'm basically a stranger to her, but she sinks into me perfectly. The smallness of her body contrasts my bulk.

Does she not know about Clyde's alter ego? A few months ago, SmorgasSmut blew up with some rumor about him. It felt like everyone knew. We found a true gem if Isadora comes into this without the influence of social media. I wasn't even sure that was possible these days.

Clyde says, "Don't worry about what anyone says. We'll take good care of you."

She cranes her neck, smiling at me. "That's what I'm hoping for, that you'll take *really* good care of me."

# Four

## Isadora

Snuggled into Knox's side, as I've learned his name is through brief introductions, I take to the intimacy as if we've done it a million times, aside from the butterflies in my stomach, the weakness in my knees, and the adrenaline rush of thinking my dream might come to life.

My snap decision not to reveal that I follow Hardwood's social media page should be fine for the four hours we'll spend together. I don't want to be dishonest, but it's not like I'll ever see these guys again.

I'm simply going to see if we can swap favors. Is that too flippant of a way to think about sex? My grandma cautioned me not to be dependent on a man. She didn't say anything about using them. I'm in uncharted territory.

They escort me to the back of the room and ask if we can speak outside, which is heading exactly the direction I want this to go. I excuse myself to grab my coat.

My nerves are completely frazzled, then again, it's not every day that I plan on asking three men to take my virginity. Technically only one of them can, but I'll get a lot more experience than I planned. Luck is on my side.

With Clyde's social media presence, I expect him to be the outgoing one, but while he's as muscular and handsome as he is online, he's reserved once we get outside.

Luke speaks first, "We're going to be honest with you."

Not the first words I was hoping for in light of my omission. I nod politely.

"Our donation stands no matter what you say to what we're about to propose. Is that clear?"

"Okay." My imagination runs wild that the farfetched thought I had about losing my virginity tonight might not be complete fantasy—or rather, it's three fantasies rolled into one.

My eyes rake from Luke's confident brawn to Clyde's rugged handsomeness to Knox's bearded thickness. I force myself to take a breath when I realize I forgot I need oxygen.

"We don't want you for the types of chores that were laid out in the auction. Our bid was planned. We were going to win you. It was deliberate. And like I said, our donation stands. You're under no obligation to do anything for us. If you say no to our offer, we'll consider your part of this deal fulfilled."

It occurs to me that he paused, so I nod and swallow hard as I process the implication.

"We'd like you to spend the night with us for sex." Knox blurts out.

"Smooth, real smooth," Luke says.

"You were rambling. I want her to know what she's in for."

"Thank you. Clear communication is important, right?" I feel ridiculous saying that, but with the comments I heard about Clyde and this just being a social media stunt, I question who's using who.

Clyde's never done anything tacky on his platform. But, if his numbers are down, would he push the limits? At worst, he might ask me to adore him. No faking required.

But Knox clearly said sex. Will my lack of experience become an issue?

The sensation that wove its way through me when Knox's arm was wrapped around me makes me feel safe at levels I didn't even know were possible. How can that happen? This is just about sex, not feelings.

I mentally shove aside the connection. This is nothing more than a glorified booty call. We all get what we want if I go home with them. It's safe. After all, the whole town knows they just bid on me, and their names are documented on the winner's sheets.

This will be fine. Totally fine. What could possibly go wrong?

"Are you in?" Knox asks nervously.

Getting to have sexual experiences with three guys instead of one meets my goal three times over. "Let's do it!"

# Five

## Clyde

The three of us drove to the auction together, figuring we had room in the truck to take Isadora home. As I sit in the back seat with her, it's hard to believe that we pulled it off.

I've managed to keep from having a blazingly obvious erection the whole evening, but my cock has been thick and long against my thigh, waiting for her, anticipating my first time.

Not just with her—this will be my first time to ever have sex. Knox and Luke are going to die laughing when they find out. Admittedly, it's hard to believe I make a living being eye candy but have zero experience with actually pleasing women.

On the drive home, small talk covers things like where we live, that we've been friends since our time in the military, and all three of us needed to get away after the horrors we saw. Which was how we landed so remote. We've seen strife in other countries and wanted to be as self-sufficient as possible. We live off the grid, grow a bunch of our own produce, and hunt our own meat.

I'm happy to stay at a safe conversation level until I figure out how to deal with revealing my virginity to everyone. Isadora leads with a lot of questions, not giving us time to ask about her. I'm convinced more and more, with each passing second, that she doesn't know what I do for a living.

I describe my job as marketing and she doesn't ask for more. Knox explains that he's a financial guru. Luke restores cars.

With each passing mile, my lack of sexual experience weighs heavier on me. It's not that I mind having sex for the first time in front of my brothers. I trust them with my life. But I'm worried she's going to laugh. Fuck, that bugs me.

Thankfully, the other guys don't detour to dirty talk. It's like they instinctively have my back because they sure as hell don't know I haven't had sex.

When we drive up to our set of cabins, I'm sweating bullets. I have to get her alone and tell her that I'm a virgin, so she can laugh or ask whatever questions she has.

I don't know why I care more about what she thinks than them, but I do.

"Does the helicopter actually fly?" Isadora cranes her neck as the car turns.

Her mind is in a drastically different place than mine. There's a landing pad behind the main garage and it's clearly visible as the headlights scan past it.

Luke answers with pride. "Yeah, I'm a pilot, but there won't be any flying in the storm that's headed our way."

Not to be selfish, but I need to get her alone. Hopping out of the truck, I dismiss talk of helicopters and lead her to my cabin. "I can give you a tour of my place."

"We go where she goes," Luke says.

"I just figured I could show her around then you could each show her your cabin, and she can pick where she wants to hang out for the night."

Knox laughs. "You want to get first dibs, but we should let the lady choose."

"I promise, we'll just talk while I show her around."

"Nope, we're all coming," Luke confirms as everybody heads to my cabin.

Then it hits me. I don't have to hide things from these guys. If she laughs, they'll have my back. Or not, and I'll live. I lean into my normal lightheartedness as I open my door. "You know what would be really funny?"

Luke shrugs.

"If someone in the group hadn't had sex before, and we all got to witness their first time."

Luke studies me. "Are you saying..."

Isadora whips her head my direction, from surveying my cabin, and caresses a hand over my shirt sleeve.

My dick thickens. I'd love to get her into my bed and close the other two out—I'd only need about half a minute of my dick in her pussy. Damn this is going to be embarrassing.

"Are you a virgin?" she asks.

"Yeah." No point dragging this out.

Knox cracks up as he closes the door. "Wait. Our manly-man lumberjack, who's always boasting about putting women's names on his wood is a—"

"I am what I am. Accept it and move on." My words are curt as I cut him off, and replay everything he said.

He didn't reveal that I have a social media presence, just described it.

Isadora smiles and tugs at the sleeve of my red and black flannel shirt. "You do look the lumberjack part. And if it makes you feel any better, you aren't the only virgin in the room."

# *Six*

# Isadora

Knox and Luke coughed and sputtered, which tells me we're all surprised by Clyde's revelation, which is such a contrast to Hardwood, Clyde's online persona.

I pull off my best effort to keep cool. After all, I don't want to be judged for being a virgin.

There's a difference in perception of male versus female virgins though. Aside from guys who want a woman who knows what she's doing, some guys want to be a woman's first.

I don't know if they think at least for that one time, they will be the best sex she's ever had, even if it sucks. Or if men are more insecure than they let on and love the idea that there's no comparison. Or in longer relationships, unlike tonight, there would be something truly beautiful about taking that step.

Tonight is just sex, though. Get the first time over with. Don't worry about it. That's my goal. Do it with a guy who knows what he's doing.

So, Clyde isn't my guy, but it will be kind of cool to be his first. Based on the followers his comments make on his posts—the way they talk about him like he's a piece of meat—I'm sure many of them would take one for the team.

But he and his friends, or brothers, chose me.

The gimmick comment from earlier plays through my mind. Possible, but not a problem. I'm keeping this transactional.

Knox rubs his hands over his face and takes an abnormally deep breath.

Luke rakes a hand through his hair. "Okay, this is interesting. I'm a V-card-carrying member too."

Knox blurts out, "What the hell? All of us? Seriously."

That's exactly my thought, *Seriously?* They have to be lying. Maybe Clyde, but not the other two, especially not Knox. I'm sure a ton of women have tangled their fingers in his beard and pulled that mouth down to where they most want it.

I need to cut off any silliness. "Okay, guys, I really am a virgin. I was hoping to get bid on by someone who would help me with my virginity."

"Help you?" Luke says.

"I don't date. I'm not good with relationships. I haven't... Never mind, it just seems easier to do it like this and get it out of the way." I rub a hand over the back of my neck and scan the room while avoiding the uncomfortable topic of my distrust of men. No Christmas decorations, could we talk about that instead?

"That's fine, but I'm not joking about being a virgin," Knox says.

We all turn to him and he tosses his hands up. "I fucking live up here in the mountains with you guys. Have you ever seen me bring a woman home?"

I glance at them, my head swiveling as if I'm a tennis spectator. There's no disagreement to his question. This evening may be more transactional than I imagined. We all serve a purpose. Defile each other!

Knox adds, "Have I ever mentioned having sex?"

They shake their heads.

"So maybe the fact that none of us ever brought it up is because none of us have ever done it?"

Luke says, "I didn't think of it that way. I just kept quiet and you guys both kept quiet. I figured you were respectful about your experiences."

Knox says, "I never wanted to use a woman for sex. I wanted a connection."

My mind whirs, and not just from all the head swivels. What the hell is he saying? The whole point of this is sex, not a...*connection*.

An emotional weight in the room shifts. I defensively turn to Clyde. "Why don't you have a Christmas tree?"

Silence fills the room.

Knox finally says, "We've got Christmas trees growing all around us."

"But you didn't bring one inside to decorate." Am I going to ruin this incredible chance to have sex?

"No," Clyde says as if he's confused.

Uncomfortable conversations simmer close to the surface. I desperately want to keep the conversation away from why I don't do relationships.

"Do either of you have Christmas trees?" I waggle my finger between Knox and Luke. They each shake their head.

Luke says, "I guess we enjoy them in all their natural beauty, kind of like you. There's nothing we would need to change. You're perfect."

Here's my chance to get back on track. "Well, except that virginity thing. Can we get to that?"

Am I the only female on the planet who's effectively landed herself in bed with three sexy lumberjacks only to find out that they're all virgins? Good thing *having sex* takes priority over finding a guy with experience.

# Seven

# Luke

Isadora got fidgety when she mentioned the 'no relationships' thing. Maybe that's something we have in common.

My problem is that I've had this idea of the woman I want, and until meeting Isadora, that woman didn't exist. But now, I have to take a breath when I realize she's in my grasp...my dream woman.

"So how do we do this? I could get naked and whoever's ready first gets to go?" she asks.

She tries to come across as fearless about her decision, but I sense something more fragile on the inside. I will protect that with everything I have. And someday, if she shares whatever that is, I'll know that I'm worthy.

"Rather than just get naked and jump on each other, why don't we play a game? Can I use your computer, Clyde?"

Clyde motions to his desk. A moment of panic flashes through me as I turn. If his light ring and tripod are out, Isadora might ask questions.

A quick survey allows me to notice the light ring tucked in a corner, presumably with the tripod. His desk looks pretty normal, with a laptop and general office supplies. Nothing to elicit questions.

I know his password so I log in and search for a list of sexual conversation starters. Skipping past the ones that have super kinky questions, I print one that remains basic. Another search leads me to a list of ways to touch a sexual partner.

While cutting the individual items on the pages apart, I toss them in two piles in the middle of the floor and explain, "One of these is an intimate question. The other is an intimate act that doesn't involve sex. It's mostly touching your partner, lips on the ear, fingers caressing the thigh... We can pair a question with touching the person we're asking it to."

Everyone sits around the piles as they agree that it sounds like a simple icebreaker.

"Why don't you go first, Isadora?" I say.

She pulls a folded piece of paper from each stack and takes a second to read them. "Fingers in your partner's hair. Who do I do this too?"

"Your pick."

"All right. This is your game idea, so I'll choose you."

I scoot closer, lacing my fingers through her silky hair.

"Am I supposed to touch you, or do you touch me?"

"For this one, we can do both."

189

"Agreed." She runs her fingers through my hair and I want to sink into her. I want to hold her even closer. Her touch is what I've been missing my entire life.

My cock is hard, but when I glance around, there are two other hard cocks in the room, so that's not as embarrassing as it could have been.

"What's the question?" I ask.

She doesn't have to look. "This one's pretty easy. How many sexual partners have you had?"

My laugh comes out decidedly indicating that I'm relieved. I don't know what I'm relieved from other than being able to give her an easy answer.

"Zero."

"Same. Okay, do you go next?"

Pride swells through me at getting a twofer with her to start the game. Pulling two papers from the stacks, I can't stop the grin from spreading over my face. Things are about to heat up.

I reach my hand forward to cup her sex in compliance with the directions, but she bats it away.

Before I have a chance to explain, she says, "Oh no. I may never have played this game, but with icebreakers, you have to pick someone other than the person who picked you. That way it transfers through everybody."

Fear grips me. I didn't think about touching Clyde and Knox. I glance at both of them and they're wide-eyed, perhaps as shell-shocked by her statement as I am.

"I don't know about that."

She smiles mischievously. "I don't see any other way this can work."

"We could rotate turns with you?" I suggest the obvious.

"But when we're doing this tonight...the whole sex thing...you guys are going to touch each other, right?"

I'm not the only one avoiding agreeing with her as nervous glances are exchanged.

She worries her lower lip and says teasingly, "What if I want you to touch each other?"

Fucking hell. I would do anything for her...even touch Knox and Clyde. Swallowing hard, I say, "Then I guess I'll have to ask, which of you two wants me to touch your junk? I'm going to make this sweetheart happy."

Both men rise to their knees to make themselves available. Clyde is closer and grabs my hand, putting it on the strain of his erection. I'm not ready to admit this out loud, but my dick twitches and dumps a spurt of pre-cum.

Isadora's eyes are glued to our contact.

"All right, time for the question, Clyde. What's your favorite sexual position?"

"Wait," Isadora interrupts. "We both put our fingers in each other's hair. You could touch each other."

I shrug as if her request doesn't have my heart pounding from the swell in Clyde's cock. He deliberately slides his hand over my jeans-covered shaft before tightening his grip. My clothes have become painful, but I'm nowhere near ready to do this nude.

Clyde must sense my stress and answers the question. "I suspect my favorite position will be having this little lady on top of me riding my cock so I can watch her titties bounce and her pretty face while she comes."

She fans herself and says, "I think I'll like that too."

Clyde withdraws, picks two pieces of paper, and leans to Knox's ear. "It's you and me, buddy. Tell me about a time you walked in on your parents having sex."

Does Clyde realize he could have chosen Isadora?

Because I'm more interested in Sweetheart than what those two yahoos are doing, I'm keenly aware of how hard she flinches.

"Bet you wish he picked you." I think I'm being clever, but she diverts her gaze and shrinks back.

Wringing her hands together, she says, "Maybe we shouldn't play this game. I'm ready to move on to the sex. Really, really ready."

If only her words matched her demeanor. "Are you sure? It's like we told you at the outset, the donation stands no matter what you agree or don't agree to this evening. We'll drive you home right now if you're uncomfortable."

"I don't like this game." She composes herself and undoes the top button of my shirt. "Let's get to the part where three sexy-jacks take my virginity."

Her nervousness is gone. She undoes another one of my buttons, and I strip off my shirt. "Then let the fun begin."

Clyde asks, "Did you just combine sexy and lumberjack?"

Her laugh confirms she's relaxed again. "Not on purpose."

"Works for me," Clyde says, undoing his shirt. Knox rushes to join the undressing.

She teases a finger through my chest hair as she takes a second to watch them. "Ooh! A show, this is getting better all the time. Take it all off, you sexy-jacks."

Clyde tosses his shirt at her. "I'll be your sexy-jack any day."

I'm with him. I'll be anything she wants, but my mind starts to put together a few pieces of the puzzle. I'm pretty sure we're getting used.

Yeah, I'm fine with that.

I'm also determined to prove to her that she can't leave after one night.

# Eight

## Isadora

I can't believe I freaked out. Did I cover fast enough? Sitting on the couch, I make a show of sliding my hands down my calves to unbuckle my shoes.

The guys comply with my request to get undressed, and I suspect I smoothed over any weirdness. I don't want to talk about relationships. They're pure fiction. My family is proof.

I was effectively orphaned when I was eleven. My mom was killed in a car wreck and my dad has been missing for far longer. My dear grandma raised me and drilled it into me that women need to be independent because men want one thing from them. That's why I have to be careful. That's why I didn't date teenage boys my own age. Those relationships are destined for failure.

I'm dedicated to school and my career and being self-sufficient...and not dying a virgin.

Grandma scraped by, barely making ends meet at times because my worthless grandpa wasn't in the picture. Not even when she took custody of me.

Those concerns wither and die amongst the chest hair and sculpted pecs in front of me. Tonight is about checking a box...or doing other things with a box. Not about fantasies of happily ever afters.

All three sexy-jacks being as inexperienced as me has an odd appeal, even though it's the exact opposite of what I wanted. I'm empowered. I never thought I'd be anyone's first.

The likelihood of growing into a spinster with my little dogs no longer weighs on me. I can do whatever I want. This evening is already giving me so much more than a bargained for and I'm not going to stop the clock at four hours if Luke, Clyde, and Knox don't.

This is my big chance to tackle sex and walk clean away.

With my shoes off, and three gorgeous naked men standing in front of me, I rise from the couch and lift my arms over my head.

"Okay, sexy-jacks, ready to put your wood to use? I'm wearing exactly three articles of clothing and there are three of you. Coincidence?"

Luke steps forward, trails his hands down my sides making my curve seem exaggerated, then he tucks his fingers under the bottom of my skirt lifting this slinky fabric. The other two men stare and absent-mindedly stroke their cocks.

Clyde is next. He rubs his hands together as he circles behind me and tucks his fingers into the waistband of my panties before Luke has the dress pulled over my head.

I wiggle my arms to help get the dress off, while Clyde lowers my panties, nudging a foot to lift so he can strip me. For a moment, I'm not sure where his hands have gone, then they slide up the front of my legs, only his pinky fingers grazing my curls.

My body's so sensitized, he might as well be lighting matches the whole way. My breath stutters as Knox steps between Luke and me. The length of his body is pressed into mine, towering over me. His hand tangles through my hair, slowly tipping my head up so he can look into my eyes.

I lift a hand between us and twirl a finger in his beard. The smile my action causes creates a warm comfy feeling in my heart. This isn't right. It's supposed to be carnal passion, bodies slapping.

"I can barely believe you're real, Isadora."

I'm supposed to be getting laid. Do they think I want this?

His hips rolling into me save me from the mushy feelings.

I grab his ass and pull him closer, pressing his erection harder into myself.

He stares adoringly. His hands trail through my hair, down both sides of my neck, over the dip in my collarbones, and down my shoulders. How is it not weird to be nearly naked with these guys?

We're fully on track as his fingers detour behind me and fumble with the clasp of my bra. After a moment, he succeeds in unhooking it, all the while, Clyde continues kissing me from behind.

The parts of my body that Knox can't reach are easily handled by Clyde's lower position.

Knox drags my arms forward as he steps back and pulls my bra off. His head falls forward and he huffs, lingering on my fingertips.

Bringing my arms around my waist, I ask, "Is everything okay?"

"It's better than okay. You're absolute perfection."

Luke steps beside us. "Alright, how are we going to do this?"

"Is there a pecking order?" I ask.

"I guess that would be a pecker order." Clyde laughs.

"Maybe we shouldn't put it like that," I look over my shoulder and narrow my gaze at him.

"Do you have a preference," Knox asks.

"I don't know how to decide. I only toyed with the possibility of being won by one guy."

"We could draw straws?" Luke offers.

"No short straws here, right guys? I'm assuming the long straw goes first." Clyde says.

Would that be wise? Maybe the shortest first, or thinnest...that evaluation wouldn't go over well. "Let's keep it easy. How about we see who can guess my favorite flavor?"

"Pumpkin spice." Clyde blurts out as he stands and kisses the side of my head.

Cliché, but reasonable. The firmness of his body and the weakness in my knees have me inclined to declare pumpkin spice the winner.

Knox saves me from the little white lie by guessing, "Chocolate."

Luke cocks his head and smirks. "You guys aren't paying attention. It's vanilla."

"She's anything but *vanilla*." Clyde poses an interesting assessment of me given that I'm ready to have sex with three guys. The fact that I'm a virgin speaks otherwise. The real answer remains to be seen. But my soon-to-be-learned sexual preferences may not align with my flavor choices.

Luke narrows his gaze at my poker face. "When I held her close, I smelled vanilla. It's in her perfume, a warm, rich vanilla, so laugh all you want, but it's the most educated guess in the room."

"Am I right?" The possessive tone of a man who knows he's right and is willing to leave the power in my hands has my sex aching to be filled.

"You are. I forgot about my perfume. Vanilla has a stigma for being plain but it's amazing." An intensity washes over me that I can't place. Is it just the knowledge that Luke will officially be my first, and I'll be his?

"I'd be happy to lick every inch of you but it won't be your perfume I'd enjoy."

The knot in my belly is impossibly tight. "I wouldn't object except I doubt these guys want to wait that long."

His wink wrecks me. How can it do that, and what is he thinking? A moment passes before he grabs my hands. I want him to grab so much more. How can he remain so calm when all I can think about is that bead of pre-cum on his erection?

He calmly says, "Do you want me to take you to my bedroom, or Clyde's since we're in his cabin?"

"Let's leave vanilla to my favorite flavor. We have the rest of our lives to have sex in bed. Tonight's the night for exploring."

"All right." Luke motions around Clyde's cabin. "Any preferences?"

"Kitchen sex seems hot."

"If you sit on the oven," Clyde jokes.

"Would you knock it off?" Knox bats him across the chest. Their cocks bobbing in front of them send shivers through me.

"Okay, kitchen sex it is. We've got the counter, the table, the bar..."

"If I stand up against the bar, you can take me from behind." I'm more nervous about the intensity of how everything feels with these guys than the physical act, so I want to avoid staring into his eyes. Is that terrible? Am I disconnecting? Doing my normal, 'don't get attached' stuff?

"If that's what you want, that's what you get." He leads me over and I place my hands on the edge, anticipation pulsing through me.

His hands wrap around my waist and he turns me to face him. "Not so fast, Sweetheart. Let me enjoy you for a second before we do this."

He cups the back of my head and pulls me in for a kiss. It's tender as if gauging my acceptance. How clear do I have to be? Maintaining a calm demeanor, my insides are screaming, *I just want to get laid!*

I'm playing Whack-A-Mole with the feelings welling up in me. I've never felt so close to someone. It's the best thing I've never asked for. Red flags are flying all over my brain, and a few on my heart. No. No. No.

His other hand slides down my back, cups my ass, and pulls my hips tight against him. The thick shaft of his erection is sandwiched between us. If it's this amazing pressed on my outsides, how will it be inside of me?

He wants this as badly as I do. Why is he dragging it out? Let's get this over with. But is *over with* what I really want?

The warm, swirly feelings waking up inside of me are too tender, too intimate, too connected.

I see why Grandma warned me that sex complicates things. I thought I could stop the feelings.

Crap! This is out of control. I'm thinking of my grandma while naked with three sexy-jacks. I hope she's not a ghost watching from the other side.

A shiver runs down my spine and I can't tell if it's Grandma's ghost sending me a message or from Luke's lips trailing kisses over my neck.

Wait. There are more than two hands on me. Clyde and Knox are beside me. One of them ran a hand down my spine. That's good. Less chance Grandma sent me a confirmation that she's watching.

I have to focus on my mission or I'll be a virgin forever.

I pull back and tap a finger to his lips. "There will be time for that later. I've been waiting to lose my virginity all day long."

A wicked grin creeps over his face. "I've been waiting for a lot longer than a day. I just had to find you."

"You're ours now, Princess," Knox whispers the words into my ear. His hot breath funnels straight to my sex.

"Relax and let us take care of you," Clyde says.

Ahhh! Why won't they stop being so stinking perfect? My hands have ended up tied behind me in the failed game of Whack-A-Mole. All the wrong feelings rage wildly inside of me, tearing apart boundaries that have defined me and kept me safe. I can't get entangled in his kindness.

Oh no! My hands aren't figuratively tied behind me. Someone, I think it's Clyde, pulled my hands back and is holding them.

I wiggle one free, brushing it over Clyde's erection on my way to Luke's. Stroking his thickness makes me crave him even more. A new shudder moves through my body. The right kind. The kind that says we're going to have insane sex all night, then walk away in the morning, as long as I'm able—to walk. Emotionally, I'll be running for the hills.

I'll deal with that later.

This is a purely transactional venture to make four V-cards ancient history. Nothing more. I'll stay in control, or at least regain control as soon as I get back to my apartment and my two little dogs who rely on my income for food.

It's important that I get a good education and can pay my own bills. The giant attempt to remember why I can't fall prey to fantasy is complete. Now back to the erection stroking in progress.

I trail my fingers from his balls to his tip, sliding the bead of pre-cum along my finger. After we get all of our first times out of the way, I'll have to see if one of them will let me watch him come. I have so many questions.

Spinning between the three of them, I turn and brace myself on the bar taking a wide stance, and rise onto my tiptoes. "That's as high as I can get. Can you make it work?"

Grumbles from Knox and Clyde indicate I'm doing good.

The possessiveness of Luke's hands on my hips challenges my authority. His legs bend against mine.

"I can make this work." His tip prods at my entrance. "I want this to be good for you. Speak up if anything isn't right."

"Will do. I'm a big girl." I sound more convinced than I am. There are so many things that already aren't right, and yet, my world has never felt more right. I try to shove that dangerous thought aside but Luke keeps making it harder to do.

"You're precious, and I don't want to hurt you ever." His tone drops an octave.

Booty calls aren't precious. Why are the guys reading so much into this? And why does the world feel a little less ominous every time they say something like that?

Wiggling my ass at him seems to unlock him from the tenderness. Thank goodness. Capturing my hand in his, he maneuvers our laced fingers so that my hand is on top, as he brings us to my center.

"Show me what you like, Sweetheart."

Relieved to be back on track, I guide him to dip inside of me. The presence of his finger causes my sex to contract. My logical mind spins out of control. The warm, comfy feelings are gone as passion takes over.

I moan wantonly. "Right there, please, keep going. I need to hold on."

Hold on to what? The bar? Control? The newfound sense of belonging to somebody?

I return my hand to the bar, and he takes over with ease, doing exactly what I've shown him.

"Put your cock in me."

His subsequent fumble to grip his cock and guide it to my pussy lips gives me a second to breathe. He manages to keep his fingers on my clit, loosely doing their job while he enters me.

The slow thrust of our bodies merging is enough to lock down that sense of belonging, and he hasn't gotten himself all of the way in.

"Fuck, Sweetheart, I love you."

My body stiffens, then bliss—from my orgasm, not his love—relieves me of the need to respond. I fall apart on his cock and hand. Besides, his words are the kind of thing that's said in the heat of passion. They don't mean anything.

His growls, the tightening of one of his hands around my hip while the other falters on my sated clit, and the intense swell of his cock inside of my already stretched channel, secure the biggest, longest orgasm of my life.

My body lurches forward as new waves of my release render me spent. I slump onto the bar while the orgasm wrecks me. Everything fades away except his erection pumping in and out. His body stiffens, stutters, then thrusts with carnal intensity.

Then he collapses on me, regrouping to keep his weight from being too much. We're in full contact.

I wish we were in a bed and could relax while we bask in the afterglow. I wish I could have this forever—

What the hell? I shake my mind from the warm blankets tempting it. Snuggling leads to conversations and intimacies I'm not ready for. A deep breath helps me accept the perfection of our business agreement.

Turning my head to Knox and Clyde, I say, "You two want to figure out who goes next?"

# Nine

## Knox

Clyde grins. "Save the best for last, right?"

He's taunting me to declare that I'm the best.

"All right. I guess I'm next."

His mouth falls open when I don't take the bait. He played himself with that one. He also underestimates my desire to make Isadora mine.

I was certain we were going to win her at the auction by pooling our resources. And even though the three of us planned on sharing her, she could have limited us to casseroles and cleaning.

All of us would've respected that decision, but I had no intention of letting her walk away after four hours. I had a whole game plan on how to woo her. And right now, I'm beside myself that she's standing here, naked, offering her pretty little pussy to me. Soon she'll know this is much deeper than just sex.

My plan involved sending her flowers, telling her how amazing the food she cooked was, and asking if I could take her on a date.

Of course, during the four hours of her donated time, I would have talked to her incessantly, much unlike my normal self, to find out as much information about her as possible.

Instead, I just watched her have sex with Luke, and it was oddly hot, but I want privacy, and not just because it will be my first time. I want to be the only thing in her world when we do it.

"That was pretty fast, Luke. Guess you have enough energy to go prep a campfire. Why don't you help him, Clyde? We can snuggle up and toast s'mores after each of us make good on pleasing our Princess."

I've never used that nickname with a woman. It generally comes across as silly to me, but I want to serve her, so I'm sticking with it.

Luke is hung up in his post-orgasm fog, barely lifting himself off of Isadora. "I'd like to see you hang on any longer. She's meant for us. You'll understand when you're inside of her."

Clyde is the one to shoot me down. "We can get a fire going later."

Just as I didn't take his bait, he's not taking mine.

I try again, a bit more desperation in my voice. "Do you have wood collected?"

The transparency of my façade is doing nothing to insulate my intent.

He shakes his head and points a finger at me. "You remember how I was hoping to get her alone earlier? We're not going to let you do it either."

Luke takes a seat at the kitchen table. His cock is shiny with their mixed release, and still kind of hard. That's hot. I shift my gaze to Princess. The white mixture dripping out of her sweet pussy ignites something in me.

Luke could have gotten her pregnant. She must be on birth control. She didn't say anything.

My brothers and I would be good with getting her pregnant, but there's a nagging in my core that I need to be the one to do it. The longer it takes to put my seed in her, the more of a head start Luke has on making the first baby.

She spins around, propping her elbows on the bar, acting oblivious to the cream pie I just witnessed. I drop to my knees in front of her.

"I want to know all the ways to make you happy. Tell me if I do this right." I've watched plenty of videos, taking notes ever since seeing the information about her in the auction. There's a learning curve to eating pussy, so I get started.

First, I use my thumb, sinking it into her slit, finding that swollen little nub that brings her pleasure. Her body language is easy to read, I don't have to ask questions and she doesn't have to verbalize answers. They're revealed through every gasp, moan, and shudder.

Then I go for it with my mouth. It's crazy that some people say, "Grab a mango and try," but I can tell you, there is nothing like sinking your tongue into a woman's pussy. The scent, the taste, the heat.

It's decidedly not mango.

In moments, her fingers are pulling my hair. Mangoes don't give you that kind of feedback.

"Knox," she cries out as her release coats my face, drenching my beard. That's fifty-fifty with mangoes, they make a damn big mess, but they don't say my name.

Vague recollections of other things I want to do with her float through my mind, but this is a good start. I ease off, not wanting to make it too intense for her. I've read that can be a problem. She needs time to come down.

It's the same for a guy. I need a minute after the intensity my own hand offers. I can't begin to imagine what it will be like with Princess making me come.

I sit back on my heels. One of my hands holds her waist because I want to hold her forever. The other hand is on the front of her thigh, my thumb stroking over her sex. The light passes cause her to shudder, and I stare at the beautiful vision of her face, her eyes closed, her jaw slack, and her pink beaded nipples.

I lift a hand and massage her breast, rolling the hard peak between my fingers. "I want to do a lot more of that for you, Princess."

"I don't think I would stop you." Her eyes flutter open and a weak smile curls her lips. "We better finish up here so Clyde doesn't have to wait."

Damn it, I was all for her saying we needed to hurry with the games and hurry with Luke, but it's my turn, and I want it to last an eternity.

"I still get to make love to you."

Refusing to let me drag it out, she says, "Didn't you mention that you wanted me riding you? Shall we head to the bedroom?"

She pushes off the counter, but I grab her hand, and in one motion shift into a chair and pull her onto my lap. Her legs reflexively straddle mine. My shaft presses up against her curls and belly.

"Right here will be fine."

"Okay. I'm ready." The checklist tone of her comment tears at my heart.

I pull her in for a kiss, holding her body tight against mine, and those beaded nipples rake over my chest. Her breasts flatten against me over and over again with our heavy breaths until she leans back and drags her fingers through my facial hair.

"Sorry, I made a mess of your beard."

"Nothing to be sorry about, Princess. I'll be enjoying your scent for a long time."

"Or at least until you shower." She says it playfully, but if never showering again means I keep wearing her scent, I don't need showers. I laugh on the inside at how unpopular that decision would be.

In a heartbeat, the mind-blowing sensation of her pussy lips parting around my tip gives warning that nothing could prepare me for this. No matter how many times I've fantasized about her, envisioned how our first time would go, or dreamed that I could muster the willpower to make this last, I rush my hand to her clit. I'm going to need her to come fast so that I don't beat her to it, after razzing Luke.

Thankfully, she's ready to go, her moans reaching a fever pitch after only a few passes of my finger. Luckily, I just educated myself on exactly how she likes it. When she gets to the point that I think she's about to lose complete control, I thrust inside of her.

"Let that pretty pussy come on me, Princess."

Motion from beside us cuts into my tunnel vision. Clyde is stroking his cock, frantically grabbing a napkin from the counter, and blowing his load into it. Princess doesn't see because her eyes are closed.

What the hell is he doing? Not my problem, except that watching his muscles flex as he comes pushes me to the brink.

I'm about to unload inside of Princess when her walls spasm. My orgasm explodes. I fill her with my seed until our bodies are sweaty and spent against each other. Her weight drapes over me, and I wrap my arms around her, ready to fight anybody who tells me I have to let her go.

I don't know how much time passes, but Clyde is decent enough not to say anything immediately. Reality has started to return when he speaks, "Do we need to set a timer?"

She laughs, and the pulse of her body against mine warms my heart. I love her little smile. I love how comfortable she is, how confident she is that she wants this, and I don't have to wonder what she's thinking.

Or do I? She's set on sex, more so than conversation and connection. I can deal with that for our first time, but I fully intend to learn everything about her.

"I tell you what, Princess. I'll let you go whenever you're ready. But I'm by no means done with you."

# *Ten*

# Clyde

Isadora pushes off Knox's chest, and I toss the napkin aside and take her hand to steady her as she stands.

Making a royal, rolling motion with my hand, I bow, and say, "Okay, *Princess*, I believe it's my turn to honor you with my cock. I promise to do so for more than four seconds."

"Don't use my nickname for her," Knox says.

"Fine."

Knox continues, "But damn, is that why you just jacked off? So you can last longer?"

No shame. I return to standing. "Hell yeah. I want to spend a lot more time inside of her than you guys did."

Little Lady's eyes are wide. "Did you really?"

I nod. "Don't worry. I'm ready to go again."

She pouts, "I wanted to watch."

"I can make that happen, but right now, I need to be inside of you."

She doesn't understand that even though Knox used the royalty nickname, all of us are willing to bow down to her. I'd like to say I feel it more, that I'm the best for her, but I'd be lying. My brothers have never been so smitten with a woman.

There's no way they'll let me be the sole one to claim her unless that's what she asks for. Which makes me wonder if she's sampling us. Is there a possibility we won't end up as a foursome?

"How do you want to do this?" she returns to her hurried, methodical demeanor.

"I'll leave it up to you. It's not often we have royalty in the house."

She glances around, then looks at my erection, then at the kitchen counter.

"Would it gross to do it with me sitting on the counter?"

"It's my house. And hell no, it wouldn't gross me out."

"All right. I'm so short, it lets me be taller. And my legs are kind of tired."

"I can help." My hands wrap around her waist as I gently lift her to the counter, keeping her close to the edge, so I can position my tip at her entrance.

Her eyes rake over me. I love it, don't get me wrong. I can sense her hunger. But there's something about the way she does it that feels disconnected, that she's holding something back.

Or maybe that's just the way I see it. Maybe she's permitted herself to do whatever she wants, and maybe she doesn't want forever. My chest tightens.

I stroke a thumb over her cheek, then across her lips. "Thank you for trusting us."

"Thank you for buying me." A hint of sass returns to her voice.

"I'm serious, Little Lady. You wanted to lose your virginity, and that's fine. But if it's at all possible, I don't want this to end after tonight." I'm a total failure at keeping the appearance of casual sex.

"Let's not worry about the future."

Why did her voice waver? I long for her to say she'll accept us. It may be Christmas, but forget the Sugar Plums, visions of Isadora dance in my entire future.

Reining myself in, I recognize how she can be cautious. She's standing here with three naked lumberjacks asking for eternity.

"Will you at least stay the night instead of just four hours?"

"If you guys keep doling out orgasms, I could be persuaded."

"We can handle that."

Then I remember I have to get on my social media in the morning. I've got one of those stupid drawings where I choose a woman's name to write on a piece of wood and make lewd comments.

I respect the women who subscribe to my platform, and the schedule I've created, but I don't want to log on ever again.

My heart and body belong to Isadora.

But I recognize the look in her eyes, that I'm eye candy, and perhaps nothing more. My stomach knots. I have to get her past that. We won her in an auction and asked for sex. How can she possibly believe there's more?

"What you did tonight was amazing—putting yourself up for auction, not knowing who would buy you, and being willing to donate four hours of your time to raise money for the fire department. You have a kind heart."

"I also have *needs*, if you know what I mean."

I lower my finger to her sex and dip inside. Holy fuck, she's so slick, hot, and tight. "Do your needs have anything to do with this?"

Her hands slap onto my shoulders. "Yes, please have sex with me."

"What if I want to make love to you?" I put my heart on the chopping block.

"Let's not complicate this."

Why is she holding back?

"All right. Tonight it's sex, but after this, I'm going to prove that I love you."

"Says the only virgin in the room," she teases.

I growl at her, then realize what I've done. "You are going to be the death of me."

"Then we better hurry and have sex so you don't die a virgin."

I can't hold back anymore. I slide my cock into her, keeping my finger on her clit, making sure she's going to come before me. It is one hell of a fierce race. I thrust as slowly as I can, giving her time to build up another orgasm.

Pressing my lips onto hers, my tongue and my erection are inside of her. My sanity is shot. My world will never be the same. I want to devote myself to her.

I'll give up my Hardwood persona. I just have to figure out how to replace my income so I can be her provider. Then...fuck...all of the distractions I'm trying to put in place fall apart.

As her fingernails dig into my shoulders, her body lurches, and her pussy milks me. I give in, pumping stream after stream of hot cum into her. The sloppy sound of wet sex fills the air and I can no longer think.

All I can do is stand there holding her, praying that even though I went last, my sperm will have the most determination to make sure she has my baby.

# Eleven

## Isadora

"Fuck, it's ten o'clock. You better get moving, Clyde." Knox whispers too loudly, waking me.

We're in a tangle on Clyde's bed and I clamp my eyes shut against the morning light. I'm surrounded by warmth, happiness, and security. I'm exhausted from several rounds of sex. Some of which were starting to last more than a few seconds.

Happiness fills me that I got to share my first time with these three incredible men who made themselves vulnerable giving up their virginity in front of each other.

Clyde quietly grumbles. "Does it look like I care?"

He pulls me closer.

"You have your...*thing*." What is Knox being discreet about?

I cringe into myself when everything starts to register. If it's really ten, Clyde is supposed to announce the next winner in his extremely popular contest. He makes a short video where he draws a follower's name, writes it on a piece of wood, and makes puns about having her name on his wood, how hard it is, and all sorts of other hysterical things that suddenly don't feel funny.

He doesn't know that I know about it, because I planned on being long gone. Tension grips my body.

"It can wait," he says in Knox's direction then kisses the top of my head.

What am I experiencing? It can't be jealousy because I'd rather have his arms around me than my name on a log any day.

My brain wakes up a little more. We're snuggling. Those feelings of comfort and security aren't what I was trying to accomplish. But I like them...a lot. Too much.

A lump forms in my throat. One more orgasm and I might be willing to throw my dreams away. Grandma would be so disappointed, especially if I gave up all of the hard work I put into being self-sufficient over the passionate declarations of sexy-jacks.

There's an easy way to put this dilemma to rest for Clyde and me.

I roll and stretch. "It's fine, Clyde. I know about Hardwood. I follow you—just like all of the local girls. It's fun to have a celebrity in town. Go ahead and do your drawing. It's not like I expect any of you to quit your jobs because of me."

I force myself to stop talking because my thoughts are getting jumbled. I'm only here for a night. No one needs to think about spending so much time with me that they can't go to work.

Clyde's arm that's over my chest goes stiff. I could have handled the reveal more gracefully. Too late now.

"You know about that? Is all of this so I'll pretend to draw your name?" The Arctic blast in his tone is a polar contrast to the rest of our time together. I should have kept my mouth shut.

I shake my head but he's not looking. I manage a soft, "No."

"Quit moping and get your damn job done, Clyde." Knox is sitting and shifts me onto his lap.

"You just want time alone with her. Fine. You can have it." Clyde throws the covers off and rolls out of the other side of the bed.

Luke stretches as he wakes. He blows a kiss when his eyes land on me leaning over Knox's shoulder. Can he tell that my smile is forced?

"I'll come out to help like always," Knox offers.

Attempting to lighten the mood and keep this superficial, I say, "How about we all go? We can cheer you on."

Clyde stares out the window. "Fine, let's go."

He's the first to throw jeans and a flannel on, even buttons it, which is weird because I'm one hundred percent certain that even when he's had a shirt on in a video or photo, it hasn't been buttoned.

Luke hands me a blanket. "You can wrap up in this if you don't want to get dressed."

"Thanks. Will I be able to see from the porch? I only have my high heels."

Clyde must have been listening. "You can wear my slippers."

He ducks into his closet and pulls out big, brown, furry slippers, complete with claws.

Not what I was expecting.

He shrugs, "Or don't wear them. I don't care."

I stand and reach for them but Luke intercepts and kneels in front of me. "Allow me."

Cupping the back of my calf, he lifts my leg while Knox steadies me from behind. I'd think Luke was putting a glass slipper on my foot with as much care as he's taking. By the time the second foot is covered, I have two oversized Big Foot style feet. They're plush enough that even though they're at least six sizes too big, they might stay on if I walk carefully.

But that's not an issue. Knox scoops me up, Luke tucks the blanket around me, and all I have to do is snuggle in. How did I let it go this far? I should be at home with my pups.

New-fallen snow blankets everything, creating a pristine, magical environment. Tiny flakes continue falling, and I extend a hand beyond the edge of the porch to catch some. Knox moves forward so I can reach easier then directs Luke to set up the tripod.

Clyde knocks the snow off of a section of log that he sets on the chopping stump.

My chest tightens. I don't enter his contests, so my name won't be drawn. He'd have to fake it. Not that I'd want him to. Besides, his process is transparent. He uses one camera to stream the footage while holding the other camera up to show the random number generator he uses for the drawing. Then he scrolls down through the comments on the entry post and finds the winner.

There's a heaviness in his demeanor. He's usually rowdy, taunting every single woman who's watching with bated breath—at least that's how I watch.

Again, silly, since I don't enter. I guess I don't want to come across as a fangirl when I know that he lives nearby. My fantasy brain must have held on to the idea that someday we'd meet in real life and...well, I messed that up.

Naked, wrapped in a blanket, snuggled into Knox's chest while I twirl my fingers in his beard, I'm already agonizing over having to leave.

"Number one-twenty-three." Dryly, Clyde scrolls through his phone, skipping out on the normal banter. He looks toward the camera and Luke, who's standing behind it, motions as if excited.

Clyde regroups.

"Hey, hey, hey, ladies!" Clyde taps into his normal excitement. He grabs the piece of wood from the stump, making a show of partially wrapping his sizeable hand around the log.

"I've got a thick one for a lucky lady. This hard piece of wood is for you, Keaton."

He glances my way then pulls the marker from his shirt pocket, uncaps it with his teeth, and writes her name on the end of the log. When he holds it up, Knox is waiting with his cell phone to snap a picture that Clyde will use to send an autographed photo to the winner.

Returning the marker to his pocket, and his attention to the streaming camera, he keeps up the show. "Ready for a pounding?"

I imagine this Keaton chick is squealing with excitement that he said her name in a stream and that he'll send her an autographed photo. It doesn't matter that it's just his job, or that I'm getting something much more precious than an autographed picture.

Placing a hand on my belly, I wonder if biology will be on my side—and what that means. Do I want Grandma's lessons about the fertile and infertile times of the month to be correct? That outcome weighs heavily on my mind. That outcome would mean I can walk away from this and get back to my normally scheduled life.

Against all of my better judgment, I allow a niggling of hope that Grandma's teachings were wrong in a lot more ways than biology. Maybe there are trustworthy guys out there.

Clyde's icy glare catches me daydreaming.

The blanket and Knox's body heat are no longer enough to combat the chill.

# Twelve

# Luke

My heart is crushed when Isadora reveals she's one of Clyde's fans. I suspected it. Why didn't I trust my gut? Is anything that happened since the auction real?

I help Clyde make the video. It's how he pays the bills. But today, there's an edge to his tone no matter how much he attempts lighthearted jokes. He cuts it short too.

Do I stand any chance with Isadora or is she just a Hardwood fan who snuck her way into his life? Everything about last night felt real to me.

Set on winning her over, I say, "Why don't we go inside where it's warmer?"

I kiss her forehead while she's snuggled in Knox's arms. She leans her head into me instead of returning the kiss.

Will an explanation help? "Now that we got Clyde's job out of the way, ready to have more fun? I don't have to work today. I made sure to clear my schedule in case you agreed to stay."

I want to show her that I thought about this, that she means something to me.

"I should get dressed. My dog sitter leaves town this afternoon. I texted her last night, and she said she could stay till noon, but I have to get back."

"Your dog can't be alone?" I ask.

"I have two small, very high-strung dogs, and they'll bark incessantly if I don't get back. They stay with my neighbor when I'm at school or work, so they don't make the other neighbors grumbly."

"Could we pick your dogs up and bring them here?"

"I have to study and…"

"You have to study over Christmas break?" I glare at Knox when he opens his mouth to comment. He may be holding her, but this is my conversation.

"I have to study for work. I have this amazing internship, and I'm always signing up to help with projects. Sometimes I don't have all the knowledge I need, but I work like mad to learn. There's this big project—"

I put my finger to her lips. "Shh. We'll take you home if that's what you want."

I'm telling myself she needs time to process this amazing bond between us. My fear is that if she keeps talking, she'll end up revealing that she got what she wanted, and she's done with us. I'm not ready to hear that.

She glances at me from under her lashes. "Thank you."

"I want to see you again, Sweetheart."

Clyde is done putting his stuff away and heads over. "She won four hours, and we already did a lot more than that. Let her go."

Pain oozes from his words. If there's any chance of calming everyone down, he needs time away from her. Once his bruised ego lets go of her being a fan, he'll come around. We all knew it was a risk.

I bridge the divide, giving everyone space. "The auction gave us a starting point with you. We all want more."

She clasps her hands. "I'm sorry if I misled you. I just wanted to lose my virginity."

Ouch.

Clyde steps toward the door. "Done. I'll get the keys and drive you back. You've got a busy life. Might as well admit what this was."

Despite him offering what she asked for, she seems taken aback by his statement.

"Thanks. I still have my Santa's helper job. I'm just really busy, and I know you guys have to work, so that was sweet of you to take off for me, Luke, but look at the bright side, you're going to have the whole rest of the day to work." She tries to sound optimistic, but every word out of her mouth is a blow to my heart.

Why couldn't she just leave the possibility open?

Knox follows Clyde, and I'm last to go inside. Knox says, "I can do my job anytime. I also planned to take off today, so I'm not missing anything if you want to hang out longer, and I'd love to meet your dogs. What are their names?"

Nervousness flashes over her face as she shakes her head.

"If we get involved in each other's lives, it'll be too hard."

Hard? This was perfect. Something isn't adding up.

Clyde continues with his irritation. "Look guys, she fit us into her busy schedule. We're grateful for what we got, right?"

Knox and I stare at him dumbfounded.

"Fine. I'm grateful even if they aren't. Thanks for the fun." Clyde is uncannily callous.

Isadora wiggles and Knox puts her down. She grabs her clothes and rushes to the bathroom.

"I'll grab the keys." Clyde heads to the bedroom.

"What the fuck is happening?" I ask Knox.

"I think Clyde's losing his shit.

"I hate to say this, but we need to talk."

"We can't let Clyde drive her home if he's going to pout the whole time."

"Right. I also think there's something big going on with her. She says she wanted us for sex, but part of her wants more. We have to figure out how to help her find that part."

Clyde and my sweetheart return, so I address him, "We're going with you."

"I've got this," Clyde says.

"Not if you're going to be a jackass."

"It's okay," Isadora says. "Clyde and I need some time alone."

My blood pressure rises, but if that's what she wants, it might be our only chance for the two of them to sort out their bullshit.

"Be nice to her, Clyde."

"Got it." He holds his keys up and heads to the door.

# Thirteen

## Isadora

I should have kept my mouth shut about Hardwood. What was I thinking? Everything is so much more awkward now.

I need to get home. I can't think straight around these guys.

Instead of a leisurely morning followed by me asking them to drive me back to my car, discreetly parting ways without exchanging phone numbers, or only getting their numbers and telling them, "I'll think about it," I've created a total mess.

My damn feelings got in the way while I was sleeping. I had dream after dream of a life with them. I even imagined how wonderful it would be having *three* men so that if one failed me, I still had two more to fall back on. An odd compromise I'm not sure Grandma would agree with if she was still alive.

Even as I woke up, I hung on to the fantasy. I still want to hang on to it. I feel like I'm making the worst decision of my life as I walk behind Clyde who's snow-shoveling our way to the garage.

"We'll take the truck with better snow tires, just in case they haven't plowed yet."

"Thanks. I'd hate to end up stranded." But the truth is I want to be stranded with them. I want my decisions taken away so that I can pretend that there really are princesses and happily ever afters.

We head to the triple bay garage near one of the other cabins, and Clyde lifts the door revealing a truck with beefy tires.

A Firebird at the other end of the large garage catches my attention.

Luke and Knox are a few paces behind.

"Is this your garage, Luke?" I ask, noticing a bunch of toolboxes that I presume a car restorer would have.

"Yeah, but we share vehicles."

"Is that Firebird for one of your customers?"

"That's my baby. 1978 black body with a gold hood chicken. Not useful in the winter, but it's my dream car. I'm restoring it to its original condition."

"That's my favorite car too." I purse my lips. If I'm trying to disconnect, I can't make more connections with them.

How can I follow through with my plan to be a strong, independent woman focused on my classes and my job if I can't get my mind off these sexy-jacks? I chastise myself for enjoying my word that perfectly describes them.

Luke says, "When the roads are clear, I'll be happy to give you a ride."

I force myself not to take him up on the offer. I need time to think, and the only way I can do that is to get away from them.

"All right. Well, thank you." I extend my hands to hug Luke and do the same with Knox, then hop in the truck. "Thanks for donating to the auction and fire department. They won't need to do another fundraiser for a good long time thanks to generous people like you."

My monologue is overly stiff so I can hide my turmoil.

Before I know it, Clyde's driving me home. After he navigates the switchbacks down the mountain and pulls onto the smoother stretch in town, he says, "Why didn't you just say you were a fan?"

"I didn't do this because I'm a fan."

"I'm supposed to believe that?"

"I really did want all three of you, once I realized what the offer was."

"You should have just said something up front."

"Would you have gone through with last night?" I'm sure he wouldn't have. No way he would have revealed to a fan that he was a virgin.

"Doesn't matter now. You got what you wanted."

"I'm sorry if I hurt your feelings."

"Fuuuck." He groans, mutters to himself, and slumps. "I can't be mad at you. You have nothing to be sorry about. I let women ogle me for a living. People in town know what I do. I should be the one who's sorry. If you'll come back, I'll quit.

I'll help Luke restore cars. Or Knox could teach me how to do some of his financial stuff. I don't want to lose you. I'll quit if that would show you that I care about you."

Crap. All I wanted to do was patch things over, not have him upend his life for me.

"I don't want you to do anything drastic. It's really important that I get my degree, finish this internship, and get a glowing recommendation because they'll probably hire me, and I'll be able to support myself."

"You don't have to. We'll take care of you." He's decidedly more optimistic, but his words are exactly what Grandma warned me about. It's all good in the beginning, she said.

How much am I ready to reveal? I sort which facts I can deliver with minimum confusing feelings. "I don't have good role models in my family. Everybody's divorced. I need to know that I can take care of myself. I hope you can understand."

"How can I possibly understand what it's like to be afraid of love after I've met you, Isadora? But I will try if you'll let me."

I cringe. "I'm not afraid of love. I just don't want to be dependent on a man and live out another ugly divorce like everyone else in my family."

"See, you're teaching me already." How can he stay positive when he's pushing all of my nervous buttons?

"My internship...it's in the city. It's a drive even from Peach Bottom Valley. I couldn't do that from the mountains every day. And how would I get to school and have time to study if

I'm hanging out with you guys? My schedule's too busy for a relationship."

Stating it so clearly was supposed to feel good. It doesn't.

"Not all relationships mean that you have to give everything up. We could find ways to make it work. We all love you."

I'm not falling for that. If I stay with them, no amount of birth control could stop their efforts to fill me with a baby. And what would I do on winter days like this when my car couldn't get down the road? It simply can't work.

"Let's be honest. Even if there was such a thing as true love, it doesn't happen between four people. It'll be easier for all of us if we make a clean break. Maybe a booty call once in a while. If you guys want something more permanent, there were a lot of women at the auction who seem to wish you would've bid on them."

"We don't have interest in them."

"I'm sorry, but a relationship isn't something I'm ready for right now." My keys are already in my hand, and I hop out as he pulls up next to my car. This has to end quickly because my determination is dangling by a thread.

# Fourteen

## Clyde

The closer I get to home, the more I know I fucked up. Isadora might have started as a fan, but that's not what she ended up as.

She wants so much out of life, and I'm convinced that I can provide it for her if she'll let me help. I don't know how, but I can, especially with Luke and Knox because there's something about the four of us that works.

My brothers call multiple times while I'm on my way home, but I turn my phone off and make the drive in silence.

We need a game plan. Going after her right now isn't going to work. My temper flared. Her temper flared. I was hurt. She was hurt. Even with my apology, her defenses stayed up.

I'll regret until the day I die, and then some, having gotten mad at her. That's why I need a game plan to win her back, to show her that I can protect her and care for her, that *we* can.

She can still have all of her goals and aspirations and dogs and have us too.

Knox is outside splitting wood. It's his go-to physical activity any time he's stressed.

I park the truck in the garage and get out.

Luke's facing the Firebird. His elbows rest on top of the car and he leans into his fists.

"Why the fuck did you insist on taking her home?" he says, without turning around.

"Because everything fell apart. I panicked. I thought she was doing this for the wrong reasons. I was mad at her for deceiving me."

Luke spins around. "Did you at least get her phone number?"

I shake my head no, frustrated that I was so caught in the chaos that I forgot.

"Why the fuck couldn't you have just chilled? We could have worked it out."

"I talked to her on the way home. She needs time to think, and so do we. What is our goal?"

Luke scoffs. "We went over this before the auction. We want her here with all of us."

"She's afraid she'll end up dependent on us. We have to come up with a way to respect her concerns, and we can't do that by smothering her."

"She could have been part of the conversation if you didn't rush her home."

"Look, I expected to like her, but..." I tap my chest. "There's something in here I can't explain. It's too intense. It scared me

235

how much I wanted her, how much I needed her. When she confessed to being a fan, I worried that she wanted the idea of Hardwood, not the reality of me, or us. I love her too much to be a toy."

I didn't realize Knox was standing in the open garage door. "I know what you're saying, man. I had a thing for her. I wanted to keep her around. Then suddenly it was like I understood my life with her in it. I don't know how she did that to us, but we have to get her back."

"We will."

Knox asks, "So what do we do, Luke? You're the action guy. You have a plan?"

"She's a fan of Hardwood and knew about the 'naming the wood' drawing. Do a mock drawing, write her name on a piece of wood, and profess your love to her on a video. We could all get on camera to do it."

It's all wrong. I'm trying to think it through so I can present it in a way they'll understand. "Okay, first of all, what I do online as Hardwood is fantasy. I don't feel anything special with any of the women there. I don't want the feelings I have for Isadora to be mixed up in that in any way. I don't want to trivialize what I feel for her by putting her name on a fucking log."

"Women eat that up," Knox says, "It would work."

Anger boils inside me at the thought of minimizing her.

"It wouldn't." But I have an idea. It's going to involve a tattoo, but I could put her name somewhere special, an act that will never be a part of my social media.

Knox continues, "I think you should do it. She'll see it. Everybody will go fucking apeshit on there if you say you fell in love. And Isadora isn't a common name so it's not like there's going to be any mistake who you're talking about. I bet you'll have all the women scrolling through every set of comments trying to see who she is."

I shake my head. "I have a plan and I'm going to need some time to pull it off. Give her some time to get through this holiday season—"

"You're kidding me," Luke says. "Let her go through the Christmas season without us?"

"I don't like waiting any more than you, but she cares about her job, her internship, and college. This woman is smart, so how she ended up with us is beyond me. If we don't come up with a plan as to how she can keep pursuing her goals, she's not going to be game for anything we say. We can't just do everything for her."

Luke picks up when I pause for a breath. "So instead of steamrolling into her life, we need to show that we care who she is, and give her time to learn that we're here for her in every way."

"Exactly, or we're going to lose her."

Knox sulks. "It feels like we already did."

# Fifteen

## Knox

There's a searing pain through the center of my chest. I'd swear I'm having a heart attack, but I just miss Isadora.

I'm not happy that Clyde has a secret plan. I want this all in the open, but he swears he'll tell us, and ultimately, I trust him.

We spend a few hours brainstorming, then meet up at Clyde's cabin to see what we've all come up with. It had to be Clyde's cabin because that's the only place we've ever had Isadora so it's the closest we can be to her right now.

"What did we come up with?" I ask once we settle in Clyde's living room, where we first saw Isadora's perfect naked body. My cock gets hard with the memory.

Clyde says, "We have to address her dogs, and how she gets back and forth to school and her internship. The Santa's helper job will be over soon, so that's not as big of a deal."

I blurt out a concern. "I don't like her wearing that skimpy dress while letting single dads ogle her under the guise of taking their kids to see Santa."

"Me either, but you're going to have to let her make her own choices," Clyde says.

Luke offers a point of logic. "She was a virgin when she came to us. It's safe to say we can trust her."

"Trusting her isn't a problem, but I still don't like it."

"Don't run her off," Luke demands.

I pull my brain back to the obstacles. "I'll build an enclosed area for her dogs. I can even make a heated section."

"Great. Next, she has to have a way to get to the city." Clyde nods at Luke, and I immediately realize what he's thinking.

Luke does too. "Already on it. Free helicopter rides for the princess."

"I'm not going to warn you again. Stick with your own damn nickname for her," I growl.

He regroups. "Free helicopter rides for my sweetheart. I checked with a friend in the city. He owns one of the buildings with a helicopter landing pad. I can fly her to town and then pick her up when she's done. He agreed that she can keep a car in the parking garage. How does that sound?"

"It's fucking outlandish but I love it. I think we've got to go big with her."

Luke says, "Go big or go home. She's worth it."

I nod and say, "Is it that easy? Did we figure it out?"

I put my fist forward and the other two meet it for a fist bump.

"What are you doing for her?" Luke asks Clyde. Good question. Clyde didn't reveal his secret yet.

"You two have the basics covered, but I've got a drastic backup plan."

"Which is…" Luke says leadingly.

"Going to stay a secret unless we need it. But there's one other problem. How to get hold of her."

Luke says, "I don't remember the blonde chick's name from the auction—"

Clyde interjects, "Maggie was first with the stepbrothers, then the blonde was Roxy, and finally our sweet Isadora."

Luke adds, "Yeah, all three of those ladies were friends, and they had a fourth friend who was too shy to be in the auction, but from what I heard, she was serving soup one minute and getting railed in the principal's office the next."

"I heard the same thing. News travels fast." Clyde raises his eyebrows.

"Well, Clyde, if you stayed off SmorgasSmut, it might not travel quite as fast because I hadn't heard that." Then again, I'm last to hear most gossip.

Luke waves a hand between us. "Back to my point…Roxy went home with Mac, the new billionaire who moved into the Cherry Ridge foothills just down the mountain from us. I tracked down his number through the realtor who sold him the house, then texted and called him to see if she has Isadora's number."

Damn! We might figure this out sooner rather than later. I sit back in my chair and lace my fingers behind my head. The pain in my chest is almost tolerable. "I'm warning you, Luke... When we get her back, I'm going to fuck her on that Firebird."

"What the hell?" Luke looks offended.

I raise my eyebrows. "I saw the way she looked at it, her favorite car and all. I'm going to make every fantasy that woman has ever had come true. If we scratch the paint job, you can put your skills to work to fix it.."

Luke shakes his head, "Fair enough. If we have to throw in 'sex on the Firebird' to win her back, let's do it."

His phone dings, and when I see that it's Mac, the searing pain in my chest is reduced another notch.

"Hold on guys. I got a text from him. Maybe this is Isadora's number." He's full of hope.

He clicks the screen, then his expression falls flat. He shakes his head and holds his phone for us to see. As I read the message, the searing pain rips my chest in two.

Mac told Roxy, she checked with Isadora, and Isadora said not to give us her number.

# Sixteen

## Clyde

A week passed with no word from Isadora. The only good thing about that is my tattoo had time to heal.

Unable to wait any longer, I reached out to Mac and urged him to put me in touch with Roxy. Perhaps because Roxy and her three guys worked it out, I was able to convince her that we're serious about Isadora.

That paved the way for Roxy to invite Isadora over to visit, which was secretly a setup for Luke and Knox to pick her up—which is where they are now.

Desperate to show Isadora that she has nothing to worry about when it comes to me writing women's names on wood, I made the bold move of getting *Isadora* tattooed on my cock. I flew in an artist with penis experience and rented a space in a local booth so the guys wouldn't know what I was up to.

There are exactly two people in the world who know what I've done. And as the minutes tick away, it occurs to me that Isadora might think I'm a total idiot.

I've never been this insecure about anything. Needing to stay busy, I grab the cocoa powder, sugar, vanilla, and milk, so I can make my grandma's super-rich hot chocolate. I've never bothered with her secret ingredient, but tonight, I'm adding it, because adding 'love' to a recipe doesn't sound odd when I'm about to reveal to a woman that I tattooed her name on my cock.

They park in front of my cabin as I'm getting mugs out.

Two layers of nerves peel away when I see her smile. One, she agreed to come home with them. Two, she's happy. So far, so good.

Rushing to meet them at the door, I swallow her in a hug. "I've missed you so much, Little Lady. Thank you for coming back to hear us out."

"They didn't tell me anything in the car, so let's get started. I have something to tell you too."

My brothers and I freeze but when she doesn't elaborate, I walk her to a chair in the living room then the three of us guys sit on the couch. Giving her space sucks. This better work.

Luke says, "We respect that you don't want distractions in your life because you're passionate about finishing your degree and working as a chemist. We also, can't get past how badly we each need you in our lives. So, we've come up with a plan."

Knox interrupts, "Princess, we aren't whole when you're gone."

I nod, wondering if my insane tattoo will diminish how intense this situation is. While Luke continues, I dole out the hot chocolate.

"Here's the plan... Knox will build a heated, enclosed area complete with grass and sunshine for your dogs. Luke will fly you to school and work any time you need him to. And I can tend to your pups while you're gone."

Which I hope isn't often because being away from her for a week was torturous.

"Wow, that's quite the offer. What about sleep? You guys gave me quite a workout." She hides her smile behind her cocoa mug.

"We're here for you, and will respect your need for sleep if all-night sex is a deal breaker." I pause while everyone laughs, including Isadora, and my world starts to feel whole again. "We're committed to your happiness."

"Not sleeping would be a deal-breaker. Thanks for being so considerate. But I have to ask... What's in the cocoa? This is the best."

"It's my grandma's recipe," I say.

"There's something special about it I can't quite place. Is there a secret ingredient?"

Shifting my gaze between Knox and Luke, I hope they won't razz me about this. There will be plenty of razzing to dole out when I reveal my tattoo.

"My grandma always said to add a heavy dose of love."

Isadora's smile fades. Crap. Was that a bad call? Did I incorrectly assume that the thing she has to say is that she loves us, or possibly could?

"It's hokey, I know, but other than that, it's a pretty standard recipe. Maybe it's just the vanilla you like."

Knox and Luke shift nervously beside me.

She closes her eyes for a second, takes a deep breath, and says, "Actually, your grandma is wise. Love makes all the difference. That's what my grandma didn't know about. It's why she cautioned me that men only want one thing. But she never got the chance to meet amazing men like you."

"I'm sorry about your grandma," Luke says.

"It's okay. She lived a good life. Made the most out of what she had. And maybe it's because of her that I found you three. I wasn't ready to say this sooner, but I love you. All three of you. That's what I needed to tell you."

We rush around her chair and hug her as tightly as possible without spilling the cocoa she has both hands wrapped around. My heart's about to explode with happiness.

"Have you taken a pregnancy test yet?" Knox asks. Nothing like getting right to the point.

She shakes her head.

Realizing there's no perfect time to tell someone their name is on your cock, and wanting to remove any fear she has that I'm fully invested in her, I go for it. "Before you take one, I want to remove all shadow of a doubt that I'm fully committed to you."

"What more can you say? You're offering everything I could want. Even the best cocoa ever."

"Don't ever think that because of what I've done online, I have anyone but you in my heart." Standing and tucking my thumbs into my sweats, I shove my pants down to mid-thigh. Too soon. I meant to explain the tattoo first.

Isadora spews the cocoa she's sipping and they all gawk at my penis.

# Seventeen

## Isadora

Isadora covers her mouth and sets the cup down. "I'm choosing not to think about how this happened. Does anyone else have one of these?"

Luke grabs a napkin and wipes the spray while he and Knox explain that this is the first they knew of Clyde's tattoo.

"Hands down, that has to be the most sincere and the craziest gift anyone's ever given me." I'm not sure how giving a blowjob to my name is going to feel, but I guess I'll have other things on my mind while we're intimate.

He pulls his pants up after we inspect the tattoo, and says, "I have another surprise."

Gathered around the tree they didn't have last time I was here, Luke scoffs, "Anything you come up with after a cock tattoo is going to be anti-climactic. You probably should have led with this other surprise."

"No, it had to go in this order." Clyde reaches behind the tree and pulls out three envelopes without names so they must all

247

be the same. He doles one out to each of us. The guys flip them over and open them with as much curiosity as I have.

A gift certificate for a tattoo. My stomach knots. Crazy thoughts run through my mind as I nervously glance at Knox and Luke's envelopes, which they're also pulling tattoo certificates out of. I meet Clyde's gaze. He's beaming with pride.

I don't want to cut him down and tell him that I am not putting anyone's name on my lady bits, but before I can get a word out, Knox gives a very clear, "Hell no, man."

He shifts his eyes to me. "I love you Isadora, but there ain't no way I'm letting someone poke needles in my dick."

"Fair enough, because I'm not keen on getting three names down there. The boob, the butt, maybe. But no, not the sensitive bits."

Luke waves his certificate. "Yeah, Clyde, I think you're the only one of us that's crazy enough to get a tattoo like that. You're on your own, man."

Clyde busts out laughing. "I had a feeling that would be the case. I'm not asking anyone to go to the same lengths as me. What I'm proposing is that we tattoo wedding rings."

Clyde grabs one more envelope from behind the tree. "One for me too. Is everybody in?"

He opens the envelope he's holding and pulls out pictures of lock and key tattoos that people have gotten as rings.

"Oh my God, I love it, Clyde. That's amazing. Yes, I'll do it." This may be the weirdest proposal ever, and just as I'm realizing

I should make it clear that I will marry all of them, not just Clyde, he studies the paper.

"And right here..." He points at a drawing of the tattoo and holds it closer to me.

What the heck? It says LICK across the top. "Why does it say lick?"

What kind of perverted hell am I agreeing to? And why does this perverted hell feel so perfect? I've missed them so badly since I stormed out that day. Being away from them didn't make life easier. It got harder day by day, as I slowly worked through the myriad of emotions and potential changes in my plans.

"Lick, seriously? Why? The lock and key are great, but not 'lick'." Knox shares my concerns.

"It's our initials."

Silence fills the room for a beat before we all crack up. Clyde throws his arms around me, Knox is next, and Luke has to shove them aside to work his way in and says, "I got a sexy dice game for us, which kind of seems childish in light of a Christmas marriage proposal complete with tattoos."

Knox says, "Wait. Are we all in on this marriage thing? Because Princess, I need to hear that you will marry all of us."

"I will."

"I love you, Isadora. Thank you for coming back to us," Knox says, and we all exchange I love yous.

I shed some tears. The guys suddenly cough a lot. I don't press, but I think my sexy-jacks might be a little teary-eyed over our engagement. It's okay. We can be ourselves when we're together. They don't have to be manly and sexy all the time. With a lifetime ahead of us, I want them to be real because there's no other way we can be.

"All right, Isadora, time for the present I got you." Knox grabs his phone out of his back pocket, taps the screen, and hands it to me.

An investment report. "This has my name on it. I don't understand."

"You want to be sure that you're never dependent on anyone, that you can always take care of yourself, so I set up an account with a nice little nest egg for you."

"That's a lot of zeros."

"Five to be exact."

"You gave me a hundred thousand dollars? I don't understand."

"It's all yours. And because I don't want you to feel like you're dependent on me to manage it, there's an advisor's name at the top. She'll be your go-to person if you have any questions. It's one hundred percent yours."

"I can't believe you're doing this."

"Me either," Luke rubs a hand over his face. "You guys could have warned me what you were doing."

Knox smiles at Luke then turns back to me. "It's to show you that we want you, but we don't want you to feel trapped. But rest assured, I will go to my grave making sure you're cared for, Princess."

"I don't feel like thank you is big enough." And I didn't come prepared to swap presents.

"Your smile is all I need."

"I'm so embarrassed. I didn't get you any gifts."

Luke grins. "You gave us something much better... You're here. And there is one more gift." He reaches under the tree.

"Oh, the dice?" I ask. It's a box that could reasonably hold a dice game.

"No. Open this up and you'll understand."

I peel back the paper, immediately realizing that I'm holding a pregnancy test. "I don't think it can work this soon."

"There's one way to find out, Sweetheart. We're all dying to know."

Nervousness wells up in me. I wasn't on the part of my period where I should have been able to get pregnant, but if there's anything to be said for the many efforts that night, a miracle might have happened. And it would be a miracle I'd readily accept, being connected to these guys forever.

I open the box and pull one of the tests out. "I'll take this on one condition."

The guys scramble to express their concern in a jumble. "Of course, anything you want. Whatever you need, just let us know."

"I get to pee on the stick alone. I get privacy in the bathroom, now and always. The door has to be closed whenever someone is on the pot. Is that clear?" Once again, we're all laughing, and it's the best sound in the world.

Even if I don't want them in the bathroom with me while I'm doing my business, we can still be happy together. I have my limits.

"All right, but there's one thing I have to know before you take that test," Luke says.

Clyde elbows him. "Can't it wait? I'm dying to know if we're dads."

"Hold on." Luke reaches under the tree again and hands me another small box.

I open it, finding the dice game. "This is what you need to know?"

"Yeah, roll those dice because I need to know how I'm going to take you on the Firebird to celebrate what I assume is going to be a positive test."

# *Epilogue*

## Isadora

### Three Years Later

Luke leads me to his garage workshop, and Clyde and Knox
follow along. I suspected he had something going on out there
because he hadn't opened the bay doors recently. And every
time I wandered that direction, the guys conveniently detoured
me away.

Since I love their surprises, I didn't sneak a peek when they
were gone. Plus, it's rare that one of them isn't around. When
they said they would be there for me and take care of me forever,
they meant it. They all work from home, which is great since we
have a toddler and another one on the way.

Clyde gave up his Hardwood persona only to realize he
missed the social aspect. Thus, *Dadvice* was born. He uses his
social media savvy to openly discuss the joys and struggles of

being a dad. He limits his followers to men, the best he can, so that dads have a safe space to discuss their reality.

The flexibility of Dadvice allows him to be there for our little one while I'm at work, which is almost entirely from home now that I'm working as a theoretical chemist. But the sanctity of focus time can never be overestimated, so he treats my work time as if I'm in the city.

And while I loved getting to see the mountains and valleys from Luke's helicopter rides, I love being home all the time even more.

In their spare time, they've been building 'the big house' as they call it. We won't have to swap between their three cabins much longer. The monstrosity they're building for our growing family is a truly luxurious mountain home.

I stare at it as we walk to the garage. It's almost finished, with huge walls of windows and a wooden deck surrounding the entire house. I feel so blessed to have ended up with them.

They say we have to have at least three kids so that they can each inherit one of the cabins when they grow up, and live near us forever.

Luke undoes the lock I hadn't realized he'd put on the bay door. "Did you think I was going to peek?"

"Just making sure, Sweetheart." He slides the door open and there sits a gorgeous white and red Firebird with a big red bow on it. His black and gold Firebird is awesome, but this is the color combination I love.

My hands are over my mouth and I'm shaking. "Is this for me?"

Luke says, "It sure is. It's fully functional with safety features updated. But we have to christen it."

"I like your thinking."

He points to a small box up by the windshield. I unwrap the package expecting it to be keys, but I'm surprised by a set of three dice.

"More games Luke, really?"

"I guess I just need more escuses to fuck you."

Knox and Clyde grimace because we've been trying to use less profanity.

"Good thing the baby's not here," I chastise him.

"I watch my mouth when she's around."

"I know you do." I rub my hands over my eight-month-pregnant belly. "So what are you proposing with these dice? Were the old ones not good enough?"

"Take a closer look."

Knox and Clyde step closer as I lift the green one. I read the different sides: *mouth, cock, hand*. Nothing crazy. Then I grab the blue one: *pussy, butt, mouth, hand, tit, belly*.

Luke taps the green one. "That's what we're going to use. And the blue one is where we're going to use it."

"And the black die?" As I lift it, I realize that it has their three names.

"I had them custom made. You'll never have to fret over who goes first again."

"Mind if we start now?" I'm always horny around my guys, and the pregnancy hormones aren't helping any.

The shop is heated, so as soon as we close the bay door, it'll start warming up. Plus, baking this baby tends to keep me pretty hot.

Luke lowers the door. I step to the work table and roll the dice. "Okay, it came up as *cock*. Now let me roll who...*Knox*."

He strips his clothes and says, "I like the way this is going."

I roll the third one. "In my pussy, sounds perfect."

"Damn straight it's perfect." He helps me get naked.

While the other two are undressing, Luke grabs the bow from the hood and positions it on my lower back while I roll again. "As always, you're my favorite thing to unwrap."

I angle my head to Luke, "I rolled cock again. Is this loaded?"

"My cock? Yes. The die, no."

I roll the placement die and get *mouth*. "Okay, cock in mouth, that's a blow job. Cock in pussy, so far this works." I roll for the person. "Luke is the lucky winner of a blow job."

He rubs his hands together. "All right, this is working out. Let's see what Clyde gets."

I fully expect the body part to show up as cock. I'm convinced that Luke, in getting the custom-made dice, had it loaded. A smile creeps over my face at the thought of Clyde's cock, and of course, the tattoo. I'm fairly certain it will remain the most dedicated thing anyone ever does for me.

And if I stand to his left, I don't even see the tattoo since it's on the other side of his cock, thus I'm able to embrace pockets of normalcy.

Rolling the green die, it comes up with *mouth*. And when I roll the location, it's the *tit*—lovely that he called it tit and not breast or nipple. Oh well, it doesn't really matter. The bottom line for all of this is that I'm about to be one very happy girl.

"Get on the hood Luke. That will put you at a good height, and I'll suck your cock while Knox gets me from behind. Clyde, can you manage from there?"

"If it means being with you, I can manage from anywhere, but be warned...my cock will be inside of you before we leave this garage."

"I'm counting on it." Because I have three wonderful sexy-jacks who are living proof that fantasies can come true.

And we live happily ever after!

If you're reading in order, you probably already know this...a bonus scene is available exclusively to newsletter subscribers!

https://SylvieHaas.com

# Holidays and Handcuffs

## A Reverse Harem Romance

Sylvie Haas

# *Blurb*

**I just won three fire fighters in a charity auction...it must be time to heat things up!**

A bad breakup.

A big inheritance I'm supposed to donate to a worthy cause.

A charity auction with three hot fire fighters, who happen to be members of the local MC.

What could possibly go wrong?

For starters, I could insist in front of everyone that I need the guys I just won to assist me with yardwork right away.

Then, instead of noting that it's nighttime, they could agree.

Then the alcohol could wear off AFTER they take me home and I confess a few secrets!

What's a girl to do with three chiseled fire fighters who are DTF? (Doing Their Fundraising, of course)

One option would be to salvage my reputation. The other...isn't as easy as I thought it would be to walk away from.

If you love dirty-talking men who have over-the-top ideas of how to please their woman and want to give her babies, you'll fit right in at the Christmas Cherry Auction!

# *One*

## Sasha

My anxiety level rises as each minute passes in the Christmas Cheer Auction, or as it's jokingly called, the Christmas Cherry Auction.

Will I be able to go through with my plan to bid on the three firefighters? If I do it, will people judge me, and make assumptions about what I want from them?

I figure I can put them to work fixing up the house I inherited from my grandma, but naughty thoughts of what I'd rather do with the firefighters make me tingly.

I give myself a mental shake. Me winning three guys won't be much different from the craziness that has gone on so far.

Three mountain men bid on Izzy, Maggie was bought by her three stepbrothers, and three millionaires or billionaires, or whatever they are these days, won Roxy.

Maybe I can get lost in the shuffle.

Will groups of women be teaming up to bid on the firefighters I have my sights on? Am I foolish to think I can win all three? I have the advantage of the huge inheritance I'm obligated to donate to charity.

I reflexively open my bank app to check that the money is still there even though I know it is.

My life has been part dream, part nightmare lately, so checking the account is my equivalent to pinching myself.

I never knew that my grandmother was rich. She lived so frugally, I assumed that she had to. Even in her dying years, she never *enjoyed* her money, not the way she could have.

It wasn't until the reading of the will, that I found out she was wealthy. Her request was that I donate fifty percent of whatever she had left to charity, and I could keep the other half as seed money for my own retirement.

I'm eternally grateful for her generosity.

That's half of the story of how I've landed at the Christmas Cherry Auction, sitting at a table with friends who promised to egg me on if I get nervous about bidding on the fire hunks.

I tug at the hem of my skirt, which is a useless act since I'm sitting on it.

The auctioneer is taking a small break. I glance at the exit. I could leave and simply write a check to the fire department for their much needed safety gear. They'd get more money that way since they'd get my grandma's money and whatever is raised this evening.

And I could keep from embarrassing myself by being up close to these men. Winger is the oldest with a strong vibe of having his shit together. Purge is thick in a *hits the gym* kind of way, and seems to be the most casual of the three. Tank is the burly and broody baby of the trio, but still almost a decade older than me. Word has it that he's been burned in more than one serious relationship. I'd like to—

"It's going to be fine," my support friend, Scarlette, says.

A deep breath helps me focus on a white lie. "Yeah, I'm just ready for them to get on with the show."

"Then why do you look ill?"

My heart's beating so fast, I don't know if I'm going to be able to pull this off. The mere thought of brazenly bidding on the rugged, tattooed guys has me feeling so much more exposed than just my bare legs.

"I'll be fine." I fan myself with my bidder paddle, then set it back on the table so I can close my bank app. In doing so, I accidentally bump my finger on my text messages icon, and John's name sits at the bottom of the screen.

That's how newly single I am. I've barely received enough messages since his breakup text to bury it. My friends tell me I should just delete it and move on. The only reason I've saved it is to remind myself that he really did break up with me by text after a year together.

Part of his final text is on the screen. I never replied. Might as well reread it and bolster my confidence to have fun bidding tonight. My finger hovers over his name.

What he doesn't know is that the day he sent that text, I'd gone to the store and bought a cute little piece of lingerie, red and lacy with white fluff across the top. It was something sexy that I thought we could have fun with because I was finally ready to have sex.

A few carefully worded mentions of things I'd read about in romance novels had caused him to roll his eyes. A few other attempts to get him to do things like chase me and take control of me had run into brick walls.

It seems anything related to romantic play, or that didn't immediately lead to sex was lost on him.

I'd worried that my sexual desires had been tainted by what I read. So I waited. And waited. Hoping my fantasy world could be appeased by lying flat on my back while he grunted on top of me—and I would be able to accept the standard first time.

What a twist of fate that on the same day that I lowered my standards enough to accept whatever he had in store, he sent me the breakup text. Which means, I'm a virgin with a wild imagination, and I'm about to bid on three fantasy guys.

That's going well. I fidget with my hair then tap his name on my phone screen.

His break up glares at me: "This no sex thing is too vanilla for me. I need more. We're over."

My heart catches a pain reading it, even though I don't want him back. I just can't believe he ended it with a text message.

Scarlette slides my phone away from me. Then Amorette, her sister, reaches over and pours a tiny bottle of tequila into my club soda. I catch her eye, and she winks.

I say, "We're not supposed to have alcohol in the high school. Don't get me in trouble. I haven't officially graduated."

"Then you better get rid of the evidence."

Famously terrible advice, but I lift the cup and let the liquid courage slide down my throat.

In a way, I have graduated because I've taken finals and I know I passed, but I haven't gotten my final grades. I'm one of those odd December graduates.

I saw no point in riding out the spring semester when I had enough credits to get the hell out. Not because I'm a stellar student, but because there's a bare minimum and I met it.

The auctioneer, Jefferson, draws our attention back to the stage as his deep voice booms over the PA system.

"Next up is a big change from the lovely ladies who raised three times the amount needed. Let's see if the guys can do the same. Winger is the first of the firefighters to auction himself."

Winger struts on like he owns the place, which I happen to know he doesn't own the high school. But he can own any room he walks into.

He freaking owns my heart right now, and he owns my virginity if he'll take it. And that's where this gets complicated. My sex is far too tingly.

265

I'm only nineteen and Wingers' got to be around forty. I'm sure he has no interest in someone like me. With his lean athletic build, overt sense of confidence, and steeled features, I'm sure he has women clamoring for his attention.

But he's auctioning four hours of his time, and I can use that for a little fix up on my grandma's house so it will sell for a lot more. That's why I'm bidding on all of the guys.

To fix the house, not my virginity status. I'll keep reminding myself of that.

Women start waving their paddles in the air, and their catcalls make them far more vocal than the men were about misconstruing the obligations of those being auctioned. I have no room to judge.

Poor firefighters, don't they do enough by running into burning buildings? They have to put up with ogling too? I tuck my fantasy back in its place and take another sip of the doctored drink.

Jefferson is talking up Winger and his physical prowess and how he's a former military pilot, has been a firefighter ever since then, and sows his wild oats in the local biker gang.

Apparently I can ovulate on command.

I've always been a lightweight when it comes to alcohol, and the buzz takes hold. Amorette's fingers wrap around mine and she raises her eyebrows. I can't believe I'm going through with this.

It would help if I wasn't so turned on by the firefighters. They're all older by at least ten years, and I'm sure people are going to have suspicions.

If I still had a boyfriend, it would be less obvious. But fresh out of my relationship, it'll look like I'm ready to sow some wild rebound oats.

The saving grace for me is that when John moved on, he didn't badmouth me. As far as I can tell, there's nothing on the SmorgasSmut social media page. Those people love rumors. So the fact that I'm a virgin appears safe even though there are rumors about my intentions at this auction.

I give a slight nod to Amorette and she helps me lift my hand because I can't do it myself despite the alcohol.

When I start to lower my number and Jefferson immediately acknowledges another woman's bid, a streak of boldness hits me. I lift my paddle higher, not needing Amorette's assistance anymore. These guys are mine.

And it's safe to say the tequila has arrived for the assist.

The auctioneer speaks too fast for me to keep up, so I listen for the intermittent clear numbers he announces. It's a frenzy, I'm having a blast, and I'm going to win.

Suddenly Amorette's pulling my hand down. I grumble at her.

"You won, silly."

"Just want to make sure they know I'm in it to win it."

We share squeals and excitement as reality sets in that my first mission is accomplished.

Tank takes the stage next. Time for mission number two.

My heart goes into a weird pounding flutter, and I'm pretty sure my panties melt right off of me.

Tank has dirty blonde hair and his bangs are long enough to frame his face, tucking in around his jaw. He often pulls it back, not necessarily in a man bun, but it's not long enough to be a ponytail. He just kind of puts a band on it and doesn't make a fuss.

Like he gives zero fucks what the world thinks. That defines his entire personality.

I've only seen the tattoos that are on his hands, and I'm imagining that if I had the pleasure of seeing him naked, I'd enjoy the full expanse of his body art.

He's into jewelry too and wears a couple rings and some bracelets that look like some metaphysical thing, so I don't know if he has a belief in that, but he wears it so well, I have to catch my breath before raising my paddle.

Laughter booms over the PA as my other hand tips my cup to my lips only to realize I've consumed the whole drink. No wonder I'm feeling flushed.

Jefferson says, "Okay, I guess we need to end the introductions because we're already getting bids, Tank."

Oops. I halt my cringe by proudly waving the paddle.

I lock eyes with Daisy, another eager bidder and nod. I love my newfound boldness, and I fully intend to go home with all three of these guys. With half a million dollars of my grandmother's money at my disposal for this auction, I'm not worried that anyone will be able to win these guys out from under me.

Daisy raises her paddle. She's notoriously single, never having found a boyfriend who could meet her needs. But she won't be getting any of the biker-firefighters alone this evening. Well, not this evening, but for the four hours they owe the winner.

A few other women join in the bidding, which doesn't surprise me because Tank is absolutely swoon worthy. His beard. Did I mention his beard? Oh God, his beard leaves me dying to find out how that and his mustache would tickle me with a kiss anywhere on my body. And I mean anywhere.

The fluster of trying to watch who's bidding against me, just about leaves my head spinning so I look at the stage. At Tank. And he's staring at me.

Deliberately. Shamelessly. Seductively.

Letting the world fall away, I keep my number in the air and lock eyes with him.

He has soulful eyes. I don't know what he's been through. He's reserved and nobody seems to know anything other than he's had some bad breakups. #soulmates

I can only hope. And before I know it, I've outlasted the other bidders and he's going home with me as well. I really need to stop thinking that. I need to respect that these men have their own lives, probably have their own women as they would term them in the MC.

But yeah, I'm ready to take them home tonight and get my four hours as soon as possible. What I'm not prepared for is that Tank gives me a wink and a sly smile before he leaves the stage.

The crowd goes wild...as they say. Were his wink and smile part of the show, keeping the audience amped to open their wallets? No worries, I've got this covered. Thank you, Grandma.

It takes a few seconds before Purge comes on, which gives me a chance to fan myself.

Instead of leaving my paddle up the entire time for him, I have fun with the other ladies, running the bid up because I know I can afford it.

When I lower my paddle, I realize that Purge is staring at me, and he shakes his head. Does he not want me to put my paddle down? Curious if I read his head shake correctly, I lift the paddle a little bit.

He nods and smiles.

Next thing I know, he's off the stage and he's coming my way.

# Two

# Purge

I'm chilling backstage, not paying attention to the auction. Just scrolling through my phone when Winger and Tank come back.

"You're up, man. Better hope she didn't spend all her money on us," Winger says.

"She, who?"

"That chick that the rumor was going around that she was going to buy all of us." Winger acts like I should be up on this.

"Except it ain't no fucking rumor," Tank says.

"So one person buys all of us. What's it matter?"

"Did you look at the picture of her on SmorgasSmut? She's the tiniest, most fuckable little thing I've ever seen and she planned ahead to buy us. Tell me you didn't check her out." Winger leads me to the edge of the stage.

Tank's staying his broody self but there's a glimmer of something in his eyes that I haven't seen in years.

"You know how I feel about this. I'm good with serving my country. I'm good with the MC helping out in ways law enforcement can't. I'm happy with volunteering my time as a firefighter. But you sound like you're ready to fill her with baby sauce. Our commitment is only to..."

Winger pulls back the curtain. "The rosy-cheeked beauty—"

I wave him off, not wanting anything to interfere with me soaking her in. The room is packed but she shines above the rest.

"She won both of you? I hope she's thinking what I'm thinking." I don't want to be left out of whatever she plans with Winger and Tank. And I hope it involves us worshipping her.

Winger asks, "And what would that be?"

"I'm not going to disgrace the high school with the things I want to do to her."

Tank shakes his head. "So it's not just me?"

I'm stunned by his admission. "I thought you swore women off years ago."

"I did until I laid eyes on her."

"So you think she's bidding on us for more than wrapping presents?"

"I think we can talk her into it." Winger's never short on confidence, and while I question if he made the proper assessment here, I'm willing to try.

The fact that she's choosing all of us rallies something primal inside of me. Part of me wants her all to myself like in a wicked bad way, but part of me thinks she deserves all of us.

I head onto the stage and give Jefferson a nod. He monologues through my intro, and the bidding starts. I lock eyes with little moneybags out there in the audience. I don't know where the hell she got enough money to win all three of us, but I'm hoping this is real. Not one of those things like you hear on an eBay bid where people run it up super high and then can't actually pay.

What the fuck? How can I fathom letting her pay? I want to be with her, and not out of a charity obligation.

She lowers her bidder paddle and I wonder if maybe she actually does have an upper limit and just ran out. I can't bear the thought of another woman winning me, so I shake my head hoping she'll catch on that she needs to keep bidding. I can't let Jefferson close out the bid. Not that he is, since he's still rambling numbers.

When I shake my head, Moneybags lifts her paddle, the furrow in her brow relaxing when I nod my approval.

I've got enough cash stashed away, I'll pay for myself. But she doesn't know that.

I jump off the stage with my sights set on her.

Murmurings rumble through the room, and gasps erupt around me, but I only have eyes for number thirteen. Nothing unlucky about that. I snake my way between the tables, barely paying attention as people clear the path for me to pass between them.

In this packed house, it's like I've manifested my place next to her when I see an empty chair, possibly the only empty chair in the whole place. People are standing along the back and the sides.

I lean down to whisper in her ear that I'll foot the bill, but she giggles and flinches as my beard touches her jaw and neck. I drag my tongue across my lips and instead of telling her I'll pay for it, I say, "Want to find out what else I can tickle?"

She raises her paddle and I let my lips brush her cheek as the bidding resumes. Every inclination I had that she's perfect is on fire inside of me now that I've touched her and smelled her, which brings up concern...I smell alcohol.

Come to think of it, her actions are ever so slightly slowed. What do I make of that? Nothing for now.

I grab the empty chair, spin it around backward, straddle it, and sit with my knee brushing the side of her thigh. Crossing my arms over the chair's back, I lean forward. She takes another sip of her drink, but best I can tell there's nothing left in the cup.

Mayor Barnes joins in the bidding and there's no fucking way I want to spend my four hours with him. He's been reaching out and making efforts to work with the local bikers who are pretty damn handy for bending a few rules to keep things straight in town. His daughter can be thanked for enlightening him about how useful we are.

But I don't owe him anything.

I lean close to number thirteen's ear again and whisper, "I'd much rather find out how many orgasms I can give you in four hours than spend that time shaking hands with a politician."

She shivers and her eyes dart to me then to the mayor.

Realizing I got distracted, I say, "I'll cover the bid, whatever it costs, just keep that paddle up."

She turns towards me and my lips brush against her cheek with her unexpected move before she flinches backward. The fire inside of me flares.

"That's not how this works," she whispers.

"Why not?"

"I have to donate the money," she says.

My fists clench. Is she trying to say this is nothing more than a charitable donation? Winger, Tank, and I read it wrong? Hell no. "Then you just keep that bidder paddle up and make sure you win me because you already got my heart, Moneybags."

From only a few inches away, I continue staring at my little sugar mama, only diverting my gaze to glare at the mayor. He seems to take the hint that I'm not amenable to him continuing. Or maybe his daughter does because she leans toward him to say something. He lowers his paddle, waving off the auctioneer.

My entire world rotates around Moneybags until I hear Jefferson declare, "Sold...to number thirteen. I guess it's her lucky number because she snatched up all of the firefighters."

I take a breath. I was too worried someone else was going to win. I have to be hers and hers alone. I take her hand, lift it, and guide her to the winner's table so we can cash out and get the hell out of here.

# Three

## Winger

"Hell yeah. She won all of us. What do you suppose she's going to ask us for first?" I say as Tank and I make our way to the winner's table where we'll sort details.

"Get your mind out of the gutter, Winger. Just because we're into her doesn't mean she bid on us for sex. It's not like this is a sex auction. It's in the fucking high school, dude."

"I know, but look at you, letting your guard down for the first time in several years." I jab him with my elbow.

"Who said I'm letting my guard down? I'm just doing my part, raising money so we can get new gear."

"You don't have to fake it with me. I know you'd tap that if given the chance." I almost feel bad for razzing Tank, but he's been raked over the coals in relationships and what I see in his eyes tells me he's finally ready to leave his bad experiences in the past.

For a nanosecond, I consider talking to Purge about backing off, so Tank can resurrect himself, but I can't. That nanosecond is over before I can even finish processing it.

When we get to the table, Purge is trying to pay the bill, but Sweet Pea waves him off. That's weird.

I turn to Tank. "Why don't you go find her coat and let's take her outside and figure out what's going on."

It's my generous attempt to let him be the gentleman in this scenario because that skimpy little get-up she's got on isn't going to be warm enough, not that we won't be pressing our bodies into her if that's why she's doing this.

Tank asks her where her coat is and what it looks like, and then he's off in a heartbeat, returning with it by the time she's filled out all the paperwork. She stands and he wraps it around her shoulders. It doesn't do anything for covering her legs, but at least it's something. And he looks like a real gentleman doing it, which is not something he looks like very often, so that's good.

"Why don't we head outside and discuss what we can do for you." I give her a wink.

She tugs the coat closed in front of her and says loudly, "I should put you three strong men to work on grandma's yard right away. Let's go make a plan."

The slight bit of slur to her words, and as I move closer, the faint hint of alcohol tells me we have a problem. She's not in a position to make the decision I want her to make right now.

We head out the back door of the school while pies are being auctioned. That will buy us time alone with Sweet Pea before people start rushing outside.

Purge lifts Sweet Pea and sets her on his bike. She's worrying her lower lip. With his voice light, he says, "Yard work?"

She looks up at the moon and shrugs.

I clarify, "Moneybags, you're drunk. We're going to need you to sober up if this isn't actually about yard work.

Sweet Pea says, "I don't think I'll be able to let you do yard work if I'm sober."

I smooth her silky hair behind her ear, then grab a fistful just enough to turn her head my direction.

"They may let you write a huge check while you're drunk, but we won't let—"

She interrupts me. "Right, consent and all. I get it. Can we please avoid the explicit details and capitalize on my liquid courage to live out a fantasy?"

My dick stiffens in my pants. She just put it out there, everything we're hoping for. I stare into those pretty dark blue eyes under the mixed glow of the full moon and the garish light from the fixture we're under.

Composing myself, I say, "If we're going to play out your fantasy, you're going to want to remember every second of it."

Purge jumps in, "He's right. For now, the only DTF we're going to accept from you is being Down To Fundraise. We need you to sober up before we do anything else."

Tank gives me an irritated look before leaning closer to Sasha. "But there's nothing wrong with you telling us what you want us to do."

# *Four*

## Sasha

I've seen each of these men in public, but I've never been this close. And I've never just purchased them.

Sitting on what I presume is Purge's bike with the three of them huddled around me, Purge and Winger in front, and Tank at my back, I feel so small, and tiny, and delicate.

There's a big size difference physically, but their confidence and their ruggedness amplify it in a way that I think my math teachers talked about. Exponential stuff. Math stuff I never understood. If they would've done it in terms of three guys, three bikers huddled around me, I think I could have understood exponential growth.

The brisk air takes my intoxication down a notch, and a flicker of sanity rushes into me. Am I crazy to toy with the idea of telling them my fantasies? This can't possibly be real. They'd probably jump back a hundred feet if they knew I was a virgin.

A vanilla virgin at that. I clamp my eyes shut to force John from my mind. I'm not vanilla. I wanted things he thought were ridiculous. Things these guys might be willing to give me.

I want my first time to be memorable. To be with experienced guys who will do it right. Not to be lying in a bed with a guy slogging over me like some of my girlfriends have talked about. I want to be an active participant in having fun, and I want them to have to chase me and want me and claim me.

Tank circles around in front with the other two.

If I tell these guys my fantasies, will they make them come true? Or will I get in over my head way too fast? I'm pretty sure the tequila is the reason for the first thought. The second most likely aligns with reality.

I put on a pretty smile and say, "You're right. I should sober up. I'm not normally the type that does this sort of thing. I can have my girlfriends drive me home and I can send you the address to my grandmama's house."

Purge puts a finger on my lips. "That's not what we meant, Money. You wouldn't have liquored up to place the bids if you only wanted help with yard work."

He nudges his leg between my thighs, and oh my God, he's thick. His leg, that is.

I squash the desire to find out if he's thick in other places. I wouldn't even know what thick means. I've felt my boyfriend's erection through his pants but that's all, just his. I can hear my biology teacher emphasizing the importance of sample size.

I squeeze my thighs around his leg, and he tucks a finger under my chin, forcing me to look up.

He says in his rich, deep voice, "Go ahead and tell us your fantasy."

Winger lifts my hand before I can answer. "You're still wearing your class ring. How old are you?"

"Nineteen."

Winger coughs. "And you're drinking?"

"My friend wanted to help me calm down."

"Your friend could have gotten you in trouble," he chastises.

"Everybody breaks rules," I say defensively.

His expression goes dark. "You ever get fucked behind the school?"

He nudges Purge out of the way and lifts me. I'm caught off guard, so my legs wrap around his waist and I lose hold of my coat while I grab his shoulders. Thankfully my coat is situated on my shoulders enough that it doesn't fall.

This is going to make it very hard not to tell them my fantasies. In fact, this is my new fantasy. Our age difference doesn't seem to be a problem. I'm not sure if this is spiraling toward a really good point or a bad one.

I'm so lost in his expression that I don't even realize he's walked me toward the brick wall of the school until he backs me into it.

"So have you?" He rolls his hips into me. I'm pretty sure he's sporting a major erection.

I have to play back what he asked me...about having sex behind the school. That's a definite no, so that's easy to answer.

"I haven't."

"Do you want to?"

"I... Maybe?" If he means right now, that's going to be a no, as much as I'd like to say yes, I don't think we should do this while half the town is inside the school.

Tank sidles up to us, his breath hot on my ear, "Come on, Tiny. Fess up. Tell us your wildest dreams. Was there a guy who didn't live up to your standards? Was there something you wanted to do that your boyfriend wasn't willing to try?"

That's a convoluted answer.

Purge closes in from the other side. I don't know what to say, so I settle for vague statements.

"I haven't been very naughty. My boyfriend made me think that what I want is bad." I can't believe I said that but it's out there, and I swear all three of their bodies go hard.

"How bad?" Tank reframes 'bad' to flip the script.

"I don't know. Just maybe role-play instead of lying in a bed. Is that a thing?"

Purge nudges Winger to turn so that I'm no longer against the wall, and Purge is behind me. He reaches around and takes my hands from Winger's shoulders, lowering them behind my back. He's close enough, he presses his body into me so that my coat doesn't fall off, as one of his hands grips my wrists. It's gentle, but I know that he's in control.

His other hand pulls my hair behind my ear and he leans down. "Bad enough to need a safe word?"

My sex is so knotted and tingly, my legs grip Winger's waist. I wonder if they can tell that my entire world is going a little bit swoony. It will be easier to have this conversation now than when I'm sober because I am certain I can't talk about safe words without tequila.

I blurt, "Bonbon."

Winger says, "What?"

Tank nods my direction. "That's her safe word, fucker." Then Tank adds, "All right, bonbon. Now, what kind of bad do you want to be?"

The fact that he accepted my safe words so openly, there's no discussion, there's no worry, no nothing, I run with it. "I want to be chased."

"Chaste?" Winger asks.

If I properly made out the subtlety of his pronunciation, it was chaste as in not sexy, as opposed to chased as in I want to be caught.

Before I can clarify, Purge says, "You need a fucking hearing aid, old man? This is chased as in she's my prey and I'm going to stalk her."

It sounds so *not right* when stated that way, and yet a hundred percent right, because that is what I want with every non-vanilla bone in my body.

"I read it in a romance novel."

"You never tried it?" Purge asks.

I shake my head. "And do any of you have handcuffs?"

Thank you, tequila, but for fuck's sake, what am I getting myself into?

Tank's voice is low and raspy. "You want me to hunt you down, handcuff you, and fuck you like the bad girl you are?"

I raise my eyebrows. When he puts it that way, tequila doesn't show any sympathy. "If you're up for it."

Without wasting another second, Winger takes control. "I'm going to drive her back to my house in her car. I'll leave my bike here. You two meet us there."

I can't believe Winger is in my car, driving me to his house in the Cherry Ridge foothills. I'm torn between saying something to pass the time on the drive, but I'm worried that anything I say could kill the mood.

I sit with my hands clasped in my lap and focus on breathing in and out over and over again, while I process that I've just asked my three dream guys to chase me, handcuff me, and have sex with me.

It would be prudent to make a game plan on how to reveal the little tidbit about my virginity. I mean, it's not like I haven't used a vibrator, so I've had penis-shaped items complete with veins and vibrations in my hoo-ha.

Perhaps it's the tequila throwing its rally cap on, but I make the decision not to tell them I've never had sex. I want to find out what it's like to be taken.

# Five

## Tank

The ride to Winger's house didn't help me cool off. If anything, knowing that he got to be in the car alone with her skyrocketed my jealousy.

Tiny opens the car door as I roll my bike to a stop. She takes one look at Winger's cobblestone driveway and pulls her high heels off before hopping out. Shoes in hand, she rushes around the car and lets him guide her to the front door.

While he's unlocking it, I step behind Sasha, grab her hips, and dip my fingers toward her sex so I can tease the sensitive spot at the top of her legs.

How can I be holding my future when I swore off relationships? Trusting my gut on the job has been vital. Trusting my gut around women, not so much.

The wiggle of her hips against me has my dick hard. Her fantasy has taunted me from the moment it rolled from her lips.

She's different. She's what I've always needed.

Winger shoves the front door open, and steps inside, turning the light on. Purge positions himself between us and the door as if inviting us to enter.

Leaning down, I say into Sasha's ear, "You better run."

She startles. "What?"

"You said you wanted to be chased, and I wasn't joking about finding you and fucking you."

"Here?" Her bold request contrasts the hints of innocence.

I'm holding too tightly for her to get away, but I didn't expect her body to go rigid. She's not trying to escape. Which creates a real problem because I don't want her to. I've already found her.

"It's your fantasy, you get to pick." I motion toward the open door. "Inside or out?"

She looks over her shoulder, and her playfulness returns. "You'll have to let go to find out."

My heart is pounding so hard, I can't believe I'm able to stay laser-focused. I've never played like this before, and to say I'm aroused is an understatement. My cock is pumping pre-cum into my underwear. I'm more alive than I thought possible.

My senses heighten to take in every shuffle of feet, every shift in the breeze, every twinkle of a star, and every scent of her shampoo, perfume, and sex...her sweet, addictive sex.

"Ready?" I ask.

She nods and wiggles but my grip stays firm. I have her where I want her, letting go is counterintuitive...except for some deep, primal need that's salivating at the thought of giving her a head start, tracking her down, then claiming her.

The rush is already intense.

"You have no idea how hot this is." I loosen my grip.

A second passes before she laughs and slips through my fingers. My chest swells, adrenaline shoots through me, and I force myself to stay put to give her the lead.

How did I not know this was an option for foreplay?

My—our—fantasy crashes into a brick wall when Purge throws his arm out as she tries to enter the house.

"What the fuck?" I'm pulled from the moment so hard it takes me a second to process that Purge hadn't heard my whispers to her. "We're starting the role play."

Winger looks at Sasha. "Not until you're sober."

Damn them. She's barely got a buzz.

"I'm sober enough."

"There's not going to be any fucking until I'm sure," Winger says as if he gets to make the rules.

My anticipation feeds into anger. "Who made you boss?"

"Maybe if you'd been with a woman in the last six years, you wouldn't be so desperate." Winger's jab is a low blow. The only desperation here is to find out if a game of cat-and-mouse can be a normal thing with Tiny.

"My sex life is none of your fucking business. I'm just trying to please the lady." I've covered the ground between us and cup my hand around the back of her neck.

How can she fit so perfectly every time I touch her?

"You want to be pleased?" I ask.

She looks at me with doe-eyes, which heightens the air of innocence that has my balls in a stranglehold. When she nods, I pick her up, crash my lips onto hers, and push past Winger.

My compromise, to keep from ending the evening in a brawl, is to take her to his couch instead of turning her out for a chase. We'll get there. She seems pretty sober, and her consent is more than clear.

With her legs splayed over my lap, her skirt has ridden up to her hips and my hands slide underneath. Silky panties. Nice, but they're in the way.

"I need to ride your pussy bare."

"We shouldn't..." Her eyes flutter shut as the rock of my hips distracts her.

"When I said I was going to find you and fuck you, I should have added that I plan on keeping you forever. So no matter how you planned on ending your thought about what we *shouldn't do*...trust me...we should."

Her fingers dig into my shoulders and little moans escape her. If she was paying attention, I just gave her a lot to think about. It wouldn't take much reading between the lines to understand I intend to knock her up.

If my cock wasn't so painfully constrained inside my pants, I'd swear it was sunk deep inside of her. Can her orgasm face be any better than watching her dry hump me?

"But..." Her eyes flutter open and meet mine. She still can't form a coherent thought.

"We're all healthy," Winger says from beside us. Purge is on the other side. They're both caressing her body with their hands, and she's totally into it.

I don't want Winger's comment to kill the mood, so I run with her fantasy of being bad. "Bad girls wouldn't overthink it. You know you want me to fill you with cum, don't you, Tiny?"

"Uh-huh."

Her cunt's so wet, my cock's getting soaked even though we're still shamefully clothed. I drag a finger through the moisture and rub my thumb over her covered clit.

Her gasp sends a shockwave through me. What will she do when I rub her clit with my cock? I taunt her. "Bad girls get wet just thinking about sex."

"Damn straight," Purge says. He eases his hand under her skirt and nudges mine out of the way.

I lean close enough that my lips drag over hers while I ask, "Are you ready for that game of chase now?"

She nods, and Winger grumbles.

"Kiss him, Tiny. Show him how ready you are." I lean away so the two of them can lock lips. The front-row seat to watch them connect assures me that I want this to happen between all of us, not just Tiny and me. But I want her first.

I've never watched like this. Never wanted to see *my* woman satisfied by another man. Never believed that I could be happy sharing.

But with my psuedo-brothers, it's crystal clear that this is the only way.

When he lets her pull away, I set her on her feet. "The guys and I are going to step outside. We'll give you a few minutes to explore the house then I'm coming for you."

"Really?" She strokes her hands over mine.

"Really." I lower a hand to her pussy and rub it through her dress. "Then this is mine."

# *Six*

# Sasha

Standing in front of Tank, Purge, and Winger while they're seated, is the only chance I have of being bigger than them, being taller, having the upper hand, and yet there's no sense of pressure or that they'd do anything I don't like.

They're humoring this whole chase thing because I asked for it. I question my sanity for a second.

"You okay?" Winger says.

"Yeah, I'm fine." I'm getting everything I asked for so I should be, but have I overstepped?

"You look kind of nervous." I shrug. "I just bought the three of you in an auction and announced that I was going to take you home to do yard work in the middle of the night. So basically, I just told the whole town I'm going to have sex with you."

"And we're damn happy you did," Purge says.

Winger ads, "If this evening got away from you, it's fine to back out, Sweet Pea. Just know that we're all in."

"That's what's so hard to believe. None of you balked at my fantasy."

"We'd be fucking idiots," Tank says.

John balked. He hadn't even considered for a second that I was telling him about the scene from my book because it turned me on. He made me feel dirty and unworthy. These guys make me feel like a treasure.

I back up a step and wave my finger. "Okay. I guess I better orient myself."

The men stand in unison and I'm suddenly small again.

Tank says, "Get yourself oriented. Find a place that gives you options.

Winger interrupts. "Anywhere you want."

Purge adds, "First to find, first to fuck."

"I *will be* first." Tank drags a finger across his lips, pausing when his fingertips are under his nose. "I've got your scent and I'm coming for you."

I force a smile because I cannot produce a single intelligent word.

Tank motions to the door. "She can't hide while we're standing here watching."

The three of them practically march out in sync. Each one looks over his shoulder at least once before exiting. Part of me wants to just sit right here so when they come in, they can have me. I don't even know if the chase is part of my fantasy anymore. I give myself a mental shake. No, it definitely is.

I don't know how long I have before they'll come back in. Quickly exploring the nearby doorways, I find a closet and a bathroom. Recalling the shape of the house from the outside, I head the other direction.

A long hallway with several closed doors reveals bedrooms and a workout room. How do I pick where to go?

I find Winger's bedroom at the end of the hallway. He has a huge closet where I can easily tuck myself behind his hanging clothes. But if I hide first, I'll miss the chase.

My hands are shaking and not just because I'm a virgin. I have full faith that my vibrator has prepared me for this, except it's going to be better because it'll be a warm body and I don't have to do the majority of the work. Plus, I won't have room-temperature silicone in my sex, I'll get hot, throbbing man meat. What the hell? Hot and throbbing man meat? Have I gone bonkers?

There will be so much more to enjoy...hands, lips, and bodies slapping together. I can't wait.

I rush back to the other end of the hallway, but instead of standing there ready to run, I strip my panties off and drop them. Then I rush back down the hallway to Winger's bedroom.

I don't want them to know where I am, but I want to hear them find my panties.

Safely inside the main bedroom, I peek down the hallway. A click signifies the front door opening. Being careful not to bump the open door, I turn my head to hear better.

"Ready or not..." Tank's words trail off.

There's a single clapping sound, like hands being brought together, followed by laughter. "All right, Money, where are you at?" It's Purge's voice.

The flurry of footsteps becomes muffled as they step onto the carpet. I'm doing everything to control my breaths including opening my mouth in hopes of making my breathing less noticeable.

My chest heaves up and down. My palms are sweaty. My legs are weak. I wonder if I'll be able to rush to the closet when they get close. I wonder if I care. After all, the bed is closer than the closet.

"Oh, Moneybags, you are a bad girl. Look at this, guys." Purge's voice has moved distinctly closer.

I'm sure he's found my panties. If only I could see. I'm imagining him squatting down, lifting them, no doubt cupping them to his nose.

Part of me is mortified—the part that had the boyfriend who thought wanting to be chased and taken control of was insane and deviant.

The other part tells me that I've met guys who get me, and I'm going to have the best first time ever.

All three of their voices draw closer and they argue over who gets to keep my panties. But Purge clarifies, "Finders keepers."

The click of multiple doors opening and rooms being searched causes my heart to beat impossibly fast. Almost not even a beat anymore. Just one exaggerated pulse that's surging blood through my body, that has my nerves on edge, that awakens my most basic instincts.

Have I waited too long to move to the closet? When I rush across the room, will they catch the flash of my bright red dress in the doorway? With three of them moving in and out of rooms, I can't tell who's where.

In a mad dash, I rush to the giant closet and quietly slink behind a couple of bins on the floor and Winger's suits hanging above them. The wardrobe diversity surprises me because I've never seen him in anything but jeans, T-shirts, and leather vests. Maybe there's another side of him I don't know.

Someone enters the bedroom. I can't see who. Then the closet darkens as one of them stands in the doorway.

"Oh, Tiny, I can smell you from here."

Can he? Is that a good thing? I worry my lower lip.

Excitement swirls through me that it's Tank. I was hoping he'd be the one to find me. I don't know why. I just want him to be my first. I squeeze my legs together to counteract the ache in my core.

My attempts to stay quiet have caused me to take impossibly shallow breaths. How embarrassing will it be if I hyperventilate, or will I pass out? Maybe lack of oxygen is already clouding my ability to think.

"You know you're trapped, right?"

A squeak escapes me, and he chuckles.

"Then again, I don't think you want to escape me, do you?"

I'm now holding my breath. It's the only way I can keep from making a sound, but I'm about to bust with anticipation. I can't see where he is, but I can feel his presence, and hear him moving closer.

He's got to be standing right in front of me. With a whoosh, the bins are shoved to the side.

A hand reaches through the suits and grabs my waist, spinning me as he pulls me through the clothes, securing my back to his chest.

The clatter of fabric and hangers bumping barely registers. A suit falls to the carpet with a soft thud. My front is pressed into the suits, swinging them back slightly.

His other hand grabs my wrist. Where I thought I'd topped out of excitement and anticipation, I'm now ten or maybe a hundred times higher.

He's moving my arms behind me. Something hard presses against my hand. By the time I interpret the metallic feel, he's slapping a handcuff on my wrist.

Exactly like he said he would.

My other hand is poised to be cuffed, but he lifts my restrained hand. I turn my head but he shoves me into the suits as he lifts. Then he guides my free hand upward, and in a swift move, has me handcuffed over the closet rod.

My vulnerability hits me like a freight train when his hands pull away and there's nowhere for me to go. The chase may have been short, but this is everything I thought I was wrong to want.

My world opens up as he shoves the clothes away from me on either side.

"Since you're not wearing panties, I guess there's nothing in the way of me making you mine, Tiny."

I don't know what to say. I've never made it this far into the fantasy. My mind always flits to a bed at this point where I imagine John grunting on top of me. This is so much better.

*Bonbon* wiggles through my mind as nothing more than a reminder that I have control. My lips are sealed.

I taunt, "You think your friends are going to let you have me all to yourself?"

He wraps an arm around me, securing his hand over my mouth, then presses his lips to the top of my head.

"You're mine first."

Based on the maneuvering behind me, I assume he's unfastening his pants with his free hand. He yanks the back of my skirt up, and I'm suddenly aware of my own wetness dripping down my thighs.

This is better than I fantasized.

He positions a leg between mine, loosens his grip on my mouth, and whispers, "If you don't say your safe word, you're mine forever."

Silence.

We're role-playing. I shouldn't be thinking that forever actually means forever. I wish it did.

"Fuck," he mutters and nudges his hot, thick cock at my entrance.

His breaths become deliberate and heavy as his tip parts my slick lips. My heart catches in my throat as he moves another inch and stops. Can he tell I'm a virgin?

Impossible. That might be the word of the moment because the stretch is an impossible mix of pain, fullness, perfection, and danger. I don't have to ask him to give me time to adjust. He must be able to tell that I need it, and he gives it. Or maybe he's taking it for himself. Stopping and smelling the roses.

Why the hell am I thinking about flowers? The sensations are taking my mind in a million directions as I try to process what we're doing. I tug against the cuffs and savor the confinement.

I belong to Tank.

He keeps his hand over my mouth. His friends are still exploring based on what I can hear.

Winger calls out, "Any luck?"

Tank firms his hand around my mouth, and presses his head into mine, kissing my hair.

He turns away and says, "No luck," as calm and cool as I can imagine before his deep, possessive whisper resumes, "Tiny, are you a virgin?"

A jolt of electricity shoots through me. Oh my god. He can tell.

"No, I..." My words can't get past his hand. Will my truth end this?

He loosens his hand on my mouth and I try to lighten the mood. "Yes, but I'm a bad virgin."

The low growl that vibrates from his chest into my back and the slight thrust of his cock against my tight walls has my body on fire in the best way.

"Please don't stop," I say, although it sounds more like I beg.

He inches further. "You should have said something."

"I didn't want you to turn me away."

"That's not a reason to turn you away, but there's no way I would've risked either of them finding you first if I'd known." He thrusts a little more.

A garbled sound escapes me as I'm stretched to my limit. It's good. It's painful. I want more. I shift my hips and moan.

"It's so good, Tank. So good. Fuck me. You promised you would fuck me."

He slaps his hand back over my mouth. "Keep quiet."

Then he meets the motion of my hips with deeper, faster thrusts.

The orgasm building inside of me is bigger than I've ever given myself. My entire body is a knot. I have a feeling I'm about to find out what it's like to be ruined.

# Seven

# Tank

A bad virgin. That still means virgin. Fucking insane is what this is. Her moans will alert the guys to where we are. They're going to figure it out pretty quickly anyway, but I want this moment with her alone. I want to make her come before either of them find us.

I'm helpless against the movement of her hips. I won't last. I wrap my hand back around her mouth and give her what she wants.

She can't possibly have any idea what she's asking for. Although, she's game for her first time to happen when she's handcuffed in a closet, so maybe I'm not exactly flying a freak flag in her eyes.

As much as I want to caress her entire body, I lower my other hand to her clit. Her pussy is tightening around me. I want to plunge her over the edge while I'm as coherent as possible.

I work her little nub until her body convulses. Holding my own release back, I memorize every flinch, every contortion, every moan as she comes undone on my cock.

Then there's no holding back.

She's mine.

I growl through my thrusts, as I hold her body against me, as I lose control and explode into her. Our juices mingle as I release my seed, shooting it deep into her womb until it overflows and drips down her legs. Her scent and mine become one the way we're meant to be.

I'm so lost, my head jerks to the side when I realize Purge and Winger are standing beside us. They've clearly been watching.

Purge smirks.

I'm so lost in the mix of our scents taking over the entire closet that I barely notice. I'm only jealous we're not at my house where her scent could infiltrate every piece of clothing I own.

I inhale deeply, my eyes heavy. Winger and Purge have stripped out of their clothes.

A flicker of possession washes through me. I don't want to share. And yet I do. I want to watch them. I want to watch them do this to her. I want to watch her pleasure, and then I want to sink inside of her again.

"All right, you had your turn, Tank. You ready for round two, Money?" Purge says.

"Yes?" Her answer is more of a question.

Winger steps forward and lifts her chin. "Do you want to stay handcuffed?"

"Yeah."

"And you're sure you're ready?"

"I am." How can she be ready? *I'm* not ready. I don't want to pull my cock out of its warm home. It belongs there, inside of her, making babies.

I narrow my gaze at Purge. "Just wait a damn minute."

"You finished. What's the problem?" he asks.

"The problem is I said I was going to keep her forever. That doesn't mean I'm going to blow my load then rush off to grab a sandwich. Give me a second. Give *us* a second." I nuzzle my nose back into her hair. She smells like heaven.

I'm the only one who knows her secret, only her secret doesn't apply anymore. She's no longer a virgin, but she's far from experienced. I'm torn between telling them so they don't hurt her and respecting her wishes.

My cock hardens again at the thought. My body tightens. Hell yeah. A double charge. My cock hadn't softened, but it gets even harder inside of her, swelling against her walls.

She leans her head back so I lower my lips to her ears and say, "I need you again. You okay with that?"

She shudders and giggles. Not what I was expecting.

"Your beard tickles."

That's a damn relief. I thought she was laughing at me wanting her again. "I can put this beard anywhere you want it…and I will before the night's over. But for now, I need to come inside of you again."

"I didn't think guys could do that."

"We're all learning stuff we didn't know tonight, right?" I let it go that she doesn't address my comment about the rest of the night. That doesn't mean I didn't notice. I take it as the reminder it is…women leave. She'll leave. And I can pretend that anything I say in the heat of role play wasn't real.

She's chuckling, while I'm giving myself a pep talk on not falling for her. Whether it's simply her nature or if the women's empowerment revolution gives her confidence, I respect that she didn't come into this thinking she was at our mercy. She came into this with her mind made up that she deserves the best. I sure as hell hope we live up to her every fantasy.

I thrust inside of her again, dragging myself in and out of her sweet walls, pumping our previous combined release out of her, probably pumping some deeper in. Who knows? It's a fucking sloppy mess as cum coats us, creating that sound of wet bodies slapping together.

Purge rakes his hand through his hair and shakes his head. I lock eyes with him.

"Yeah, she's that fucking good, guys." Then I fill her again.

# Eight

## Sasha

When Tank relents and pulls out of me, it's like I've lost my purpose. How can our bond be so consuming already? Purge steps closer, strokes his fingers from the handcuffs down to my shoulder, then leans around and kisses me.

"Are you sure you don't want to get your arms down?"

"If you uncuff me, I'll run."

"Do you want to run?"

I confess, "I'm not sure I can after what Tank just did to me."

"Fuck." Purge pivots behind me, puts his hands on my hips, then nestles his cock between my legs. One of his hands slides around my front and circles my clit.

I'm barreling toward another release. My body's impossibly sensitive. I feel like I'm falling and he tightens an arm around my waist. I'm secure as he presses into me, and I'm stretched once again. Nothing's the same as that first time, but this is just as perfect.

Purge is more vocal, grunting and groaning, but I think Tank had attempted to keep the other guys from finding us.

"You ready, Money?"

"Yeah." I can barely form the word.

He tightens his grip on my hips and thrusts hard. It feels so fucking good, I can't last. As my body surrenders to his ministrations on my clit, to the way these men fulfill my fantasy without question, we come undone.

When we're sated and he pulls out, Winger moves in. I'm spent and dripping with not only my cum, but both of theirs.

Winger holds me gently and eases himself inside.

"Are we making your fantasy come true?"

"It's better than I thought."

"You're better than we thought."

My world becomes a blur as he gives me two more orgasms before filling me with his seed.

I don't understand how this can feel so right when the thought of sex with my boyfriend never seemed right. Do I need this type of behavior? Am I deviant? I'm hooking up with three men.

Self-doubt's feeble attempt to take hold falls away as Winger cradles his arms around me while Tank unfastens the handcuffs and lowers my hands.

My arms almost feel as weird and stretched as my other parts. Purge takes my free hand and plants kisses around my wrist.

I turn my head and notice the red mark, no doubt from how limply I hung. I've never been so sated in my entire life.

Tank lifts me and I almost fall asleep against his chest despite only being there for a few paces. He walks me into Winger's bathroom, a huge expansive black and white marble room.

Winger's ahead of us and has turned on the tub. He's testing the water while Tank steadies me on my feet. He and Purge strip my dress. How can I be so comfortable with all of them?

"Christ," Purge says from in front of me. "Your tits are as perfect as the rest of you. I can't believe we didn't even get you undressed before doing that."

I glance down, confirming that my bra is still on. "You were focused on what I wanted."

A strange, irritated sound comes from behind me. Why didn't Tank like that? His fingers are hot against my back as he unhooks my bra. Purge takes hold and slides it away from me, tossing it onto the counter.

Then he steps back and slowly rakes his eyes down my body, all the way to my toes, smiling when he gets there. Does he like my manicure? The bright red that perfectly matches my dress? I did that on purpose. It also happens to match the lingerie my boyfriend never got to see.

Purge lifts his gaze, stopping at the sight of Tank's hands wrapping in front of me. One hand crossing my chest, cradling my breast and rolling my nipple between his thumb and forefinger. Tank drops his other hand to my sex, sliding back and forth, smearing the cum into me.

Purge lowers his gaze to watch.

"If you boys give me a bath, you're going to wash this off."

My back is pressed against Tank's chest, and he leans his lips into my hair. "We're going to put more in there, don't worry." Then he lowers his voice, "Besides, I already got you pregnant."

Purge strokes his cock, which is decidedly thicker and longer than it was a second ago. He likes watching. I like him watching.

Is this another level of my deviant desires? Did something in the universe tell me I'd never be satisfied with my boyfriend? That's why I held out?

It's almost a shame that I'm giving John brain space while I'm here with these amazing men, but the contrast is how much more right this feels than anything I felt in the time with him.

I don't want to fall prey to false beliefs. I asked for role-playing. I asked for chasing. They gave me what I wanted.

I protect myself by saying, "We only have four hours. If you're going to clean me up and start over, we better get going."

I step forward and dip my toe into the tub. Tapping into my bold streak, since these men seem to like a high confidence level, I drag my finger through the hot mess between my legs and tap it on Winger's cheek as he reaches for my hand to help me step over the edge of the tub.

Immersing in the warm water, I say, "The temperature's just perfect. Care to join me?"

# Nine

## Winger

I don't know what to make of Sasha. I've never met a woman like her. Is it just the generation gap? I rake my hand through my hair when she settles into the tub. I used to date a lot and women weren't so bold.

I've never felt a connection like this. There's an underlying sense that our souls have already intertwined. And apparently, the magic includes my two best buds.

Maybe that's it. Maybe there's something in the thing between the four of us.

With her invitation, I lick the salty mix from my lips and step into the tub. I position myself in back and lean her against my chest. My legs wrap around hers, my arms wrap around her body, and she's exactly where she belongs.

I look down and can't think of a better sight in the world than seeing her protected in my arms, for a sweetly intimate scene. For a different kind of intimacy, there's a very different best sight in the world...her riding my dick.

"Is this part of your fantasy?" I ask.

"I never really got this far."

"You never played it out in real life?"

"No." Longing fills her short answer.

"Why do you say it like that?"

Sweet Pea and Tank share a moment. His jaw flexes. What the hell does he know about her that I don't? I tighten my embrace.

She says tentatively, "Until tonight, I never had sex with a guy."

Water sloshes as I sit upright and lean beside her, so I can look into her eyes. Is this more role-playing? Did she fail to mention that she was playing an innocent virgin being chased by three guys? Was it part of the MC thing, rather than us being firefighters? I mean, we don't have that kind of MC, but some clubs do.

"You were a virgin, as in Tank was your first?" Purge asks.

She nods, and the doe-eyed innocence of her big blue eyes seals the truth of her revelation.

"Why didn't you tell us?" I ask.

"It wasn't your business."

"Yeah, actually, we're having sex. That's something that we deserve to know."

"Do you?"

Tank rushes over and sits on the edge of the tub. "Look, it's her decision whether to tell people or not. She knew what she was getting into, and while I agree with you, Winger, I would've liked to have known before we started, it wouldn't have been the same. So I can see where she's coming from."

Purge says, "I'm going to go grab some drinks. We all need to cool off about this."

I settle lower in the tub again, wrapping my arms around her, cherishing her even more.

"Sorry. I overreacted, but I'm not used to women wanting to have sex quite like you did, especially for their first time."

Tank scoffs. "That's because you're an old fucker."

"Yeah, well, I know how to treat a woman. I know how to make her happy." I slip my hands between her legs, circling her clit.

I listen for her moans and settle into a slow rhythm.

"You may have been the first to claim her, but I'll be the first to give her bath sex." I may sound overly competitive. I don't know if that's a thing, but part of me is desperate to show her something she's never experienced. I'll take anything I can get.

While I'm easing her into her next orgasm, and her body writhes on top of me, I ask, "Are there any other fantasies you want to play out?"

"Why don't I turn around to straddle you, and we check another thing off?"

"Let me make you come first."

She doesn't object. I quicken my circles and toy with her nipple with my other hand while I plant kisses on the side of her face and her hair. She's too perfect, and yet, I don't know how much of this is her role play. Is that what she planned for four hours of winning us?

I don't understand a woman like her. So while I'm having the best night of my life, I'm also terrified that this isn't anything more than a game to her. I'll lay down my life for her, and she might be toying with us.

# Ten

# Sasha

Having sex in the bathtub is undeniably incredible. Something about feeling buoyant and surrounded by all that warmth, it's just special. Not that I'm an expert on locations or positions, but it was the other parts of the bath that were equally captivating, like having someone drag a washcloth over my entire body, fingers rubbing through my hair, massaging the shampoo, and then the conditioner, and of course, the gentle rinsing.

Who knew that these men that are so intimidating in real life with all of their tattoos, their broody features and attitudes, and their stoic-ness as they roll into town on their motorcycles en masse—I mean, they are kind of terrifying. They're big and thick, and did I mention tattooed? Oh, it makes me swoon-ey just thinking about it, and yet they're gentle.

Winger lifts me out of the bathtub and hands me to Tank and Purge who cooperate in wrapping me with a bathrobe that swallows me. It's one of those super thick, white, fluffy robes that you'd expect from a hotel. Then I catch an emblem on it. Not a Holiday Inn or Motel 6. Too rich for my blood.

It serves as a reminder that they have lives. They've served in the military. They fearlessly run into burning buildings as volunteer firefighters. I truly can't wrap my brain around what mentality it takes to do that, but what's most intriguing to me is this flip side to them.

My boyfriend was never like this. He never shampooed my hair. I think I knew he wasn't the one. He was comfortable. He was convenient. He was safe, but he wasn't right.

Winger, Purge, and Tank? They're so right. But what girl wouldn't think that?

I wish I understood what makes us click. Or if we have anything special from their perspective. I'm not about to mess this up by asking and appearing clingy. The money I spent on them was the best purchase I ever made.

My mind flits back to them being in a biker gang. Maybe this is normal. I shudder at the thought. After Winger dries himself off, which is just a series of quick pats on various parts of his body, he grabs a brush from his drawer.

"Ready for some downtime?"

"Sure."

"Or we could make sure we can do anal and blow jobs and anything else Moneybags wants to accomplish in these four hours. But if you want to brush her hair, man, that's okay," Purge says.

I cringe at his nickname for me. A reminder that I purchased their time.

Winger shakes his head.

"Look," Tank says, "She might be more vanilla than you're thinking. I mean, seriously, the chase thing, that was pretty wild, but just give her a minute to get used to everything else."

Purge plants a kiss on the tip of her nose. "Vanilla, cherry, hot fudge sundae. Whatever you got, I'm ready for it."

Vanilla. John's text runs through my mind. Why is that word so triggering? Did he have to use that? I'm not vanilla, and yet the damage has been done. I can't get it out of my mind.

Rather than let it bug me, I attempt to own it. "Vanilla's a very popular flavor. How about you eat that vanilla right out of me and we'll see what I have left?"

"Fuck yeah," Purge says.

"How do you want to do it?" Winger takes my hand and motions to his bedroom with the hairbrush.

A chuckle rolls through me.

On the bed? Missionary? This is getting more vanilla by the minute.

Winger surprises me by flopping onto a cushioned window seat, leaning his back against the glass, and saying, "Take your robe off. I want you to sit on my cock and I'm going to fuck you while one of those two *eats that vanilla right out of you*. How does that sound?"

"Are we talking anal?" Purge asks.

"Enough with that already," Tank says.

"I just want to know what I'd be agreeing to. Hear me out..." He widens his stance. "If I'm going to be licking pussy and Winger's cock at the same time, that's something I need to know going in. As opposed to if he's getting some back door action, it might not be stroke for stroke that he's getting to embrace the wonders of my tongue."

Winger looks at me and I shrug. "Can we just keep it...regular for right now?" I don't want to say pussy in front of them, which is pretty silly.

Winger helps me position myself on his lap, facing away from him, and I swear, I don't think I can ever get used to how it feels to have an erection inside of me. Sex is so primal. I sense that everything I'm doing is right.

Purge drops to his knees. "Works for me. Time to get to know both of you really well."

If there's supposed to be awkwardness, I simply don't feel it. I want to keep going. I want to do everything with them.

There will be no vanilla left by the time we sample all the ice creams. Is that where the term vanilla comes from? Vanilla ice cream? I quickly lose concern as my orgasm knots tighter.

Winger hands the brush to Tank and says, "Why don't you give her the ultimate treatment and brush her hair while we're taking care of everything else?"

Tank settles beside us on the window cushion. For a moment, the beautiful, snowy landscape that overlooks Peach Bottom

Valley flashes through my mind, but only for a second. I shift my eyes to Purge between my legs. The sight of him going to town in pure bliss, looking up at me, can't be rivaled.

Knowing that his tongue has to be stroking Winger's cock does something to me, and it's something really, really good.

Then Tank starts to brush my hair. He's careful, starting at the bottom, working his way up carefully, and not pulling too hard on the tangles. But even the slight tug, the slight pain, when he catches one unexpectedly, it shoots some kind of connection through me, like my world is perfect.

Then I come unraveled on Winger's cock. I can feel my pussy contracting around him as I give in to the bliss. A choked sound comes from behind me.

He must not have realized I was that close. His hands flatten around my breasts and he works his hips more carefully while driving me through every iteration of my orgasm until he's spilling himself inside of me, and I can only imagine that Purge is tasting both of us.

None of them miss a beat as I drift through the amazing moment. When I can focus, Purge is sitting back on his heels, a sly grin on his face. Then he wipes his hand over his mouth.

"You two are pretty fucking tasty. Ready to switch places, or have we completely ruined you? Do you need a break?"

Ruined? They might have ruined me. I can no longer imagine how one guy could be satisfying enough, and yet, all I've ever imagined was the white picket fence.

Was that the vanilla version of me projecting itself? I didn't understand that the white picket fence was vanilla. Maybe I don't want that.

I'm clearly ahead of myself in thinking of a future with these three. Would they even be willing to settle down? Would I be willing to subject a kid to having three fathers? God, if they father half as good as they fuck, our kids would be so lucky, and they mentioned wanting kids.

It's not part of the role-play, is it? It can't be. We all know better. We all know there's a good chance I'll be pregnant before the night's over. I rub a hand over my belly and it catches Purge's attention.

"You okay?"

I don't bother to lift my head off Winger's shoulder where I've fallen back against him.

I nod and try to say, "Mm-hmm," but I'm not sure it comes out.

All I can do right now is melt into him, and Tank beside us, and Purge as he rises up on his knees and lays his head on my belly.

# *Eleven*

## Tank

When I wake up, Sasha has already left the bed, which means I'm sleeping in a king-sized bed with Purge and Winger. Not something I ever thought I would do.

The scent of sex between three different guys and one wet-as-hell woman hangs thick in the air. There was plenty of cum to go around.

But, I need her again, right now. I can't imagine how she could handle a first night so amazingly, but she did. We did our best to give her everything she wanted.

Not bothering to get dressed, I stroke my hand over my morning wood and make my way to the kitchen, where faint sounds of Christmas music come from.

Sasha hasn't bothered to get dressed either, much to my delight. Then I clue into her choice of song, *All I Want for Christmas is You*. I'll take that as another hint that I might not have to walk back my thoughts of keeping her around forever.

My chest swells with hope and pride.

Her perfect peach of an ass swaying back and forth to the music is quite a sight for tired eyes. Hearing my footsteps, she turns around, and I get to enjoy her luscious tits and pretty pink nipples, and the curve of her waist that sucks in underneath that beautiful rack. My eyes trail downward to the flair of those baby-making hips that fit perfectly in my hands and her little tuft of hair hiding that sweet spot.

Jesus. Any chance my morning wood is going to take a break is gone. I'm hard as a rock, and the smile on her face sets my soul on fire. And yet, women don't stick around. How long before she tires of us? At least I understand not to let that soul fire get out of control.

I hate myself for focusing on sex, but it's the only way I can be close to her without revealing what I feel.

I'll give. I'll take. I'll do everything in my power to walk away unscathed.

"You up for a breakfast round?" I hope the three of us haven't worn her out.

Scooting to the side, she points at the coffee maker. "I was thinking coffee and biscotti, but cock and kisses would work too."

She shrugs, tipping her head to one shoulder. So fucking adorable. I walk over, pinning her against the counter, my cock sandwiched between our bodies.

Kissing her is like being transported to the Garden of Eden. How can someone as perfect and amazing as her be in my grasp?

I've learned my lesson though. The universe will rip her away. If I hadn't learned the hard way, no one would be able to hold me back from her. I'd believe that my past heartbreaks were essential to lead me to Sasha No one, nowhere, no way would be able to keep me from her. She'd be completely mine.

I pull away, dragging her to one of the chairs in the breakfast nook, pull it out, sit, then help her straddle my lap. I keep her between me and the table in case she wants to lean back for support.

"I wasn't sure if you were finished with us." I don't want to get too specific, so I'm hoping she'll open up about her thoughts.

A foolish glimmer of hope inside my heart refuses to be ignored even though my heart is shrouded in fear. I can't stop what I feel for her, but I can hide it.

I stifle the three little words that are on the tip of my tongue.

The auction, the role play, and her willingness to take all three of us...it's too good to be true. Maybe a friend dared her to lose her virginity in this auction. Maybe she wasn't even a virgin. My cock twitches at how tight she is. How perfectly she stretches to meet me.

"Right. Finished." She looks at her wrist as if wearing a watch. "I mean, not this round, but our time is almost up. Nice of you guys to each share your four hours with each other. That made this extra memorable."

There it is. We'll soon be nothing but a memory to her. Good thing I didn't propose. I'm irritated with myself for even thinking we have a future. But, I sure as hell will enjoy the last chance to fuck her before she gets Winger to drive her back to get his bike.

Then I can move on...alone. Unless I knock her up. At the very least, I'll have our child.

Everything in me tells me that thought is wrong. The hair stands on the back of my neck. But, I'm not going to play the fool this time. I'm going to go out strong.

"You better get ready because if this is the last thing you have to remember me by, then I promise, you'll remember it."

A flash of something I don't quite understand crosses her face. Regret?

"Give me something I'll never forget." Her playful tone returns but carries a somber edge.

My cock's thicker and harder than it's ever been. I'm in so much pain it almost blinds me. But for the sight of Sasha straddling my lap, there'd be no point in seeing anything at all. Once she walks out the door, I might as well be blind.

Wanting to make love to her before the other two guys wake up, discussions will have to wait.

I take her hand and slide her fingers through the pre-cum that's made a trail down my cock. We smear it all around and I tuck my fingers inside of her, priming her with that little bit of baby sauce.

When she takes a pregnancy test in two weeks and it's positive, she'll understand how I intended to make this memorable. She'll have to come back. She'll have to accept the fact that I am forever mingled in her life.

I shove away thoughts that she's actually on birth control and that this is all fun and games, all part of the role play.

Christ. My head is a wreck. That's a sure sign I want more than a quick fuck from her. I can't get out of my head.

This woman. This tiny woman has ruined me.

I lift her to slide my cock where it belongs. And, still, after everything we gave her last night, she's warm and tight and relieves all my pain. She makes everything right. She fuels me with anticipation that I'll soon be filling her with my seed once again, a parting gift. No bath after this time. My cum will stay in there and do its goddamn job.

When I'm fully seated and she's bracing herself, I pump her up and down on my cock. Gentle pumps, enough that we both benefit from the motion but small enough that I can take her nipple into my mouth and suck on it. Then I switch to the other one and it's just as good.

It should be impossible for her to fit me as perfectly as she does, to accept what Winger and Purge and I offered without question. To be the one who initiated this whole damn fantasy.

And, yet, it happened. We may have joked about ruining her, but I'm pretty sure that when she walks out the door, she'll take all of our hearts.

*Get out of your fucking head, Tank.*

I let her tit pop out of my mouth and meet her gaze, pumping hard until her pussy begs for all of my baby sauce, and we come undone with each other.

I have no idea how much time passes with her body slumped against mine. My arms are wrapped around her. Her tits are pressed against my chest, and we breathe with each other. We exist in the same space because we're one, as we should be. Then, her head rolls to the side, her lips grazing my neck, and she says the most god-awful words anyone's ever spoken.

"I'm going to miss you."

I could ask her to stay. I could do a lot of things. They all push me to a place I swore I would never go again.

# Twelve

## Sasha

My body has melted into Tank. I don't understand how we can have something this intense, and it can feel so perfect, and yet, our relationship is over as quickly as it started.

Love at first sight. That can't be real. Not between four people, can it?

Right. It's not.

For all the times I've been grumpy about those analogies that women imprint on the first men they have sex with, I have to question if it's true. I can't imagine a life without these three.

But I know women move on. Women move on all the time, and they move on happily and strongly. I've seen it many times. So if this imprint theory is a complete crock of shit, why am I almost in tears?

I'll be strong. I'll put on a brave face and act like leaving isn't a big deal.

I roll my head to the side and kiss Tank's neck. "I'm going to miss you."

He tenses. His breaths deepen. He's probably worried I'm fishing for an invitation to stay. I mean, I could stay till lunch. I don't think anyone would complain, but stay in their lives... That gets complicated real fast.

I honestly don't know how I can ever date again.

He saves me from the spiral of despair my mind is ready to embark on and says, "You can come over for *breakfast* any time."

There's a distance, a coolness to his words. He nods toward my coffee and biscotti but I catch his drift. A breakfast call instead of a booty call? Or could I show up the night before and make sure I'm there in time for breakfast?

If my heart wasn't hurting, it would be a funny thought.

I keep up the role-play, lean back, and rub my wrist, noting the telltale red ring. Muscle memory takes me back to the sensation of my arms stretched overhead, handcuffed around the closet rod while each of them took me from behind.

I loved it all—the chase, the rush of adrenaline, of not knowing exactly what was going to happen, the pleasure-pain, the way they adored me, and the safe space they gave me to completely surrender. Everything.

"Guess I'll go back to my boring cold cereal and coffee for breakfast when you guys aren't around." I start to lift, and lament at the slow drag of Tank's still-hard cock out of my sex.

He grabs a napkin from the table and tucks it between my legs. I wish he was doing it to keep what he calls the baby sauce inside. He probably just doesn't want to have to clean up the mess if I drip all over the kitchen floor.

Then he surprises me by saying, "Well, unless you're ready to quit taking birth control I've done all I can do."

His words sting. My chest tightens. I'm pretty sure it misses a few beats. I didn't tell him I was on birth control. Confusion blurs my world.

My stomach knots. The chocolate-dipped almond biscotti and coffee have no appeal. I think I'm going to throw up.

Did they really think I was on birth control? Did they think there was no way I would go through with this if I wasn't? Did I say something to confuse them? Oh my God, what if I got pregnant and they don't want me?

I barely eke out, "I'm not on birth control."

He huffs, and I feel insanely stupid with the napkin tucked between my legs.

Rushing to the closest bathroom, I try to figure out what to do. A few deep breaths help me decide it will be much easier to process whatever just happened in the comfort of my own home. I clean myself and head out of the current bathroom, to a different one where my dress was left.

Passing Winger on the way, I say, "I need to go home. Want me to drive you back to your bike?"

"You don't have to leave. You can hang out all day. I don't have anything else to do."

"I should go. I think the mystique of the role play has worn off. Even if I got four hours with each of you, time's up, right?" I don't wait for him to answer.

While I'm dressing, I hear him rifling through his dresser. The less I say at this point, the better.

# *Thirteen*

## Winger

Sasha's a whole different person this morning. The wild and crazy woman from the night before is replaced with someone who might as well be a taskmaster. And the sole task on her schedule is getting home.

I try to talk to her while I'm getting dressed, but she cuts me off and just says, "It'll be easier if we don't drag this out."

"We can do whatever you want, Sweet Pea." I step closer, bringing my hand to her face, needy to stroke her silky brown hair again. To be close to her, to smell her. God, I don't even need to have sex with her.

I would in a heartbeat, but just being near her, I know that I'm in the right place in this world. But she stiffens and pulls away.

"You can drop the sweet talk." She keeps her gaze diverted.

"You don't need to be embarrassed. What you did rocked our worlds."

"I'm not embarrassed, I liked it. I did what I wanted." Her words are clipped and defensive as she puts intense focus on smoothing her hair down.

"Okay, not embarrassed. Do you want this to end? I mean, it was pretty incredible, right?"

"Tank said I could come back for breakfast anytime. I guess we should swap phone numbers, huh?" She turns to me but maintains a disinterested expression.

"Definitely. Let's swap phone numbers, but you don't have to rush off. Did Tank say you have to leave?"

"Look, Winger, I may be young, but I know what this is. You don't have to worry about me getting all mushy, and dependent, and gold-digging, and whatever else. I get it. Plus, I have my own money."

She tries to walk past me, and I grab her harder than I intended. Her gasp alerts me to relax my grip on her arm.

"Maybe you *don't* understand what happened last night. I'm not ready for you to leave. You don't *ever* have to leave."

"That's sweet and all. Why wouldn't I want to be three hot dudes' plaything? But seriously, all I've ever wanted to do is settle down and have a family. So this," she waves her finger haphazardly. "This isn't exactly my white, vanilla, picket fence, suburban, two-and-a-half kid life."

I can't believe she's pulling back. Time to sort out what the hell is going on in her head.

"You've got a lot of dreams built into that statement. But up until last night, you didn't know this could be one of them. So I tell you what...I'll drive us back to get my bike, and you can drive away. But we're going to be in touch. Is that clear?"

"Yeah. Yeah. All good." She stares in the mirror, adjusting her dress as if we were an old married couple and I was telling her I had to cancel on picking the kids up from soccer and she'd have to do it. A bit miffed, but she'd take one for the team so that I'd owe her.

"I just need to know something."

"Sure. Whatever." She's so closed off, she could put up a defense in the Super Bowl and no one would get past it.

I follow her toward the front door and ask, "Is there anything at all that we did last night that you didn't like?"

"Oh, contrary, you did all the things I didn't even know I liked. So kudos to you guys."

Huh. I thought maybe there'd be at least one thing. But then again, if she doesn't want to talk about it, she is solidly able to shut us down.

Thankfully, the snowplow has run by the time we head out. Her car can handle the road, and I'll be able to handle it on my bike on the way back. Alone.

We might as well have the windows down on the ride back to the school with how cold the air is between us.

My heart sinks to depths I didn't even know were possible. I'm not even sure it's in my body anymore. I feel vacant.

She gets out of the car and circles around, so I do the same. She graciously lets me give her a peck on the cheek as we pass then shirks out of my grip.

"It's cold. I need to get back in the car."

"Right." I check my phone and see that the guys texted.

Tank: *we can't let her go*

Well, I don't know that they have a choice, other than waiting to see if we managed to get her pregnant. I don't want her to want us out of obligation though.

Purge: *We have a plan B*

Now they have my attention. I glance at Sasha as she adjusts the seat and the mirror.

Me: *Bring on plan B*

With any luck, B stands for baby. There's no way I can let her go.

Or maybe I have to. She has a say. I still can't wrap my brain around the possibility that this sweet young thing bought us in an auction to use us for our dicks...and our tongues and fingers and, well, for her personal pleasure.

No, I can't accept that, and not just because I'm old-fashioned. I know what I felt between us, and what I saw in her eyes.

I don't know what she's hiding behind, or why, but Plan B will be to break those walls down and show her how much we love her.

# Fourteen

## Purge

I send Winger a text: *Give her a head start, then meet us at Sugar D parking lot if you can't imagine life without her*

A second later, a text comes back from Winger: *On my way*

Tank and I watch the road for her little red Versa. Luckily, we're able to park our bikes behind a minivan in the parking lot so she doesn't notice us. Once she passes, we rev our engines and roll our bikes toward the street.

Winger's getting close and falls in with us as we pull onto the road a safe distance behind her.

Sasha mentioned that she lives near the school, so we don't waste any time. Per our plan, I stop beside her at a stoplight.

She worries her lower lip, stirring so many memories of the night before, then startles when she looks to the side and sees me.

We lock eyes and I'm certain she feels the way we do. I motion for her to roll her window down but she doesn't.

When she and Winger left, I came clean with Tank, and he had the same thought as me. We need her. Neither of us is going to settle for breakfast. We need the whole buffet, the full menu, the drive-thru, and the special Sunday brunch. We want it all.

She glances from me to the light and I can tell she's checking her mirrors, but all she's going to see behind her are Tank and Winger. We're the only ones out on this snowy day.

I motion again and she lowers the window.

"What are you doing here?" she asks.

"We can't let you leave."

"Why not?"

"Because none of us were joking about our intentions last night. Babies. Forever. We were all too chicken to say it, but I love you. Winger loves you. Tank loves you. And not to be cocky, but we're pretty sure you love us back."

She giggles nervously and puts her hand over her mouth. "You can't know that after one night."

"Well, see, that's where you're wrong, Sasha. We can, and we do. So I've got one question for you."

"I'm not sure I'm ready to say that I... I mean, I think I do, but it's so hard to believe."

"I'm not asking you to say that you love us. Take all the time you need."

"Okay." She glances at the light, which turns green. "What's the question?"

"Do you want bonbons?"

She furrows her brow and I lick my lips in anticipation that I know she doesn't. It's whether she's ready to admit that she doesn't want them. The glint of recognition hits her eyes when Winger and Tank rev their engines.

"Bonbons?" I ask again.

She shakes her head no. Tentatively at first, then wholeheartedly, and a smile breaks out on her lips.

Then she hits the gas almost hard enough to spin the wheels of her little Nissan Versa, and she takes off across the intersection. Tank and Winger are hot on her heels while I sit there laughing.

"Hot damn," I mutter to myself before taking off after them.

Moneybags has no idea how happy she just made me. But I'm surprised when she takes the road that leads to the edge of town. This isn't where I thought she lived. She mentioned an apartment near the school but we've gone the opposite direction from the only apartment I can think of nearby.

Another chase? She's controlling the shots as she always will. My only concern is that the roads are plowed wherever she's taking us.

In minutes, we pull up to an old house on the outskirts of town. The yard hasn't been tended in a while based on the awkward shape of the snow covering the ground. The house looks like it hasn't had the most TLC lately either.

Weeds have grown through the gravel driveway.

Then it hits me. This is her grandmother's house that we heard about, the inheritance, the place she needs her yard work done.

I pass Tank and Winger, stopping beside her car. "Tell me you don't actually want us to do yard work today."

"Yard work, breakfast, I'm pretty flexible about what we do. The only thing I don't want is bonbons. Is that clear?"

"Well, technically, you just said the safe word so we have to stop."

"But I said I don't want them."

"The whole point of a safe word is that if you say it, everything stops."

"Fine. I don't want those sweet little ball things that shall not be named."

I shove my kickstand down, lean my bike to the side and hop off. I flex my hands against each other then crack my knuckles.

The other two guys are quickly approaching, so I say, "If you don't want the things that shall not be named, then I suggest you get moving."

She hops out of the car and throws up her hands as the guys catch on to our conversation and move faster.

"Wait, give me five minutes."

"I don't think that's how this works," I clarify.

She plops her hands on her hips. "I believe it works however I say it works, or I might speak of those sweet little balls that shall not be named."

"Okay, five minutes it is." I take out my phone and start a timer, then flash it at her.

"Seriously? A timer?"

"You said five minutes."

"Okay." She fast walks, not making a huge effort, but drops her keys when she gets to the top of the steps onto the porch. She's flustered, and if that wasn't enough to make my dick hard, the glimpse of her ass when she bends over to pick the keys up sure does.

I glance at the timer ticking away. I don't know what she needs five minutes for, but this is going to be the longest five minutes of my life.

# Fifteen

## Sasha

I can't believe the guys followed me. That they admitted they're not ready for this to be over, but not just in a sexual way. Well, I mean, the sexual way will continue for sure, but they want more.

We all want more.

My inherited house is the perfect option for privacy.

After dropping my shoes by the door, I head to the kitchen out of habit and toss my phone and keys onto the counter.

That's it for habits as I rush upstairs to the room I've claimed as my own. The room that was supposed to be the big revelation spot for my boyfriend, which is why I've loaded a few dresser drawers and put white satin sheets on the bed. The patchwork quilt bedspread is draped over an upholstered chair so as not to kill the mood.

Silly me. Or is that prophetic me? The current mood is far better than anything I imagined.

I pull open the heavy wooden drawer that has the pristine red and white lingerie I'd planned to wear for John. At least I have something sexy to slip into—although I'm not sure it will be *more comfortable*, as they say.

Hurriedly peeling off my dress, bra, and underwear, I lift the sexy garment.

A shudder overtakes me.

My guys are fresh and exciting. This slip of fabric is somehow tainted. And likely to bring up questions. Do all virgins keep lingerie lying around...or only the bad virgins?

I chuckle at my term. It's amazing Tank didn't run for the hills.

To the contrary...he's about to be running up these stairs.

Naked, I plop on the bed and glance around the room, trying to think of anything else I can wear. Sweats, t-shirts, and threadbare pajamas, the only other items I have here, leave me convinced naked is the best option.

Slipping on the silky sheet as I attempt to stand, an idea hits me.

I pull the top sheet off and quickly wrap it around myself in toga fashion. The fabric is decidedly uncooperative compared to the cotton sheets I've used as togas, but with a little work, I manage to get the ends tucked in just right.

From the top of the stairs, I'll be able to see the guys open the door and come in, but they won't know about the back stairwell, so I'll have a running start by the time the chase ensues.

My heart pounds and my sweaty palms are no help in gathering the slick fabric that tangles around my feet. If I'm going to have any chance of keeping a lead, I have to be able to do more than trip on the sheet.

I won't have much time when they see me. They're on the porch, probably gripping the door handle, ready to burst in. How have my five minutes not passed? It seems like an eternity.

Purge's yell answers my unspoken question. "Time's up. Ready or not, here we come."

Do I imagine that he emphasizes the last word? Well, they're not coming yet, but I'm sure they will be soon, and so will I, over and over again. Thankfully, there are no neighbors.

The door flies open.

The three of them storm in, their eyes barely initiate a scan of the house, which is completely unfamiliar to them. The many dark corners, and old green and gold furniture are a stark contrast to my brand-new white satin sheets.

And it's the shiny white that catches their attention.

All three of them lift their gaze at the same time. Tank is the first to break into a full sprint, scaling the stairs two to three at a time, before I can even register that he's moving my direction.

My breath has stopped. I'm frozen. I'm kind of terrified. Then I snap out of it. Thank god for the long, formal stairwell. I have time to get away.

My heart's beating a million miles an hour, providing blood flow and energy for the fight or flight response that carries me down the hallway. Shoving an arm out to keep from slamming into the wall, I round the corner faster than I ever have before.

The quick whooshes of the sheet as my feet navigate my path, highlight how much it impedes me. I tug the fabric higher.

I have my lead, but the harsh stomp of Tank's boots as he lands on the second floor keeps my adrenaline surging.

Another corner.

I've always loved my grandma's maze of a house, full of hiding places. Ever since I was a kid, my cousins and I would play chase through the house. The beauty of older architecture as she always said, but thoughts of her are fleeting as each man calls out my nickname.

The mix of humor and urgency is intoxicating.

Finally, I'm at the back stairwell, which is disguised by a door that's identical to all of the bedroom doors. Quickly opening the door, I step through, and keep my eyes on the corner, ensuring Tank doesn't see where I went before I quietly close it.

I stop at the bottom, making efforts to control my breath while knowing it will take him a moment to figure out where I've gone. The stairwell runs from the kitchen to the second floor, so that food and beverages could be taken directly upstairs.

Putting my ear to the door, I listen for a moment. Silence. I inch the door open and breathe a sigh of relief that the coast is clear. The irony is that I don't want to get away, and I now solidly understand the thrill of the chase.

I question if I can sneak up on the guys. Have they all gone upstairs?

My throat closes when a hand grabs me from behind.

It's Winger. Shit. He'd been silently waiting behind the door. He pulls me close. "You didn't think we'd all follow the same path, did you?"

The sound of blood pulsing through my body echoes in my ears but can't drown out his low gravel of pride. I swallow the lump in my throat.

The chase was supposed to take longer, but now that I'm caught, I squeeze my thighs together. I want him inside of me so bad. I want to drop my sheet. No. I want him to strip it from me, but he doesn't. He also doesn't announce that he found me.

He just inches the fabric up and dips the finger between my legs. "You understand that if you let us play today, you're letting us play forever?"

I take a second to think, and his grip tightens around my arm. Rather than feeling like he's pressuring me to agree, it's as if he's assuring me that he means it.

"Yes," I croak, the lump in my throat not totally gone.

"We're not joking about this. I love you, Sasha. Purge told us you're not ready to say it. We'll give you time to get there."

Isn't that a risk or contradiction or something illogical? If I can't say it, how can they know that I ever will? And yet, logical or not, it's what I need.

"Thank you."

"In the meantime, we'll do everything in our power to make you ours, if we haven't already." He rubs his hand over my belly, and I honestly hope that they have.

I want this. It's just that no part of my brain can believe it's happening. And as soon as I can accept that, I'll be able to say that I love them—because I do. What I feel for them, the trust, acceptance, and rightness, have to be love.

Winger spins me around, kisses me, then pulls back and stares into my eyes. "I never thought I was going to find the perfect woman. I gave up on it years ago. But Sasha, you are everything I want, and I'll do whatever it takes to be the same for you."

Adrenaline must fuel my boldness. "I can't believe I'm saying this, but you already are."

"I fucking love you, Sasha. I need..."

I lose track of what he's saying when he reaches for something in his back pocket. Before I know it, there's a handcuff around my wrist again.

Perhaps I should broaden our adventures by telling them more of my fantasies, but this one's more than fine for a few million more times. It'll be different without a closet rod in sight.

He lifts me onto the kitchen counter and pulls my hand upward to an open section of the cabinet that has wooden dowel rods separating the bigger space.

Leaving my other hand free, he attaches me to one of the wooden rods.

He caresses his fingers down my restrained arm, then tangles his fingers with my other hand. "I want you to be able to touch us this time. You want that, don't you?"

Stroking the scruff of this five o'clock shadow, I say, "That's not all I want."

Tugging at the top of my sheet, he peels the fabric away, letting it fall around me as he admires my nakedness.

I'm not embarrassed when I'm with them. Instead, I'm worried that I'm too much of a sex newbie to safely navigate the precariousness of how easily the fabric slips over the counter.

Winger groans while he stares at my bare breasts, seems to make a decision, then taps my knees.

The slippery fabric makes my effort to spread my legs appear overzealous.

He remains silent as he stares at my sex. I'm fairly certain that he has now looked at my lady bits longer than I ever have.

"Beautiful," he murmurs as he strips himself naked.

Purge calls out from upstairs, "There are so many goddamn doors in this place. Where the fuck are you, Moneybags?"

"You got that right," Tank says from the other downstairs wing of the house. "Any luck, Winger?"

"Oh, I got all the luck in the world," Winger whispers.

There's a shift in his mood as he strokes his cock, from fun to determination. With one hand, he reaches behind me and pulls me forward, easily sliding his shaft into me. I bite my lower lip to hold back my cries. He's making love to me, looking into my eyes, kissing me, fondling my breast, stroking my arms.

I don't know how long we're going at it, because I'm drifting through the tail of my first orgasm when the other two guys come into the kitchen. Clothes are being thrown in places my grandmother would never have approved of.

Then again, orgasms and bodily fluids are breaking the rules as well.

I'm barreling towards my next release when my phone rings.

Orgasm averted.

The ringtone—it's ingrained in my brain and I beg the name to vacate my entire existence.

Tank lifts the phone. "John?" His face is still positioned toward the screen, but he looks at me, past his lowered brows.

"No one important."

"Oh, yeah? So I can answer it?"

"Please don't."

Winger pumps slowly, enough to keep my attention, but allowing me the ability to talk.

"Is this the boyfriend?"

346

"How do you know about my boyfriend?" Then I remember the brief conversation where I admitted he had made me feel dirty.

Purge cracks up. "So that's a yes. Because rumors were going around, rumors that you were going to buy us, rumors that you might be using us, rumors that you wanted to make your boyfriend jealous."

"He's not my boyfriend anymore, I promise."

"You broke up with him?"

"No, he broke up with me." Why can't they just let me enjoy Winger's thick cock?

Purge busts out laughing. "Nobody in their right mind would break up with you."

"Fine. He's not in his right mind. I'll give you that. Just please don't answer it." I lean my head into my extended arm, but the guys won't let it go.

I give them the Cliff Notes version while getting slow-fucked to the repeated ringtone of my ex-boyfriend. "He texted me that I wasn't enough. I was too vanilla, a boring girlfriend, and he needed more."

Winger stops, looks me dead in the eye, and says, "Let Tank answer."

Tank hovers his finger over the accept call button and says, "Are there any words you want to say right now before I answer this call?"

I furrow my brow. The ringtone starts again.

"Any particular repeated three-letter word, a sweet treat, you want to mention to shut this down?"

John doesn't control my life anymore. I finally know who I am.

Purge is already stroking his cock, and I hope they're thinking what I'm thinking.

Purge catches my ogle and says, "Let us all come inside of you, each one of us in turn. Keep him on the phone long enough for that. You don't have to tell him what we're doing. This is for you."

Shifting my gaze to each of them in turn, I stop on Tank. "Answer the call."

The tension in his face could be etched in stone until those words are out of my mouth. He taps the button. Winger picks up his thrusts. Tank positions the phone at my ear, and I try to grab it with my free hand, but he shakes his head.

Winger occupies my hand by holding it to his lips, kissing me. "Keep touching us," he whispers.

So I do.

I stroke his lips, his jaw, and I say, "Hey, John," best I can, in my heavily sex-addled voice.

"What are you doing?" he asks.

"What does it matter to..." I gasp. Winger's cock swells. His jaw is clenched and I suspect he's about to come.

"It's none of your business, what I'm doing," I say quickly.

Winger groans through his release. I can tell he's trying to be quiet, but not quiet enough.

The warmth of his seed fills me as John asks, "Are you with someone?"

"Like I said, it's none of your business." The distraction of the conversation is enough to keep me from orgasming but something I've learned in my limited sex life is that it's not all about the orgasm. The ride can be pretty fucking incredible…no pun intended.

Winger pulls out and makes room for Purge. I'm stretched, and full, once again. He thrusts hard and fast, causing me to shift back and forth. In a microsecond of a pause, he rips the satin sheet out from under me. With increased friction between my ass and the counter, he grips my hips and pumps me with the wildest look of abandon.

I swear he is going to split me in two.

I don't know what John's saying anymore.

I try to pull myself back into the moment, and John is fishing, "You sound…?"

"I'm exercising."

A smirk cracks through Purge's intense expression, a split second before his jaw falls slack. His body breaks rhythm, and he growls his release.

Holding up two fingers, he pulls out, drags his fingers through the mess between my legs, and whispers, "Two loads of baby sauce."

Winger wastes no time taking hold of the phone as Tank fills me. My confidence goes up increasingly with each minute. I can't believe they're coming so fast. My orgasm winds tighter, but Tank beats me to it. He comes undone inside of me, slides out, then drops to his knees and nuzzles his face in my sex.

As if rehearsed, the guys each hold up three fingers, and Tank says, "Your turn."

"You don't exercise," John says. "Put me on video. I don't believe you."

The thrill of the chase. The risk of getting caught. The build-up before the release. I almost don't want to climax. Almost, but the craziness of the situation is enough to let me enjoy it.

"No video. I'm pretty sure I'm the definition of a hot mess right now."

He tries to send a video call through, and I shake my head furiously at Winger. He and Purge are quietly laughing and I know they want to accept the call.

I don't think they would show John what's actually happening, but John's an asshole, and he will be an asshole for the rest of his life. No need to stoop to his level when I have something this incredible to enjoy.

The amount of control I have and the confidence my guys have given me feed into my building orgasm.

Maybe I won't stoop to his level, but I'm not opposed to bending.

"Actually, I've found this great new way to work out. It's totally *not* vanilla exercise. And hang on. I think I'm about to do one of those high-intensity interval trainings. Give me a second."

I cry out my release. I come all over Tank's face, my body's shaking. I have no idea what John's thinking, and I don't care. I drop my head back into the crook of my arm. I'm sated.

"You know what, John? It turns out there's nothing vanilla about me. You were the one that wasn't enough."

I lift my hand out of Tank's hair and tap the end call button.

# *Epilogue*

## Sasha

I just dropped the kids off for a visit with Izzy and her brood, which is a nice thing about the crazy night of the first Christmas Cherry Auction. Seven years ago, for the five of us ladies who ended up with reverse harems, a special, magical thing happened.

We've been each other's support system ever since, with wonderful role models to look up to from Eggplant Canyon, since those ladies were doing their thing, getting all their needs met, not just their pleasure, before we even held the auction.

The guys and I decided to keep Grandma's house, and with the kids gone, it's a rare moment that we have it to ourselves, on Christmas Eve no less.

I know something's up because the guys asked me to drop the kids off, instead of insisting on doing it for me. And they asked me to stop by Sugar D's Bakery to pick up donuts, with a special request of the Long Johns with the delicious cream inside.

I would swear that they're perverts, insisting on calling Éclairs *Long Johns* and being way too emphatic about them being filled with cream. It's probably a guy joke referencing the time they all filled me with cream while I was on the phone with John.

Not my proudest moment.

But it was right up there, which means that I don't have any room to judge my guys for pervy jokes. They're my perverts, and I can't wait to be alone with them.

So when I walk inside and none of them are anywhere to be seen, the anticipation continues.

"Hey, guys, anyone home?" I call out. The silence of the house is such a stark contrast to the laughter that's usually coming from our three little ones and the three dads instigating most of the laughter.

Then I hear, "You're present is on the stairs." Tank peeks out of the bedroom door closest to the top of the stairs.

"Should I put the donuts in the kitchen first?"

"Yeah. We'll get to the *Long Johns* later."

I roll my eyes.

"Am I going to need my energy later?" I laugh as I head to the kitchen, set the donuts down, then return to the stairwell.

Tank's standing outside of the room when I return, dragging his bangs back as he rakes his fingers through his hair. In only his underwear, the display of tattoos and contoured muscles never gets old. That suffices as a gift any day.

"It's been a while since we got to *play*." Tank watches as I survey the empty stairs.

Excitement bubbles through me. I love a gift as much as the next person, but I have a feeling the present he referred to won't be wrapped in a box.

"He means adult play." Winger appears from somewhere behind me and he's dressed as scantily as Tank, both sporting erections.

Wasting no time taking on my role, I taunt them and start up the stairs.

"I hope so, we've gotten kind of vanilla." The term 'vanilla', and its insinuations, no longer have any impact on me.

Winger holds back for a second at the base of the stairs and Tank patiently watches me climb.

I'm halfway up when he grins mischievously and I realize they're trapping me. Adrenaline spikes in a way that it hasn't for quite a while.

It's been a few months since we had the house to ourselves and all of the little ones were gone. But that time was out of sheer exhaustion so the guys and I could sleep after a stomach flu wore us all out.

I'm glad I set the donuts down because they'd end up ruined if I'm right about what's about to happen.

Tank steps down the first few steps, meeting me three-quarters of the way up. Presuming that the game has begun, I scoot to the side to past him and politely say, "Excuse me."

He grips my chin and tips my head up. "You're not going anywhere."

My entire body tingles.

Winger's hands stroke up my legs from behind. I'd been so focused on Tank, I hadn't noticed he'd caught up with me. Winger's thumbs catch under my ass cheeks but over my leggings.

Bummer, I didn't wear a skirt. The problem is short-lived when he trails them upward and removes my leggings.

I reciprocate the action with Tank and pull his underwear down, dragging my tongue over his tip, taking in his musky pre-cum. Free from his underwear, he sits on the step and drags his thumb over my lips, catching my lower lip as he tucks his thumb inside.

"You're going to suck my cock."

I consider saying something clever about it being better to give than receive, but I opt for a simple challenge. "Am I?"

"You didn't run."

"I didn't know I was supposed to." Nor am I sure I have the energy. The addition of kids to the household offers extra obstacles scattered haphazardly on the floor. We'd need to pick up before running through the house.

"Would you like to?"

I lunge toward the side but he steps into my path. Winger grabs my hands and pulls them behind me. With Tank on a higher step, his cock is at face level. He grips himself and taps his tip against my lips.

"Not this time, Tiny. You don't always get what you want."

We all know this statement is rarely true. And while they might have new ideas of how we can play. I want lots of orgasms and to snuggle with them, both things I'm likely to get.

Movement at the top of the stairwell catches my attention. A video camera is barely peeking around the corner. Purge steps forward with it.

On film. That's something we haven't done before. He comes closer and tosses a pair of handcuffs to Tank.

The camera had been so distracting, I hadn't noticed the cuffs. And it's not like he could have had them hidden anywhere since he's in his undies too.

"Still want to get away, Money," Purge laughs as he moves closer while watching the screen.

I try to wrestle my hand free and I give Winger a challenge, but he ends up wrapping his arm around me, overpowering me, and making it easy for Tank to slap the handcuff on my wrist.

In one swift move, they have one of my hands attached to the stair railing.

Handcuffs remain one of my favorite toys. Maybe because they always remind me of my first night. Maybe because being in handcuffs pretty much guarantees I'm about to have a lot of orgasms.

Heaven forbid I ever get arrested. I'm not sure how that would go.

Tank sits on the stair above me, reaches around, and slaps my ass.

I startle from the sting even though I liked it, and he rubs gently to soothe me, but his words offer much more than his hands.

"I don't know if you realized what you were in for when you bought us so many Christmases ago, but every day I'm with you is like a fucking holiday." He kisses where he spanked me. "Bend over and take that cock now, unless you want to give your safe word a try."

"There's a first time for everything," I tease. "Bon...appétit."

I use my free hand to steady myself as I bend at the waist, lick my lips, and lean down for his cock.

On the step below me, Winger nudges my legs apart. I think he's going to have sex with me, until I realize he's sunk down and his head is between my legs. He's eating my pussy from behind, which is so fucking hot. I don't know why that's even better than in front, but it is.

I glance up at Purge whose underwear is gone, and he's got his cock in one hand. He positions the video camera at a few different angles.

"Scoot over, Tank." Purge nudges him with his foot.

I pop off Tank's dick and let him scoot over so Purge can sit beside us. I can't wait to see the video he's capturing. The thrill that it sends through me is unbelievable and Winger has to ease up so I can get my bearings. It's only a second before we'll be back to pleasing one another.

Purge leans back on the arm without the camera and says, "Why don't you show the camera how good you take my cock?"

I lean his direction, tease my tongue over the tip, and start to sink onto him when Winger gets me to the point of no return. I was too distracted and didn't realize I was so close. My breaths are heavy and I can't keep good suction. I give up, rest my forehead on his chest, and let my body unravel.

Purge says, "I would complain that you messed things up, but that's even better. Keep doing that back there, Winger." Purge has the camera low, catching my face.

He continues, "Watching you come, fuck, we should have been doing this long ago. Tank, help me prop her up, and Money, keep that mouth open. We're going to get some *money shots*."

The warmth of Winger's huff warms my sex as the guys laugh at his joke. They lift me enough, I can get my arm back under me. I'm too sex-drunk to think about what they're doing.

Purge starts stroking his cock furiously, and Tank does the same. I've needed another session like this for far too long, which is apparent as Winger's tongue teases every last hint of orgasm from me.

It doesn't take long for me to catch on though as Purge shoots his load into my mouth, or at least partially in my mouth. Spurts of his seed coat my cheeks, my t-shirt, and Tank and his own bare legs since they're sitting so close together.

Tank groans, bucks against his hand, and catches me from the other side.

Winger gave me a reprieve and rests his head on my hip so he can watch.

I lick my lips, taking in their combined salty release.

I'm about to crumple into them when Winger stands and balances me against his body. "You ready to take it where it counts, Sweet Pea."

"Since when do you have to ask?" I wiggle my ass against him. The stair height helps balance our height difference nicely.

He chuckles. "I guess we should have known we'd have our work cut out keeping you satisfied when you tricked us into your first time."

Tank rubs his thumb over the cum on my cheek then wipes it on his leg. "I'll never forget what a bad virgin you were."

We share a laugh but Winger uses the broken tension to slide his cock into me.

Catching my breath, I manage one more bit of fun. "But at least you were game to spend the rest of the night fucking the bad virgin right out of me."

"Oh yeah, we made sure there was none of that bad virgin left." Purge tries to sound serious.

"Nothing like making sure the job is done." Winger firms his grip on my hips and thrusts, completing me in the way only these guys can.

When my body milks him for every last bit of baby sauce, we crumple into a mess on the steps and I'm surrounded with happiness.

"I love you all so much."

They share my sentiment, then Tank adds. "Merry Christmas, Tiny. You're the best present ever."

Low, sincere voices of agreement fill my ears while hands tighten around me. I drift off to sleep in my favorite place...in a tangle of their bodies where all of my cares fade away because we're one.

And we live happily ever after!

Getting redundant? Sorry, but just in case someone goes straight for the handcuffs story, and hasn't seen this yet...a bonus scene for this story is available exclusively to newsletter subscribers!

https://SylvieHaas.com

# Wishful and Wanton

## A Reverse Harem Romance

Sylvie Haas

# Blurb

**I'm too shy to get on stage and auction myself, but that doesn't stop my principal, teacher, and a coach from bidding on me.**

F stands for Fail.

That became readily apparent when I biffed my final semester of high school, and had to spend an extra semester finishing those classes.

Despite being ready to break free and never set foot in that school again, I volunteer to help with the fundraiser for the fire department, which forces me to be in the building one last time.

And it turns out, I still have lessons to learn...like that F can stand for a lot of other things, namely, what the principal, art teacher, and coach want to do to me!

But do they want to do it Forever?

If you love dirty-talking men who have over-the-top ideas of how to please their woman and want to give her babies, volunteer to help at the Christmas Cherry Auction!

# One

Positioned between the broccoli cheddar soup and the minestrone, I smile at my former English teacher and fill a cup with the latter for her.

Since I'm too chicken to get on stage at the Christmas Cherry Auction, I figured I could help with the fundraiser by serving soup. I didn't think about the event being held in the high school, a place I was forced to spend one too many semesters since I didn't graduate when I was supposed to.

Aside from spending a few more hours in my former prison, I have to deal with being pleasant to the teachers, when all I want to do is get away from them. Well, some of them. Others stir thoughts in me that students aren't supposed to have.

Perhaps it would help if I called the auction what it is, the Christmas Cheer Auction, and focus on raising money for the fire department, but the Cherry nickname hits too close to home.

I wish that I had the moxie or bravado or confidence, or whatever it is that my friends who plan on prancing across the stage have. But I don't, so my meager contribution to the fundraiser is soup ladling.

Another smile. Another ladle of soup.

A few of the parent attendees who recognize me as their kid's friend make small talk as they shuffle past.

*No, I'm not home from college for winter break. No, I don't know what I'm going to do with my life. No, I don't like answering invasive questions that remind me that most of my peers graduated in the spring and moved away, but here I am in December with no plan in sight.*

The truth is that I've always wanted to be a mom, but since I didn't date any guys in high school, I might even fail at that. At least the seasonal job I picked up as a helper at Santa's Winter Wonderland in the mall gives me a chance to be around kids.

Mrs. Dupree, the high school counselor, who dutifully informed me that I wasn't living up to my potential is next in line. Reaching for her cup, I divert my eyes and hope she'll pick up on the cue that I'm not in the mood for any conversation beyond her choice of soup.

In my effort to dismiss her, my gaze lands on Coach Curtis as he rounds the corner, one thick arm raised as he rakes his fingers through his freshly washed hair. Perhaps it would be more appropriate for me to notice the guys closer to my age who have just finished their weight training session, but they might as well be invisible.

Suddenly, I'm dumping hot broth, vegetables, and pasta on my hand. Dropping the cup and ladle into the crockpot, I yank my hands back, knock over the stack of clean cups and spoons, and cringe at the mess I've made. Yet another fail.

My ladling mishap either comes from my knees giving out or my heart beating so fast it jostles my arms. I can't tell. All I know is that Coach Curtis does that to me.

I duck behind the table to pick up the mess I've made, and to hide.

Mrs. Dupree clears her throat.

I pop my head up. "Sorry, I don't recommend the minestrone."

Mary, who's managing the two crockpots next to me puts the cover on the soup I ruined and offers to add the broccoli cheddar to her offerings.

If Coach Curtis wasn't so blindingly hot, maybe I'd have paid attention to my male peers. Maybe I wouldn't be swooning over a man ten years my senior. Maybe I—

"Let me help you with that, Jade," the sinfully seductive voice of our high school principal says as he kneels beside me.

"Principal Spears," I say, then have to force myself to take a breath since he sends my hoo-ha into an even bigger frenzy than Coach Curtis did. Instead of Coach's all-out brawn, Principal Spears is a suit-wearing, sophisticated type.

Our eyes lock and I realize he's not lost in my fantasy, he's waiting for me to say something other than his name.

But he knew my name. Me. Jade Johnson. The nearly perfect, straight-C student. It's the *nearly* part that landed me back in high school for another semester. If only F stood for Fair or Fantastic or Free...nope. Fail. It's practically my mantra.

I'm the winner of zero awards, academic or otherwise. Star nothing. So how does he know me? I give myself a mental check. He takes his job seriously, so of course, he knows my name. He was my principal for four and a half years.

"You don't have to help me. I'll get it."

"Are you okay? Did you get burned?" He tenderly lifts my hand. I'm pretty sure the gesture is supposed to be helpful, which leaves me confused because the way he strokes his thumb over my wrist is so intimate. Maybe F stands for Fantasy. I'm lost in his woodsy cologne.

"I'm fine, and really, you don't have to help."

"I don't have to help. I want to." He gathers the scattered cups and utensils.

"Thank you." I shift my gaze to the closest plastic spoon to give myself a reprieve from his intense brown eyes. If I'd known how it felt to be this close to him, I would have misbehaved in school just to get called to his office.

Gah! Why didn't I think of that sooner?

Not understanding why he would want to crawl around and help me, I manage a simple, "Thank you," only to realize I just said that.

"I didn't see your name on the auction list. You're friends with Roxy, Izzy, and Maggie, right?" His rich chocolaty voice wraps his words in a delicious package. He knows who my friends are... He's a dream. A much older, off-limits dream...who I'll go home and shamelessly pleasure myself to in the privacy of my bedroom in my parents' house.

I shake my head and lower it. "I wish I was that bold. They asked me to auction myself, and I feel horrible for saying no, but I can't get on stage in front of a crowd."

He tucks a finger under my chin, gently lifting until I meet his gaze. "Not everyone has the same skills."

His primary skill is clearly seducing me, or do all teenage girls react like this to him?

Reality check. It doesn't matter.

"You don't have to get on stage to impress me." Is that a simple attempt to comfort me or a seduction?

Obviously, I'm hearing things—Fake things.

Skills. Let me focus on those instead of how I can impress him. What are my skills? Falling in love with men I can't have? Not a good one to bring up. The flutters in my chest make it hard to focus. Falling, flutters, focus...am I still caught up on what F can stand for?

Rather than let my mind go to the F word I'd like to try with him, and Coach Curtis, I avoid embarrassing myself since there's a very important F word I need to remember.

Fundraiser—as in the one I'm at, along with most of the town.

"I haven't figured my skills out yet. Right now, I only seem to be good at making messes." I force a smile.

His expression stiffens. "High school should have helped you find something you're passionate about."

Again with the strange wording and tone. I glance over my shoulder to confirm that the soup line is moving along just fine and that no one's paying attention to Principal Spears and me on our hands and knees.

There's enough background noise, I doubt anyone can hear us.

Our little bubble of privacy, and the fleeting moment I have with him, embolden me. I'm also leaning very heavily into my imagination's take on his words...because I'm almost certain he's capitalizing on an F word...Flirting.

"High school helped me find some...thing I'm passionate about, trust me, just not a career." That statement is the boldest thing I've ever *almost* done. Thankfully I realized it's too much and switched my wording midsentence. I tip my head down and let my hair fall on either side, hiding myself from the world before I embarrass myself.

He drags a finger over my cheek, guiding my hair behind my ear. This can't be happening.

Do sparks actually fly? Boyfriends do the hair-tucking move, not *friends*, but we can't be that F-word anyway. Principals definitely don't do the hair thing with students.

"Then we failed you. I should make it up to you, Jade. I could help you evaluate plans for your future."

Ugh! Future is one of my most dreaded F words. He'll send me back to Mrs. Dupree to look at more college degree plans, then vocation and technical schools.

"The school didn't fail me. I just want to be a mom." The first statement was intended. The second—I should have kept that one to myself.

Principal's jaw flexes. He looks away. And if I'm not mistaken, I hear a growl. Probably just his stomach since he is on the floor with me instead of eating dinner.

I'm sure he's about to lecture me on women being able to do anything, which somehow people say, then instantly exclude motherhood as a viable option.

I save him from having to give his spiel. "I know. I'm supposed to want more. But I want what I want, and there's no step-by-step four-year plan or eighteen-month certification to get me there."

"It's nine." The grumpiness etched on his face and the gravelly tone are a bit overreactive.

"What?" I sit back on my heels.

He takes all of the plasticware from me and throws them in the trash can that's beside him.

Lifting me to standing, he leans to my ear. "Nine months to motherhood, and you could start tonight if you wanted."

*Fuck!*

This is hardly appropriate, yet I've never wanted to continue a conversation more. "That would require someone to get to know me and have enough interest to make that commitment."

I'm not about to tell him I've never had sex. Leaving the hint that I don't have a serious boyfriend is plenty.

He wraps his fingers around my wrist and leads me into the reception office which is only a few steps away. Of course, my twitter-pated brain imagines continuing through the area to his office, but he stops short. Closing the door behind us, we're alone, though, and that's enough to get my attention.

"Your birthday is December eighth. You didn't date in high school, went to prom with your girlfriends. You never signed up for a single club or extra-curricular activity. You—"

"How do you know all of that?"

"I know you, Jade. I respected the rules. I forced myself to give you space to find yourself or whatever it is teens do in their gap year, but instead of graduating, you came back."

That's an optimistic way to view me failing two classes in my final semester.

"Jade, I want you."

"Want me to...?" I offer the open-ended statement even though I know he said what he meant.

"I think you know."

The reception area suddenly seems smaller, more intimate, and yet leaves me completely exposed.

"But..." I falter, unable to force the words out.

"But you graduated. The rules don't apply anymore."

"I haven't graduated, final grades aren't in yet."

"You passed each of your classes. I already checked with your teachers."

This is escalating as quickly as my heart is racing. "But you're thirty-six. I'm only eight—just turned nineteen."

"Life has enough limits, enough rules...don't create them where they don't exist."

"Okay, let's say, there are no rules. What exactly are you proposing?" It's fair that I go into this rule-free zone with clarity on things like not expecting anything more than a sexy trip to the principal's office to get my bottom spanked.

Is that what I want? With the naughty floodgates wide open, my mind flits back to Coach Curtis and my long-standing fantasy about getting hoisted up, wrapping my legs around his waist, and being lost in passion as he crashes me into a wall of lockers.

Yeah, there are obvious problems with that one, like the odor of smelly socks and jock straps, the likelihood my backside would be bruised by getting crushed against a lock, and the mortifying possibility of getting caught. My imagination erases those issues—except the getting caught part. Depending who catches us and how they react, I might not mind.

The mental blur I'm lost in vanishes when Principal Spears steps closer. "Are you thinking about how much you want this to happen?"

"I...um..."

"I've seen the way you look at me. Don't let fear hold you back."

Was I that obvious? I can't think straight. Or crooked. Or at all.

His voice lowers. "You can tell me no. You can walk out that door." He motions to the one we just came through. "Or you can march your naughty ass into my office and play out both of our fantasies."

A roar of laughter filters in from the auction, pulling my attention to the door. Guilt washes over me that I'm not brave enough to get on stage like my friends, and now I'm shirking my soup-line duties.

All for what? To admit to one of my dream guys that I'm not the experienced wild child he thinks I am? To get all worked up only to disappoint him? Or maybe, my virginity would make it even more fun. And I could experience a first time with a guy who knows what he's doing.

I'm not exactly committed to my feeble effort, but I make it. "I'm supposed to be out there helping raise money."

"Of course." The kiss my principal, former principal, plants on my forehead sends electric shocks to my toes. I've never been so energized and confident. Angling my head upward, I'm ready to take a chance.

But he steps away and leaves. His absence rakes through me, tearing my heart out. A bit much for a foolish fantasy.

How can I already feel abandoned? Should I consider it lucky that I can escape further pain if I walk away now?

I pull myself together, trail a hand over the counter to steady myself, and walk to the door. There are too many people standing near the back of the room to see where Spears went. The soup line is no longer busy, and Mary lets me know they don't need me anymore.

A tinge of guilt is relieved, but did I miss my chance by not going into his office?

The PA system is alive with the auctioneer rapidly escalating the bids on Maggie. My heart, which must still be in my chest, is happy since she was afraid no one would bid on her. I snake my way through the people at the back of the room and spy Spears at the winner's table.

Bidding is ongoing, so he didn't win her. What's he doing?

I'll find out in a second because he storms back to me. My traitorous heart flips. The possessive, command in his entire demeanor has my panties soaked.

He stops barely a foot in front of me and balls his fists. "There, I donated three thousand dollars in your name. Your commitment is fulfilled."

A shiver runs up my spine. "My name? What if people wonder why you donated for me?"

"Let them ask."

For sake of sounding dense, I need him to clear up what's happening. Nothing this good has ever happened to me. "What would you tell them?"

"That you're mine." He lifts a hand but halts it midair next to my cheek before lowering it. "The only reason I'm not touching you right here in front of everyone is because you haven't agreed."

How much power do I have over him? It's intoxicating. And yet, I want him to take it all from me.

"Do you agree?" He prompts.

I worry my lower lip, and in a barely audible voice, say, "Make me."

His mouth goes slack and his breaths are heavy. "Be careful what you ask for."

Careful is exactly the opposite of what I'm feeling right now. "I want you to tell me what to do."

He thrusts a pointer finger toward the room we just left. His eyes take on a darkness I've never seen. "Get in my office right now, Miss Johnson."

I flinch. Adrenaline rushes through me. I don't like being in trouble, but my legs are practically jelly at his demand.

He's doing what I asked. And he's doing it perfectly. People around us are watching. My body vibrates with need.

"Yes, sir." I lower my head, letting my hair shield me from the onlookers, and pretend-sulk to his office. I'd swear my hearing has obliterated everything except for his footfalls and breaths, but I can't possibly hear them above the auction.

I'm barely inside the room when the heat of his body envelopes me from behind. One of his hands clamps on my waist and guides me forward.

His breaths are labored, much like my own, except mine verge on panting. I hope I don't ruin this by revealing that I've never had sex. He hinted that he knew I didn't date.

I accept that my virginity could be part of the allure, but it will be gone after this evening. Will his interest vanish too?

It will be worth it.

He reaches back to swing the door shut, and a sharp slap on the wooden door pulls me out of my head. Spinning toward the sound, I find a very angry art teacher in the doorway. Mr. Pierce also happens to be a star in my fantasies, but I've never seen him like this.

# Two

Guilt washes over me for getting turned on by his intensity and being in a room with the two of them. Pierce's hair is a few inches long and has the just-rolled-out-of-bed look, not the prim and proper short, infallible cut of Spears. Pierce's tattoos and relaxed-fit t-shirt and jeans are another contrast.

But they now have a common thread...they're both serious and stern.

Mr. Pierce composes himself enough to close the door, and doesn't leave time for me to wallow.

He practically growls, "You have no right to treat Jade like that."

He's defending me.

I had an art class with him my freshman year but told myself never to take another class with him because all of my projects ended up having something to do with a penis—in the planning stages. Thankfully, I forced myself to choose different topics.

My heart is getting a workout in all sorts of ways I'm not sure are healthy.

"Don't interfere," Spears demands, and the thickness of the tension makes me worry they could go to blows.

In stark contrast to his normally relaxed demeanor, the not-so-mild-mannered art teacher circles the principal, forcing his body between the two of us. I stumble back a step.

Dang. I'd rather be the meat in the sandwich...oops, more inappropriate thoughts. I'm a wanton mess.

"Don't talk to Jade like that ever again." Pierce is standing up to his boss.

*Oh no!* This could go wrong. Shoving an arm between the men, I say, "Wait. I asked him to do that."

"You asked to be in trouble?" Pierce's brow furrows.

Crap. Crap. Crap. "I've never been sent to the principal's office before. I wanted to—"

"Mind your own fucking business, Pierce." Spears cuts me off. "I made a private bid on her and we're going to discuss how she makes good on it."

"You're not in the auction," Pierce says to me. "I would have noticed."

Would have noticed? What is going on? Spears looks too mad to be considering a threesome. And I must be losing my mind for conjuring up that possibility.

"I said private, as in get the hell out," Spears tries to keep from raising his voice.

My chest tightens at the thought of Pierce leaving.

"You're taking private bids?" he asks me.

"I'm too shy to get on stage so it's more like a donation." I force a smile. Does he want to donate too?

The tension in his expression relaxes. "If I make a donation, I get four hours of your time."

"Who's counting?" I shrug, hoping to lighten the mood. Didn't Spears tell me not to let fear hold me back?

Did I really just do that? Being desired by these men unleashes a side of myself I've never explored.

Spears hasn't relaxed. "*I'm* counting. What's going on here is none of your business, Pierce."

He's counting? Not great. That hints that this is a one-time thing, but okay. How can I spin this to my advantage? What if I put my active imagination to good use?

"What if I wish it was?"

Both men stare at me. Spears asks, "Was what?"

"His business...like we could be in this *business* together?" My bravado fades as the statement awkwardly detours into ridiculousness.

I force myself to stop before nervously furthering the analogy to say that we could run a sandwich shop and I'll be the meat, or the filling, or well, yeah...best to shut up.

The sound from the auction is a distant ebb and flow. Everything I want is right here in my personal bubble, pressing into me from either side.

Pierce has an odd calm to his voice. "I'll donate right now if you're serious."

"I want her for myself." Spears grips my upper arm. Being objectified isn't normally something I pride myself on, but a primal part of me jumps right in line for being his. I want to be his in every way. If I'm going big, should I ask him if I can call him Daddy?

"Have you asked Jade what she wants?" Pierce challenges, tapping into another deep-seated part of me that values his consideration of my desires.

They shift their attention to me. I've never been good at being put on the spot. Nor have I been good at analogies, or sports, but I think it's time to swing for the fences.

"I want..." A quick mental check assures me that sanity must be with Elvis because it's left the building. "I want both of you."

"At the same time?" Pierce asks.

I nod.

"What happened to wanting me to tell you what to do?" Principal Spears's voice hints at betrayal.

I smile sweetly at him, praying that he'll go for it. "Every team needs a strong leader."

He nods, pride and satisfaction glinting in his eyes.

Pierce shifts his gaze between us and says, "I'll be right back."

He's out the door before either of us can respond.

Spears tightens his grip on my arm, moving me away from the door, then promptly shuts it, wrapping his arms around me, and kissing me with the full force of a man who fears he has something to prove.

And whatever that is...he proves it.

Every primitive, instinctive piece of knowledge my mind has about sex bubbles to the surface as his hands find their way under my short skirt and knead my butt.

I'm yanking his buttoned-up shirt from his slacks, pressing my body into his while trying to make space to undress him, and if he had a ceiling fan in his office, I'd be tossing his tie onto it.

How can a kiss unravel me?

Was asking for Pierce to be included a mistake? I don't want this kiss to end...except if Spears wants to put his mouth in other places. I shiver at the possibilities.

The rattle of the door handle intrudes into our perfect moment. "I'm in for four thousand. Is that enough or do I need to donate more?" Pierce booms as he throws the door open.

Wow! I'm thrilled, but Spears flinches. He's been topped. Will he be content that I indicated he could be the boss of us, and that the normally easy-going art teacher agreed?

Spears nudges me backward until I'm sitting on his desk. "Don't move."

His disheveled appearance with the loosened tie, shirt askew, and a smear of my lipstick on his lips is super hot. And his hair...when were my hands in his hair? He's always so perfectly groomed. I like this mussed, out-of-control look on him.

"Lock the door," he directs Pierce, who probably planned on it.

We're about to be alone. The ache between my thighs is nearly unbearable.

I'm anticipating the click of the door closing when a hand slides around the edge. A split second of worry passes through me that the hand will be smashed. Fear of being caught with a disheveled principal between my legs replaces the worry. My body tightens into a giant knot.

My eyes fly to Spears. Can we think of a different explanation for his appearance? My hands instinctively pat my hair. I glance at the buttons down the front of my cute Santa's helper dress to confirm it's still buttoned. What do my lips look like?

No time to find a mirror. The door swings wider as Pierce fails to overcome whoever's pushing from the other side.

# Three

Coach Curtis looms in the doorway.

*Be still my heart!* This is either about to go seriously right or seriously wrong.

"What the fuck is happening?" His gruff demeanor extends beyond coaching.

I stifle a mix of giddiness and concern. If he's willing to join in, can Coach Curtis be a team player and accept Spears as the boss of this scene? Spears is already his boss at the school.

I'm waiting for the principal to answer when I realize he's staring at me.

Maybe I'm drooling. Oh well, as long as Curtis can be a team player, I'm going for the most insane night of my life.

"Let's call this the VIP suite. Whatever you think you're seeing, you're probably right."

He closes the door, and I boldly extend the challenge.

"This is a pay-to-play event, and the bidding is at..." I turn to Pierce. "Where did you leave off?"

Pierce points toward the door. "Four thousand. Make a donation at the winner's table."

Coach chokes and pats his back pocket then steps toward me, bumping Spears out of the way. That elicits a grumble.

Pressing one of his thick thighs between my legs, he towers over me. "Let me be clear, Jade…"

A hint of a squee escapes me that he also knows my name. My mantra had been to lay low, do the bare minimum, and graduate. Failing at laying low is one failure I'm okay with.

He loops his hands behind me and scoots me forward to the desk's edge, pressing my sex against his leg. Sweet muscular Jesus. Now I understand why my peers grind on each other at dances. Absolutely sinful.

My skirt is bunched around my hips and there's a chance my soaked panties are going to leave a wet spot on his athletic shorts. I'm strangely okay with that.

He continues, "I won't be asking you to wrap presents or clean my house when I make this donation."

With my neck craned, I wiggle my hips and boldly say, "Yeah big boy, I understand. We're talking about sex."

And with that statement, my mouth just got way ahead of my experience level. As if that didn't happen a couple of guys ago.

Pierce chokes. Spears tries to move Curtis, but that's pointless.

Curtis continues as if we're the only two in the room. "You don't understand."

Crap. That's what I was afraid of. I shrug. "Well, since we're in school, why don't you educate me?"

"I'm not making this donation so I can stick my dick inside of you. I'm doing it because it will make you happy."

"Oh!" If I was built out of blocks of wood, I'd be a toppling Jenga tower. Surely the other two are on the sex page with me?

Curtis cups a hand around the back of my head and presses the lightest kiss on my lips. Not what I expected from someone who can bench press my car. "Then when I fill your pussy with my cock and make sweet love to you, there won't be any question about who you belong to."

The room sways and he pulls me into his hard, broad chest, kissing the top of my head. Now we're back on track, except for the *belong to* thing. That implies a longer term than just tonight.

"Wait a fucking minute," Spears says. "Once you earn your spot, you'll be third in line."

Curtis puts a few inches of space between us and stares down at me. I'm surprised but relieved that he lets Spears control him.

That's not what's happening though.

He slips a hand between us, goes straight under my skirt, strokes my panties, and says, "Cookie, I've been waiting for this day. I wasn't sure how to make it work, but this is perfect. These two can get your virgin pussy warmed up so that you'll be stretched and ready for my fat cock."

I barely have time to swoon over the nickname, as I process his correct presumption that I'm a virgin, and that he's aware of how wet I am and doesn't balk.

Scoffs from the other two guys fade as Coach drags my hand over the giant erection straining his shorts.

"Thank you," I say, immediately regretting how stupid that sounds.

"You don't have to thank me, Cookie. Just keep your pussy ready because I've been dreaming of it every night, and I've got a backlog of baby juice for you. I can't tell you how disappointed I was when your name wasn't on the auction list."

"Is he right? You're a virgin?" Pierce corrals us back to the obvious question.

I shift my gaze from Pierce to Spears to Curtis. "He's right. I am."

Coach grins.

I'm aware of Principal Spears dragging his hands over his face in my periphery. Pierce, steps closer. No one's addressing Coach's comment about baby juice, which brings the inherent assumption of babies, doesn't it? I've already confessed to Spears that I want to be a mom.

Pierce asks, "And you're offering to take all three of us?"

"Yes, she is. Let's give her what she deserves." Curtis winks, manages to get his erection to relax to a not-quite-modest swell in his shorts, and heads out to pay.

# Four

"Get everything off my desk," Spears directs Pierce who gets right to work.

My breasts rise and fall against Spears's fingers while he slowly unfastens one button at a time down the front of my dress. The top of it falls open wider and wider with each freed button.

Spears's jaw tenses with each reveal and the corded muscles in his neck flex as the final button is unleashed and the fabric falls away.

"You naughty girl. Did you wear sexy bras and panties like this when you were a student in my school?"

I nod, unsure which answer he's hoping for. My newly purchased matched set of a red bra and panty has me feeling extra sexy.

"Fuck." He rakes a hand through his hair and steps back as if getting a better vantage point. "It's a good thing none of the high school boys touched you. I would have had to expel them."

Pierce circles around, gasps, and stops in his tracks. "Pure beauty."

Under his scrutinous eye, I feel like a work of art.

"Will you pose for me?" His question catches me off guard but Spears has a ready response.

"We're not wasting time so you can play with watercolors, Pierce."

"It doesn't have to be tonight. I need to capture your curves, the softness of your femininity—shit! I need to capture your innocence, and that does have to be tonight. Can I take a picture of you before we go through with this?"

I glance at Spears whose eyebrows raise. So much for all the high school lessons about how dangerous intimate pictures are in the digital age. He gives a faint nod.

"Okay." I start to slide an arm free from the sleeve since the dress is still draped around me.

Pierce reaches out, stopping me. "Hold on. I want this look...and would you mind if I keep taking pictures throughout the evening?"

That's a huge request. But it's infinitely fascinating. The men all have more to lose than me if the pictures get out. My Santa's helper job at the mall ends with the season, and I doubt Yvette, my boss at Sugar D's bakery will hold it against me since she shacked up with two lawyers.

The school district isn't likely to take kindly to three of their employees railing a newly former student.

"You don't have to agree to pictures," Spears says, rubbing the backs of his fingers over my thigh.

"Tonight isn't about *having* to do anything. It's about my wishes coming true. As long as I get a copy of each picture, take all you want."

Coach returns to the office and grins. "Documenting the evening in case we need an instant replay?"

"It's for art, you dolt." Pierce has little patience.

Curtis balls his fist in front of his mouth and fakes a cough around his response. "Spank bank."

Spears positions himself between my thighs. My bright red panties and bra are the only thing between us. He trails a tender caress over my belly as he addresses the guys.

"Let's get this straight. I'm only including the two of you because she asked me to. I was the first to make a move and the first to kiss her, and rest assured, I'll be the first to lick her pussy until she comes on my face, and I'll be the first to put my seed in her. Got it."

Seed? Hmm.

Pierce angles the camera, capturing the sternness on the principal's face. I shiver at how exciting that will be to look at later. I love his possessive streak.

Curtis smirks and strips off his tank top. "Like I said, warm her up."

I stare in disbelief as his erection stretches the fabric of his shorts right before my eyes. The other two men stare also. Perhaps there is some truth to his claim of being big. Everyone in the room is impressed.

Curtis dips his thumbs into his waistband. "What are we waiting for?"

We might as well be statues as he unveils himself. The word girth always seemed odd to me, but staring at his cock, I'd say he's got girth. And even though his game plan to warm me up is going to be necessary, I'm anxious to find out what it's like to be that full.

Pierce snaps a closeup of Spears cupping my breasts, dragging his thumbs over my nipples. My head falls back, and after Pierce takes a few more photos, he sets the camera down and kisses his way up my neck.

The slow tease of his tongue over my lips, the gentle pressure as he slides into my mouth, and the delicate invitation he extends as our tongues explore, wrap me with love.

Warm breath on my ear comes from Spears as he leans in. Someone strokes a finger over my wet center, and I figure out who when Spears says, "What were you planning to do about this needy pussy?"

Pierce trails his kisses to my breasts and sucks on me through the fabric. Curtis towers at the end of the desk. His clothes are gone. His cock is in his hand. And officially, his big fat cock is the first one I've ever seen in person.

I'm trusting that this is going to work.

I loll my head to Spears and my lips graze his. When did he get undressed? Not complaining.

"Answer me." His authoritative voice melts me.

Is he being demanding because I told him to, or is he just like this? Do I care?

On barely a breath, I say, "I would have played with myself."

"Show us," he adds. That gets Pierce's attention. He slowly withdraws his mouth from my bra.

I worry my lower lip, then say, "I wouldn't have panties on. Anyone care to help?"

Spears is on top of the task. Pierce notices that he's the only guy still dressed and quickly fixes that situation.

"Do you wear your bra to bed?" Spears asks.

I shake my head.

"Then we better get that off too."

Spears's erection rubs against my leg as he reaches around me to unfasten my only remaining piece of clothing. His pre-cum slicks my skin.

For a tiny moment, I consider how many levels of wrong this is. But that tiny moment is gone. Leaning back on my hands, I'm spread on the principal's desk, eager to be extremely naughty.

"Let me have a taste of that sweet pussy before either of them gets their funk on it," Coach says.

Apparently, he's forgotten I'm supposed to show them how I play with myself, but I'd rather they do all the work, so I let it go.

Spears shoves a hand against Coach's chest. "I said I was first. For everything."

"Instead of you bossing everyone around, why don't we let the lady decide."

Coach turns, and it occurs to me that I don't want to decide. I want them to own me. I want all of my cares to go away. No worry about my future. No pressure to do more with my life. No insinuation that somehow, I'm *being happy* wrong.

I just want to be cared for and adored, just like Spears wants to do. Just like a Daddy would do. They've given me nicknames, so I go for it.

"Daddy makes the rules." I bat my eyelashes playfully.

The room, and the people in it, might as well be frozen in time again. There's a surreal moment where I can take in everything at once. My senses are heightened. I'm happier than—

"The fuck if he's my daddy," Coach breaks the spell.

Principal loosely grips my chin, gently stroking his fingers forward until his fingertips land on my lips. In the same way I sense that he wants a kiss, I also know that he wants to be my daddy. I detect with every fiber of my being that he liked me saying that. And now that I did, it's not up for discussion.

"You heard my sweet baby. If you don't like what she's saying, get the hell out."

He meets Coach's glare until it softens, then looks to Pierce, who hesitates for a moment then smiles and says, "Daddy, hmm... What's in a name?"

I love how accepting he is, but Coach is having a harder time.

"What's in a name?" Spears pauses as if struggling to understand the question. "Everything. I'm her fucking daddy. Got it?"

Pierce raises his hands in front of his chest in a show of submission. "Just having fun with a literary reference."

"I'm familiar with Shakespeare, but the old bard may have gotten it wrong because Jade calling me Daddy changes everything."

"Well, it's not supposed to matter. That's the point of—"

"Don't bother explaining, because it fucking matters." Principal shifts his attention from Pierce to me. "Just for pretend, call Pierce, Daddy."

It's a crazy thought. Pierce is wonderfully seductive in his own way, but he's not a daddy. As if I'm an expert. But far be it from me to defy my principal daddy.

Turning my head to the side and tilting it so that locks of hair fall over my face, I stare through the strands, into Pierce's eyes for a prolonged moment.

He's captivated. He already knows the name matters.

Coach steps closer, his erection leading the way.

It bumps Spears's hand that's on my arm, and elicits a cautionary, "What the hell. Keep your dick to yourself."

"Not a chance. And if you two don't get to fucking, I *will* beat you to it."

"Nobody does anything until Jade does what she's supposed to." The firmness of Pierce's statement shocks all of us. More gently he focuses his words on me. "You were about to say..."

Spears huffs. "I thought the name didn't matter."

"Just. Let. Her. Say it." Pierce's insistence is uncanny. And super hot.

His overly-controlled expression hints that he's hiding how badly he'd like to hear it. Can all three be Daddies? They each just dropped a few thousand on me.

They've all admitted to wanting to take care of me. I'm not sure how far to push this, but having the three of them to myself is worth fighting for. It's not every day I get offered a fantasy—correction, three fantasies rolled into one!

I swirl my finger through the pre-cum on Pierce's tip and lock gazes with him. "I could simply ask you to fuck me, Daddy, but I think we need to get something straight. Daddies have a big responsibility. How would you earn that title?"

Warmth coats my finger. I lower my gaze and see that a spurt of pre-cum pumped onto it. Time to kick this into high gear and find out what this supposedly salty stuff tastes like.

While he's dumbfounded, I consider my finger deliberately, then lift it to my lips where I lick it with the very tip of my tongue. The planned moan ends up coming naturally as I dip my finger into my mouth and suck.

The room is frozen in time again. I thought Pierce's photos would freeze-frame the moments, but it keeps happening in real life.

"Jade, I'll take care of you and make sure your world is full of beauty, love, and happiness."

Coach grunts and I thrust a finger to his lips.

"Shhh, big boy, you'll get your turn."

I give my attention back to Pierce. "I like the way that sounds, you're such a romantic daddy."

"Fine." Coach grips my chin, forcing me to look up at him. "Pierce can be in charge of things like candles and rose petals. But when you need to be fucked to the point of forgetting everything that stresses you, I'm your fuck daddy."

My splayed sex aches to find out what that would feel like. I clamp my legs around Spears, who kneels. Looking up at me, he says, "I'll make sure *all* of your needs are met. Remember that day you found tickets to your favorite band in your locker?"

I furrow my brow and nod. "That was you?"

"I can't say that. But I might have paid close attention to who you invited to go with you."

"So you'd know if I took a guy?"

He shrugs. "Then there was the time flowers were delivered to the school on your birthday."

"You again?"

"Can't say that...again."

"They were beautiful. All of the girls were jealous." My world is upended. I'd attributed the tickets, the flowers, and a few other goodies to my best friends feeling bad for me. I thought they were pretending to be a secret admirer.

"All of the *guys* should be jealous of this." Daddy grips my thighs, his fingers digging in, holding my legs firmly apart as he leans forward, plants a kiss on my belly, then drifts down to my sex.

Long, warm breaths keep me keenly aware of my vulnerability. They also add fuel to my fire. Anticipation to my eagerness. Then the touch of his tongue gently sliding along my slit, pressing further the moment he's over my clit, has my breaths faltering.

Pierce steps to the far side, leaving Coach at the end of the desk. Pierce alternates snapping photos with light caresses. I'm honestly torn as to whether I prefer he physically enjoy me right now or document the moment so we can all enjoy it later.

Coach doesn't split his attention. He cups his huge hand behind my head, tangles his fingers in my hair, and takes control. The tug on my hair fills me with insane need.

His lips lock on mine and I'm trapped between his kisses and his hand. His tongue explores my mouth with equal command, and I would be lost in surrender if Daddy's tongue wasn't licking me into a frenzy. Why does that feel so much better than my fingers?

A hand cups the bottom of my breast before toying with my nipple. Who is it? Without opening my eyes, I know it has to be romantic daddy. Coach isn't going to be tender like that, and Daddy's still holding onto my thighs like he's lost at sea and I'm his life raft.

Another tug of my hair is a little harder than before.

Crap. That did it. I'm plunging toward release. White heat obliterates my world. All sensations ball into euphoria. These men are the perfect combination of everything I need. Will I ever be able to replicate this night?

Reality flits back to my brain. I have a sense that time has passed. I'm still surrounded by their warmth but Coach's head rests on top of mine. Pierce's hand strokes back and forth over my belly. And Daddy's head rests on my thigh.

Opening my eyes, I bask in the glory that I'm not dreaming. Pierce is watching me.

"Your orgasm face is the most beautiful thing I've ever seen."

Embarrassment tries to rise within me, but the three of them fill me with confidence.

He continues, "Since this evening is all about you, what do you want next?"

"There's so much to choose from."

Coach rights himself and licks his lips.

With the reminder, I say, "You wanted a taste before they get their funk on me, right?"

He nods, and motions for Spears to move, which happens without a fuss.

I cover my sex with my hand so I can finish my thought. "That was exhilarating and exhausting, so I don't want to be too wiped out before we get to the sex. Just a taste."

"Yes, ma'am."

Even on his knees, he's huge. He tosses my thighs onto his shoulders as he leans in. He kisses my curls before lapping at my sex over and over again. The groans coming from his chest practically shake the desk.

Giving in would be the easiest thing to do, but I'm seriously worried if I'm up for the number of orgasms these three could give me. I tap his head.

He ignores me.

I tap harder.

He shakes his head no, which drags his tongue back and forth over my clit. Damn him. Or should I say, thank you? No. I have to conserve energy.

His hair is too short so I grab the only thing I can think of, his ears, and pull him up.

"I said just a taste."

He's cracking up by the time our eyes meet. "I'm a slow taster."

I shake my head and say to Pierce, "I suppose you want a taste too?"

"I want everything you're willing to give, and if that's just a taste for now, it's perfect." He extends the camera phone to me. "I want to know what this looks like from your position."

Eyes closed was my preference, but okay. Everyone shuffles to reposition. Pierce takes my free hand and guides me to standing. "Be the goddess you are. Stand over me. Let me bow at your feet."

"What the fuck?" Coach says.

I tap the corner of the phone to his lips. "Shhh. You had your turn."

Spears busts out laughing but I can't join him. Pierce kisses my foot and works his way up my leg.

Coach wraps his hand around mine that's hovering in the air with the phone. "He gave you a job."

I can't believe I'm taking pictures of the art teacher kissing my naked body. Kissing my sex. Looking up at me while his tongue is buried in my curls.

My attempts at fantasizing over these guys failed miserably. I had no idea it could be like this, and not just the three of them, but the way they tend to me.

I waver and Coach steadies me. Spears takes the camera and finishes the job, stepping back, presumably getting the big picture, as I come undone on romantic daddy's face.

"Hey, you said not to make you come." Coach is clearly keeping score.

I flop my head to the side. "So spank me."

"Hell yeah." Daddy thrusts the phone at Pierce.

Before I can figure out what's happening, Daddy's sitting in his desk chair, and I'm bent over his knee. I wiggle my breasts free from where they squished uncomfortably against his legs, and his hand flattens possessively on my back until I resettle.

"All right, Coach, she asked you to spank her." Principal daddy says.

"You're not going to claim the right to do that first too?"

Principal's hand slides over my exposed cheek before a thick finger rips his hand away.

"Don't you dare," Coach says. Seconds later his hand slides back and forth over my butt, then taps lightly.

"You've got to be kidding me," Principal says. The words are barely out of his mouth when Coach lands a firm smack on my ass. My body flinches. My sex flinches. I didn't know that was possible. Am I somehow wired to clamp around a cock in response to a spanking?

I didn't pay much attention in Biology, or any of my classes, but I'm certain no one ever taught that. Or why I'm so turned on at having my hair pulled, which becomes apparent once again as Spears pulls my hair away from my face, twists it around his hand, and angles my face to look at Pierce, who's taking photos of the scene.

Another firm smack taunts my body. Why on earth does that make my pussy tighten? I have to know how this will feel when a cock is inside of me.

"I need sex." Yes, I do, but did those words come from my mouth?

"You better get on it then, Spears." Coach grips my cheeks with both hands and spreads them.

Oh my. Is he looking? The fleeting embarrassment is gone before he lands a tongue-heavy kiss on my pussy lips from behind. Yet another new and amazing thing to learn that I like. This is the most intense note-taking I've done in years.

"Want to sit on Daddy's cock?"

I nod.

Spears handles me with ease, lifting and turning me so I'm straddling his lap. "I want to be able to see your face while I teach you what it's like to come on a cock."

I close my eyes, reality sinking in that my first time is going to be with my principal and with spectators.

Coach's big hands wrap around my waist as he lifts me. Daddy positions his cock at my entrance. I do what I can to balance myself.

Daddy slides his hands under my hips. "I've got her."

Coach drags his fingers slowly as he withdraws, leaving Spears to lower me while intensely studying my expression.

"Tell me if you need to stop."

"I can't imagine I'll want to." I shift my hips, moving on top of his cock, begging him to speed this lesson up.

He lowers me, parting my lower lips, easing himself into me. It's like we're meant to do this. My body stretches around him as I'm pressed to my limits, filled with sensations I've never experienced.

My walls alternate between taking him in and contracting around him. He swallows hard every time the latter happens.

"Are you trying to make me come?" he asks.

My hands settle on his shoulders. "That is the point."

"I'm not wearing protection." His words sound more like a taunt than a caution.

"I know."

"And you're not on birth control." He shifts his hands from under me to my hips.

Rather than ask how he knows, I assume he read my medical file. "Is that a deal breaker?"

"I'd rather think of it as a guarantee."

"Of what?" My fingers tighten as my body begs me to move, to slide over his shaft, to inch closer to release.

"Of you being mine."

Everything clicks into place the second his words hit my ears. This is real. He understands what we're doing. Hell, he's the leader. And I will follow.

Except where orgasms are concerned—I'm the leader there. His strokes push me over the edge. My body might as well cease to exist as the biggest orgasm of my life obliterates everything.

Pleasure becomes my entire existence. The only sensations I can detect are his cock and pure happiness. I've lost track of where my body merges with his, only sensing even more fullness as his groans invade my euphoria and he fills me even more.

It's done. We've attempted to create a child—my favorite wish in the whole world, especially with a Daddy as responsible and able as principal daddy.

His arms are wrapped around me, holding me close when I regain consciousness. I'm not sure that I passed out exactly, but I was transported to another world. The meaning of mind-blowing sex becomes apparent.

Rustling from behind me encourages me to open my eyes. Pierce is positioning a coat on the desk. "When you're ready, I want to make love to you right here."

"Laying on the desk?"

"You can do anything you want. The coat doesn't offer much cushion but I'm not taking you on the floor."

Agreed. Not on the floor. "If all I have to do is lay there and accept another orgasm, I'm game. Otherwise, I need a minute."

"I'll do all the work, Jade, as long as you're willing to carry my baby."

A soft smile curves my mouth. "Deal."

They help me onto the desk. Pierce, being the romantic daddy, stands to the side, dragging his fingers over my skin. A path of excitement follows his touch. His eyes leave a trail of love, and I've never felt so beautiful as the way he adores me.

A thorough caress from head to toe and back practically melts me. The ache between my legs is the exception. I should be satisfied after Daddy filled me, but I'm greedy and want the romance to hurry so I can get to Fuck Daddy. What have I become?

Is it ridiculous to want all three of them for myself? My brain is too fuck-hungry to care.

My legs press against each other.

"Tsk. Tsk." Pierce says gently, sliding a hand between my thighs. "Don't hide this pretty pussy."

"I wasn't..." I don't have the energy or concern to continue as he climbs onto the desk.

His shaft presses at my entrance as he lowers his mouth for a kiss, then shifts to my ear. "I don't want to rush with you, but we have to play nice."

He angles his head to look at Coach who looks decidedly unimpressed that he's still waiting. Cum drips from his erection.

"You better hurry or he might pull you off of me."

"I love you, Jade."

"I love you too," I whisper, despite finding it hard to believe this all came together so quickly.

Grumbles of love come from the other two, which heightens how surreal this is. Can we really love each other? Why not? I've had my eyes on them for years, and they've been watching me. This is fate.

Pierce slides into me, the sensation less foreign than with Spears, but new in its own way. Pierce uses slower strokes, and the partial weight of his body makes me feel even more connected.

And my sex agrees. The building orgasm swells around his cock. The strain on his face is beautiful. Motion from beside us draws my attention and I realize Spears is taking photos. I hope he captures that look.

Pierce quickens his pace, catching me off guard, and I surrender, not even trying to make this last longer. I've got one more guy to go, and I doubt any of them will be done after one time.

He cries out as my fingernails dig into his back with the intensity of my release. Attempting to let go so I don't hurt him, I can't. His cock thickens inside of me. I'm coming so hard, my release is coating us, and the poor coat. Oops.

All romantic notions are gone as Pierce ruts into me like a wild beast. Can people in the auction hear him? Coach must have the same concern because a hand slaps around Pierce's mouth, who shakes his head free, lowers it next to mine, and continues to work his hips as we grind through our release.

Can all sex be this good? The question fades as I lose myself in the floaty bliss.

Until I can't breathe. Pierce has dropped some of his weight onto me. I wiggle and gasp.

"Sorry." He shuffles upward, kissing me before climbing off.

His absence leaves Coach and his huge grin in my line of sight.

Rational thinking tells me I'm not ready for this, but an extremely carnal part of my brain has awakened, and I can't get him inside of me fast enough. Plus, I'm super lubed with my own wetness and the slick cum of the other two guys. If I'm not ready now, I'll never be.

I pull from my exhaustion and raise on my elbows. "They did their part."

He wastes no time scooping me into his arms, my body plastered against his broad, contoured muscles of a chest. He's so much thicker up close. And I'm up so much higher than normal.

The cock prodding at my sex should probably be my biggest focus, but I'm not nearly this tall and it's an interesting perspective.

Then his cock grabs my attention as he shucks me down a tiny bit and my pussy lips stretch around him. Oh my god.

"You ready for this, Cookie?"

"Mentally, I'm ready, but physically...go slow." I smile.

"I'll be good to you. Don't worry. All you have to do is let that pretty pussy come all over my cock."

"That's my kind of checklist."

He spins around, one hand under me, easily supporting my weight, and the other spanning my back as he presses me into the wall.

The security of being sandwiched between a wall of muscle and a wall of plaster is oddly invigorating.

Small pumps of his cock allow him to work his way inside of me while taking away the shock of how much I have to stretch around him. His shaft presses into everything inside of me. My G-spot. The other spot that I've heard most women don't even know about. And my cervix. He's completely filled me.

My nipples bead hard as rocks as my breasts flatten and slide against his chest. His scent, fresh from the shower does unexpected things to me.

Stimulation comes at me from so many directions, I can't think. And without thinking, I lose control once again.

My body jerks as I contract around his girth. His jaw falls slack and his eyes become slits. A growl rips through him, and I completely shatter.

Physically? Mentally? Spiritually? Nothing makes sense anymore, except abandoning myself, and I do.

*Knock. Knock. Knock.*

My mind is forced back to reality.

"It's locked," Spears whispers.

"Shouldn't you answer?" I ask.

Before he can say anything, Mrs. Dupree's voice calls through the door. "Mr. Spears, we're locking up and noticed a few cars still in the lot. Yours included."

"Well, fuck," Coach grumbles and lowers me. Pierce hands me a wad of tissues, and we all scramble for clothes.

"Working late. Thanks for checking," Spears says.

"I also saw Coach Curtis's car along with Mister Pierce's and—"

They each pipe up that they're in the office.

"And a student's car." Her voice has gone ice cold. I fumble through my buttons and curse myself when the bottom of my dress is uneven. I backtrack to the missed button.

"We're doing life coaching like you recommended."

"This doesn't feel right." She rattles the door handle again. "Are you okay, Jade? Open the door right now."

I inhale deeply to gather myself while Spears opens the door.

Presenting myself, I say, "I'm great. They didn't do anything wrong. There were some embarrassing questions I had about my future, that were best handled in private."

She raises an eyebrow. "In private with the three of them? I'm your guidance counselor. You could have come to me."

"Yes, but they seemed to get me, to understand my desires. You never thought I was making good choices."

"I'm not sure that's changed." She looks from one man to the next.

I rub a hand over my belly, hoping that changes are underway. "They've helped me realize that there's nothing wrong with my life plan."

Dupree purses her lips. "The only plan I recall you ever mentioning was to have kids. No thoughts about how you would pay for them or ensure you could support yourself if you end up divorced."

I smile confidently. "Not only do I have a plan, I have two backup plans."

"Feel free to head out. I'll close up," Spears tells her.

"May I see you alone for a moment, Miss Johnson?"

I'm fairly certain this will be over faster if I comply so I step in her direction, then follow her lead as she moves farther away from them.

"I'm concerned about all of you being alone without a female present."

"You doubt Principal Spears has good morals?"

"It's just that things happen sometimes, and I want you to feel safe."

"Trust me, I've never felt more safe in my entire life."

"I'd feel better if you left with me."

I bite my tongue to keep from saying that I'd feel better if at least one of them was inside of me. "I appreciate your concern, but we're not quite finished solidifying my plans for the future. I promise, if they do anything that makes me the least bit uncomfortable, I'll let them know, and I'm one hundred percent confident they'll respect whatever I say."

She glares at them. "I don't know what you're up to, but I don't like it."

My shoulders slump forward. That's my biggest concern...what will people think?

Spears moves beside me. "This is one young lady you don't need to worry about Mrs. Dupree. Her future is rock solid." He platonically sets a hand on my shoulder, filling me with courage, then he continues. "I'll put my word on it."

The other two step up and add their confirmation.

Is it possible to feel like our connection is magical, that the four of us are soulmates?

# *Epilogue*

## Two years later

Under the guise of my friend Maggie being free to watch our kiddos Christmas Eve morning, I suggested to Daddy, Pierce, and Coach that I would need them out of the house so I could do last-minute Christmas prep. Thus they're all currently at the high school wrapping up the semester. We spent so much time tending to our toddler and 3-month-old baby, on top of helping with the third annual Christmas Cherry Auction, that they had a few loose ends to knock out.

And yeah, I resigned myself to calling it the Christmas *Cherry* Auction as has everyone else. No point denying reality, even though it does bring plenty of cheer.

What my guys don't know is that I have ulterior motives this morning, and an important factor is that the school will be empty. The janitor won't even be there. I checked.

Sneaking into the school, I make a beeline for Pierce's art room and close the door quickly, pre-emptively lifting my finger to my lips for him to keep quiet.

He startles and scrambles to hide the canvas on his easel, but if I can trust the glimpse I got, he's painting me. Nice.

Acting as if I don't think it's weird that he freaked out, I say. "Shhh. I need you to help me with a surprise."

He rushes to hug me and eyes the closed door. Any time the guys get alone time with me, they appreciate it. "Our little secret."

"Can you cover the little window on the door?"

"I'm liking this more all the time." He has no idea how exciting this is about to get.

I'm buzzing with anticipation as it is. While he tapes paper over the window, I strip naked.

"What the..." he stammers when he turns around.

Even though I expected that reaction, it doesn't stop me from laughing. "We're going to have to work fast."

He grabs the button on his jeans but I motion for him to stop.

"It's not what you think." I ignore his disappointment. "I need you to paint something."

"I like where this is going." He winks and heads to his cabinet where he pulls out body paint, and I wonder if he's suspicious since I had him paint me for the last baby reveal.

Waiting a second for him to set the basket of paints down, I point to my belly and say, "I need a 'baby on board' sign."

His mouth drops open and he rushes to me again. "Jade, you're all that I need, but another baby...that's the best Christmas present ever. I can't believe you're pregnant again."

"Merry Christmas, but it's not that hard to believe, but enjoy it while it lasts. I'm taking a break after this one."

We share a laugh.

"Fair enough." He rubs my belly then steps back and studies me from head to toe. "Instead of a 'baby on board' sign, can I suggest a different idea?"

"Baby on board was pretty low-hanging fruit. That's all my mommy brain can handle. What's your idea?"

He brings his hands together up high, then makes a curvy motion as if moving them down my body. "I want to paint your entire body...turn you into a gingerbread woman with a little *babybread* on your belly."

He'll need to allow time for two of those babies. I glance at the generic wall clock.

"How long will it take? I have to pick the kids up from Maggie's in two hours." I cup my boobs. "Or things will get uncomfortable."

I dropped milk off for the baby but my boobs won't care. They'll produce like clockwork.

Pierce grins. "You know we're all more than willing to help you with that. We hate for you to be uncomfortable."

"I don't know what I'd do without such generous husbands, but Maggie has other things to do today, you know, it being Christmas Eve and all."

"Fine. Instead of putting a base color over your entire body, I'll only do the candy decorations, and keep them to a minimum…but would you be opposed to a shave? I want to paint a peppermint swirl there." He eyes my sex.

I'm distracted by the idea that he has the necessary tools to do that in his classroom but he explains that they've shaved arms to do simple body paint at the local festivals. The classroom has a sink, so we're all set.

Now to deal with the bigger issue. "Before you commit, I should caution you that we'll need two of the little babybreads."

His wheels turn as my statement sinks in. He encircles me with another embrace. "Fuck! This just keeps getting better."

His hard cock presses into me and I'm tempted to skip straight to celebratory sex, but I love his gingerbread idea even more than my baby on board sign, and can't wait to get started.

"So, how long will this take? You need time to shave me and paint. We have to call the other two in for the reveal. Then everyone will want to celebrate."

Pierce rubs his jaw as he stares at me like I'm a blank canvas. "It won't be my best work, but I can whip out the basics in an hour, we can do initial celebrations here, then grab the kids, and when they go down for a nap, we can finish celebrating at home."

Tossing a hand up, I say, "You're forgetting something very important."

His brow furrows.

"When the kids take a nap, I'm taking a nap, too."

"You'll get your nap, I promise. And you'll need it when we're done with you."

"Deal."

He kisses my belly then motions for me to sit on the counter by the sink so he can shave me. A few strokes in, I decide to tackle the task myself. I'll let him try a different time when we're not rushed.

While I'm doing that, he covers the classroom couch with a sheet and I get comfortable on it. This is a new addition from when I took his class six years ago, but the longer he teaches, the bolder he gets about embracing different ideas in his art classroom.

He starts with the babybreads, and it takes everything in me not to wiggle with the tickles of the paintbrush. Even if those two cuties were the only things he painted, it would be awesome, but he adds the red and white swirl on my sex.

Next, he goes for brightly wrapped candy covering my breasts, but while he's working on the second one, someone tries the handle of the door, jostling it, presumably surprised that it's locked.

We freeze, giving each other questioning glances. It has to be either Daddy or Coach.

I look toward the canvas and easel he turned away from me earlier. "Tell him you're working on a surprise."

Pierce blurts it out, a little clunky, but it works.

Spears says, "Cool. Can't wait to see it."

Then silence. Did he leave? That was easy. We snicker that our secret's safe, and he goes back to painting.

For a moment. Then the sound of a key sliding into the lock and the door clicking open bring our secret to a close.

Spears is staring at us. "Like I said. I couldn't wait. Are you pregnant? With twins?"

Shrugging, I smile. "We were going to do a Christmas reveal."

"Consider it done." He's typing on his phone, slips it into his pocket, and before he's done kissing my belly, Coach's voice booms from the hallway.

"What's the hurry?" he says as he enters the room. Stopping in his tracks while staring at my belly, he does a fist pump. "We got two in you at once! Yeah, boys, we did it!"

"I guess we can start the celebration." Pierce waves his finger. "Watch out for the wet paint."

Coach drops to his knees, slides my butt to the edge of the couch, kisses both babybreads, and dives into my peppermint center. His flurry of kisses and laps of his tongue send me into a frenzy until he lifts his face, which is amazingly not covered with paint. Probably just my candy boobs are still wet.

He asks, "What are you two waiting for? This gingerbread mama needs to be decorated with some of that fancy white stuff."

I chuckle. "You mean Royal Icing?"

"Hell no. I mean cum."

We all break into laughter.

Pierce shakes his head as he and Spears undress. "You could have at least run with the analogy and been a little less blunt."

"I call plays like I see them. If you want analogies, we'd have to bring one of the English teachers in."

I hold my hands up. "Nope. Our family is perfect, just like this."

"Other than a few more babies," Spears mutters, then louder says, "But you're right. We are perfect, and we're going to keep it that way forever. I love you, Baby."

"I love you too, Daddy." The other two no longer vie for daddy status, as they've come to understand Spear's need to be in control and that they fill other roles. That's what makes us so perfect together.

As with any time an 'I love you' gets said, everyone jumps in. When we've all restated the obvious, Pierce strokes his cock and nods at Spears. "Let's put the finishing touches on this Cookie while Coach eats her."

"Good call, I love my Cookie," Coach says, returning to my lingering urgency.

Spears fists his cock. "We've got all the Royal Icing she'll ever need."

The expertise of Coach's mouth unravels me, and warmth streams onto my belly and chest as the other two finish the decorations.

All I have to do is relax and surrender to the love and hunger in their eyes.

They've given me everything I ever wished for and more. On the surface that might be the babies and life as a mom, we're a perfect Family, but much deeper, they've given me a better F-word...Freedom from worrying about what anyone else thinks. And the promise of Forever.

And we live happily ever after!

You're probably an expert at this by now... A bonus scene with the other baby reveal and some locker room action is available exclusively to newsletter subscribers.

https://SylvieHaas.com

# More by Sylvie Haas

More Sylvie Haas stories set in Eggplant Canyon and Peach Bottom Valley can be found at

https://mybook.to/EggplantCanyon

And if you like things fast and hot, grab a seat at Sugar D's Speed Dating:

https://mybook.to/SugarDsSpeedDating

# Sylvie Haas
## Freebies

Do you love bonus content?

Sign up for my newsletter and you'll get access to all of my freebies, and I'll keep you up to date on all of my new releases and special offers.

https://SylvieHaas.com

# About the Author

Sylvie Haas obsesses over dirty-talking heroes who fall hard and fast for the women of their dreams. And usually, you'll find heroes, yes plural, in one book because she has such a hard time making the heroine choose one possessive guy.

On most days, you can find Sylvie with the wind in her hair, her fingers on the keyboard, and her mind in the gutter as she thinks up new places her characters can get frisky.

Sylvie's books will always deliver a happily ever after, and even though they're short, they'll leave you satisfied!